Tut's Queen

Also by Bela I. Sandor

Fundamentals of Cyclic Stress and Strain, University of Wisconsin Press, 1972
Strength of Materials, Prentice-Hall, 1978
Engineering Mechanics: Statics, 2nd ed., Prentice-Hall, 1987
Engineering Mechanics: Dynamics, 2nd ed., Prentice-Hall, 1987
"Mechanics of Solids," Ch.1, The CRC Handbook of Mechanical Engineering, 2nd ed., CRC Press, 2004

"The Rise and Decline of the Tutankhamun-Class Chariot," Oxford Journal of Archaeology, May 2004
"Tutankhamun's Chariots: Secret Treasures of Engineering Mechanics," Fatigue and Fracture of Engineering Materials and Structures, July 2004

Tut's Queen

Bela I. Sandor

iUniverse, Inc.
New York   Bloomington

Tut's Queen

This is a work of fiction. All of the characters, names, incidents, organizations, and dialogue in this novel are either the products of the author's imagination or are used fictitiously.

iUniverse books may be ordered through booksellers or by contacting:

iUniverse
1663 Liberty Drive
Bloomington, IN 47403
www.iuniverse.com
1-800-Authors (1-800-288-4677)

Because of the dynamic nature of the Internet, any Web addresses or links contained in this book may have changed since publication and may no longer be valid. The views expressed in this work are solely those of the author and do not necessarily reflect the views of the publisher, and the publisher hereby disclaims any responsibility for them.

ISBN: 9-781-4401-1266-9 (pbk)
ISBN: 9-781-4401-1267-6 (ebk)

Printed in the United States of America

iUniverse rev. date: 12/16/2008

To Lanny Bell, for taking me into Tut's world

1

The Queen's Hips Jerking My Jaws

I wiggled my eyebrows, trying to loosen the blindfold that my Master had put on me. "The ripe Queen, ahh," he said while pushing me by the shoulder into the entrance of the narrow service corridor. The blindfolding of me was excessive, even silly, as if I had no means of mapping our path or acquiring other useful information, but there was no choice, and I was too stunned to think clearly and protest when he sprung this visit to the Queen on me.

"Still, don't enlarge your future too soon," he said sharply, though probably smiling. He pulled on my elbow to stop me and lowered his voice. "No. You need more luck, and, more of everything. No. This splendid red fish is not about to leap yet, or ever. This is not for you to examine her body as you have been hoping deep in the night, don't jerk your head, I know you well enough, but for her to test you. Don't ask me how this came about, or even how she knows anything about you, or why she would care. Maybe the giggles and whispers of her servant girls ... how much donkey sausage have you been feeding them? And when? Sure. Like sneaking out before dawn, instead of doing your daily task of making fire with the drill. Oh, to be young and reckless ... but I warn you, don't misread her signals." He didn't finish his admonition, but threw a blanket on my head, perhaps to prevent the servants from recognizing me, and started to push me forward again.

Dust shook from the wrap into my nostrils, and his orders for me not to talk loudly, let alone cough or sneeze, made it increasingly uncomfortable as we hustled along, bumping my shoulders left and right on the walls. The horsehair blanket touched my lips, and I tried to blow away the rough and foul-tasting fabric. As before ... as the donkey blanket had been on my head, at Bahhari village, choking me, with three duck-pluckers thick in coop odors holding me down on the straw in the shed, one on the arms, while biting my neck through the blanket, a pungent crocodile breath, ready to burst into flame like an Asiatic dragon's wind from his tongue, what were they drinking, the heaviest one sitting on my feet, and the third one busy with her feather-wise fingers on my crotch, her raspy tongue is a leech giving me a scary miracle as if she was Isis raising Osiris from the dead. Finally, the blanket falls off and they let me breathe, breathe to live and run, run to cool down in good mud, but they are shrieking, "Come back, we are not done," and hoarse laughter behind me, but what exactly happened and why, why? "The same place tonight, better in the dark, then really done, boy, really stretch you out." Forever, I will spit on their donkeys' graves, but momentarily I had to push a sniffing dog away from my crotch. I blindly kicked after the dog and heard it paw the ground as it ran away.

"Calm down and don't breathe so much," my Master whispered. "You want to be presentable to Ankh, and also not bring shame on my head. I warn you." I stumbled and croaked, "Sire, please." He let me stop and relax for a while. It was good to lean against the cool plaster wall while crouching. I wondered if I was rubbing with my back against a fresh bright painting showing the royal family at a festival or something, scenes that were everywhere. If I was, I wasn't told, but that would be normal for my absent-minded Master.

Even through the horse hairs, I could detect the smell of fresh laundry, and hear singing by several soft voices, I strained to recognize them, something about being separated from their sweet brothers by the wide river and its thousand crocodiles, no doubt meaning their families or their strict masters. Sweet brothers, sweet dreams, the palace servants singing and talking about their lovers, who might be more coarse and filthy than the blanket, something that is crazy, not easy to fathom. Further on, in a side corridor, it was the bakery ovens with their strong earthy smells that could drive me crazy, time passes slowly in the midst of bakery smells, stupidly having started out with an empty stomach in my excitement, reminding me of the rumor that the Queen liked to munch on small crusty breads in the shape of fertility dolls, and large grapes, day and night. I also recalled hearing Captain Minkh of the Inner Guard saying over a sand-dwellers' dice game that he had a better personal suggestion for her, in case the bread dolls and the grapes turned out to be unproductive, so to speak. "What?" said another player who was concentrating too much on the cheaters in their game. "I will show you first, for practice," said Minkh. Where will they play tonight, and will the cat sleep by the huge beer jug on the table, oblivious to all the noise around it? My mind was flipping and twisting into another alley. Why can't I focus on the big things at hand?

We passed a room full of fruits, and another of flowers, and the barbershop of the famous Third-Sabtet, owner of nine magic fingers working rich hair and wigs, and inventor of the latest rage, the myrrh-in-tallow party cone-hats. He is good to know for his excellent clients and wig-making assistants freely offering various mysteries to a young man of enlarged curiosity. Or not so freely, old men often say. Why? What's the problem? My lips are caked with dust. Then the heaviest perfumes of the world, mixed with a latrine's stench, swirled into my nostrils. "They should learn how to hide the smells with sand, like a cat does. I have an idea on how to do that in that room," I said to Rehotep, and he grunted in approval. "Me, too," he said. "With few gawking servants, because the nobility hate to be seen with their tunics down or up. Although, such a project is not a priority now, and perhaps never will be, they are used to the stink, so don't waste your time on it. Not tonight, anyway. But, we are getting close, and this is a good place to give you more advice that occurred to me in passing. Stop and listen.

"She is three and a half years older than the King, and two years older than you are, I guess, you peasant of obscure pedigree, if any, which makes her a whole lot smarter than both of you put together. Never forget that, if you want to live to a ripe old age."

"Sire, if you forgive me, how do you know that?" My throat was drier than stable straw, and my thoughts drifted to Nubian booza beer.

"How? It's plain and simple. Because she doesn't show it to ordinary mortals, but I have seen signs of what she is made of, although teaching any woman is like carrying sand in a splitting sack. Keep your eyes and ears open, wait, hold back, you can start opening them soon enough. Here, give this charm to her if there is a good chance, a perfect chance. Dry stud-dung molded with honeycomb, a special thing for horse-lovers, you can say it is sized to fit a young hedgehog and that it's from me. Learn this, too. When a woman has too much gold, this kind of unique object is the best gift for her, even in her own eyes, but you will never know what she is really thinking and planning. Remember, royalty love to receive small gifts that tickle the crotch, it's as certain as a sunburn out of season." He pressed it deeper into my palm.

"This thing, this charm, I am afraid I cannot," my tongue froze stiff when suddenly a new sensation entered my sphere, an unseen but large presence that heated and stirred the air. The Master quickly removed my wrap and the blindfold, and I found my nose almost touching the hairs on the slowly heaving chest of a thick-oiled guard. He needed a thorough scrubbing in a hot ash-and-natron bath, but you can't tell a huge man that soap is cheap.

"He is not an advanced user of our rare words, and he will not hurt you if you behave properly," said my Master softly, but this reassurance could not stop the morning's fresh raw egg rising in my gullet against my rapid swallowing. "However, note that he differs from a woman. For him, self-assertion does not earn an evil reputation, nor does he have to rely on a sweet potion that a woman may consider as a practical weapon, if you get my drift. Now let him take you inside to the next guard, hopefully lavished with essence of lavender, and let me return to my easy chair for a quiet evening, thinking of young this and young that, even if having far fewer words but more ideas than a glass-blower has with red-hot air."

"What, Sire?" I couldn't follow his meandering words and started to turn back, but he disappeared behind the guard who pushed a door open for me, reaching over my head and nudging my buttocks with his bulbous knee. So much for the famous words of the new wrestler in the court, the crazed Asiatic man sporting the one-and-a-half ear, bragging that he could kick any local butt, any time. The brute shoved me toward another guard, indeed much cleaner.

Inside, what appeared to be my destination, I was still brushing the blanket's dust and lint from my hair and clothes when a peculiar stench and a glint of gold hit me at the same time. Is this her Scented Soft Room the girls in the laundry gossip about? The room was in low light. The glint was attractive to the eye, from a Hathor-Isis amulet on Queen Ankh's chest, hanging from a three-stranded blue and green stone-bead necklace, nesting between her breasts, which were pushed together a little by the embroidered straps of her long tunic. Did I just two months ago drill those beads in the shop as part of a test of my newly improved four-spindle bowstring drill? It is and will remain for a hundred generations the most astonishing and efficient drill setup in the eternal Two Lands and beyond, without a doubt. Nevertheless, I was happy to improve and prove the drill to my Master, without having to use it all day long, day in, day out, on millions of little stones. If I had only known where those beads would end up in the heavenly valley of these other Two Lands ... I was hoping that she didn't see me shake my head like a wet dog or an old man getting loose hairs and scalp flakes off his shoulders, but if I was hoping to be unseen, why was I here? Run. No. Focus ... where ... failure means being kicked out of the shop, then what, become a glassblower, always red-headed from effort, my head was getting redder in the shadows, perhaps from the light off that amulet.

She was sitting on a large alabaster chair covered with three or four leopard skins, taking ointment from a flower-like stemmed vessel with two long fingers, first slowly passing the fingertips under her nose, heaving her chest in the long inhale, and applying it to her earlobes and neck, apparently not noticing me, though that was not likely. She had seven bright henna spots on her hair and skin, a sacred number, of course, but why am I always counting, it's like a dog scratching, when in a tight corner? Her chair was decorated to endure, and one arm of it was slightly glowing, white stone lit up as faint yellow by a nearby lamp. The amulet of the goddess of love and beauty was a rich version of much simpler and very common fertility objects made of cords. Ankh's face was beautiful as always, exceeding the work of the best sculptors, but strangely I was more interested in her ripe ball-eyes than in her face, so I prayed that she would soon get up and let them bounce a little, something that's hugely enjoyable watching in servant girls, too, but a Queen of this quality, yes.

A blind harpist beyond the Queen's chair began playing, making a mouse scurry away from him, first trying for a hole in the opposite wall, but it was blocked by a bulb of onion against serpents. Perhaps there is gold in the idea of driving vermin from the granaries using some easily generated sound selected for the purpose, especially if it's pleasing to human ears. She softly sang a few words of the Teasing Maid, 'when the red fish leaps beautifully on my fingers,' then fell silent. I moved left and right a little, cautiously, to locate the source of the smell that hit me upon my entrance. What's roasting on the red coals in the brazier? Gourds? No. It must be a bull's testicles. The words of the famous scribe Kakhun came to life through the burning odors, 'Nemsu symptoms. It's common in women of the nobility, to hide the issue of a sore and stinking hedgehog, to say they smell something roasting. The most highly recommended treatment is to fumigate their crotches exactly with what they say they are smelling.' Luckily, she can afford the fumes from the best meat for the problem, every time. Luckily, she pays handsomely for the medical advice. So, what is the best profession in the palace, my good Master, and why am I learning anything else? Wheels, springs, bearings. Sure. The more you know, the more rounded is the belly.

Finally, she is up and moving, good. She picked up an intricate, tall lamp in the shape of a frog at the bottom, with many tiny frogs around its feet, obviously the fertility-frog goddess, I couldn't remember its name. On the head of the frog, the potter god, Khum, I know him well, is fashioning a well-endowed royal infant on his wheel. She took the lamp to a dark wall, now with her back to good advantage, but not enough vibration, to illuminate a golden statue of Hathor-Isis, similar to her necklace amulet but life-size, if there is such a thing for a larger-than-average goddess. The Golden One, Lady of Heaven, protector of lovers, patron of love, pleasure, ecstasy and inebriation had a kingly cobra on the front of her headband, a huge sun-disk on top of the head, a mandrake fruit in one hand, and a sacred sistrum rattle in the other, both to help communication with the spirit world. The Queen touched and stroked and kissed the shining breasts and belly of the statue, shook the rattle loudly enough that I looked around for more mice, touched the amulet to the statue, and returned to her seat.

She played with the beads on her broad wesekh collar, picked up a bronze mirror by its lotus-stalk handle, representative of creation, and applied red balm to her lips. She let her dangling hand touch a tall and straight Min-lettuce standing in a bowl of its own milky fluid, never enough fertility objects for assurance, and finally closed her big black eyes amid black painted outlines. What should I do? I could slip out when she is not looking, but that could not be an acceptable end to the test, whatever that was. Besides, slipping out from her presence may earn me a bad trip to the Big-Tooth-Red-Mud riverbank, hastened along by cruel bony knees from behind. For Thoth's baboon's pity, what is best to do and say? The needed words were scarcer than greenstones. The wheels in my head spun faster and faster, till all the spokes disappeared behind their own wispy veils of blurring speed.

It pays to be on good terms with Thoth. My favorite baboon's image dashed across my mind, kicking up a whirl of thoughts and leaving a single idea well fleshed out for the first move, but also making my heart pound like a redfish leaping on the river repeatedly to escape a crocodile. I crawled up to Ankh, not worrying about the scraping noises, assuming she knew I was there, and held out on my hands the dung-charm from my Master. I waited, suddenly finding the harpist annoying. I looked up and saw her slowly opening her eyes with a warm radiance, and rolling a little ball of myrrh and cinnamon and rush-nut out on her long tongue into her fingers, which placed the ball on the arm of the chair. I knew all the ingredients and taste of the chew, having talked at length to the servant girl who made them. The taste was sharp and strange but much better than those predicted for me by my ignorant enemies, the tastes of rotten bread and sour beer, or the dreams of drinking warm old beer, sure omens of suffering to come.

Ankh. I lost my head in a fleeting vision of licking salt together, and hung the charm on her golden amulet. Even more boldly, I opened up like the Eloquent Peasant, a favorite character of mine on a fading scroll, each word more firm and bold than the one before, "For Your Highness, a Spirit Charm from the Strong Stallion, an excellent dung."

In the ensuing silence I looked down, clenching my teeth not to say too much, let alone the precise opposite of the horse-dung idea, like crocodile dung, a most highly regarded contraceptive all over, but probably not welcome here at the moment, in these days of a widely-rumored need for healthy royal infant boys, none too soon. I kept looking down, overcome by alternating hot and cold flashes of fear, but consoling myself during these very-likely last moments of my life by studying her exquisite, long toes and crimson toenails. There were no hairs visible even on the big toes, not surprisingly, because the rich liked to be fully shaven, and all the nails were filed into elegant egg shapes, with the narrow ends pointing forward. I wondered how many hours it took originally to shape all the toes, and how often it would be necessary to touch them up, and what it would take to get such a job, given my substantial skills with my hands and all kinds of tools, and given the prerequisite of survival at the moment. I shifted my aching knees, to no avail. No hairs on her toes and legs, except, is that a curly-curly black hair lodged between the big toe and the gold-braided thong of the fine-fibered papyrus sandal, how long would that be when stretched out end to end, just curious, and how would I compare it to an appropriate hair of one of the finest servant girls, and how did it get there?

Her silence continued, and my back started to get stiff, so I stealthily raised my trunk a little, finding her bejeweled hands come into view, long fingers, crimson nails of similar shape as those on the feet, but longer and more pointed, the nail on the right pointing finger with an edge-crack, not surprising at all, for such a delicate beam sticking out so far. I thought of a clever device, an underlying reinforcement using other nail pieces, maybe from captive princesses of properly high blood, glued in there with my latest bull-ear-tail glue, invisible to all onlookers, except the likes of me, if any, at such a close range. Maybe that will save my tender skin if I am about to be marched down to the river as a result of my impudence. If I am not lucky and things get worse, the brute guard might say, like Seth did to Horus, 'Your backside is quite lovely.' But, thank you, Good Thoth and all your intermediary baboons, for the idea of strengthening the long nails of fine ladies. There may even be a lot of gold from making that tiny supplementary device, ten for the fingers and ten for the toes, for each Queen, and the same number for each noble woman, a very few will be fortunate to get it, besides all that plain gold, what about a ring like she is wearing on the same finger, or even better, a big signature ring for the whole Two Lands, in time, of course. I can be patient if the outcome is good and certain.

"Charm-Carver, you indeed are favored by Isis and have excellent fingers as widely spoken about, in addition to your strength and vigor every day, and you are not limping about. The charm is going to be useful for a long time, many times, more than three times a month. Rise. I only request that you make no other objects exactly like it for other women, to give this one all its available power, naturally." She briefly closed her eyes and lifted the charm to her nose, inhaling deeply. "Also, you must keep it a secret, like many other secrets that you will encounter. Tell me about the fastest stallions, I wish I had more time to spend with them, and with few people watching, until the proper time."

She studied her large ring, her eyes flashed. "The proper time, Dream-Carver, you must know from the scrolls that the big dream started in ancient times. Queen Sonefer first created a Great Female Horus, the King of Upper and Lower Egypt, the Daughter-Equal-to-a-Son of God Re, Meryet. There were a handful of others like her since her time, but not enough real mistresses of the Two Lands. Now Isis-Hathor has granted her dream and wisdom to me, to be more than a royal ornament, more than the First One Known to the King, more than the Wife of the Absent One, in good time, and you, you may be of value, become even a Great Strong Bull in the Two Lands, sipping beer with the goddess from her vessel through gold straws, in good time, so open your mind to Isis.

"The first step, driving the strongest stallions. I wish to learn it the no-hands way, like the great warrior kings are shown on the walls. Isis-Hathor tells me I too have the head and belly of a driver-

9

king, but no one is to know about it, yet. No one. We start now. Pick up those reins from that basket and wrap the ends around your waist as they should be, and talk your way through it. Make it simple talk, no Highness words to slow you down, but remember it is not for palace talk, loose or otherwise, ever. Pick up the reins!" She swept the chew-ball off the armrest, brown and sticky, it rolled on the floor for a distance of only a finger.

Her words were surprisingly quiet, perhaps to be heard by me alone, but they were echoing louder and louder in my skull. "Female Horus, Strong Bull." I reached for the reins that I found to be soft, red leather. I uncoiled them, worrying in a daze about which one should be on which side of me, but the fresh smell of the leather was reassuringly from my earthy side of the world. "Your … yes. Please hold the horse ends of the lines. Here, to drive by the belly, I wrap the right-side reins around my right waist, coming from the front, from the horse end, your position for the moment. Similarly for the left reins, but they go around my left waist first. There are options now, for the next action. For a very firm hold, I wrap them around my waist completely, one from the right and the other from the left, and finally tie them together at my back. For a relatively loose hold, which is my preference for high speed in starting off, and safety, in case of trouble and having to undo them, I stuff the reins at my back into my tight tunic or a tight belt. This is firm enough for normal usage, and yet they can be pulled out to cut loose in a hurry. This much is easy. The control of the horses with the reins tied on the waist this way is more complicated than holding the reins in the hands, and it takes daily practice to perfect it, but you can learn it, I am sure, very fast. Like this.

"When your belly, when your hips are moved forward evenly, left and right, the horses feel the reins being relaxed evenly, and on the word 'Go!' or 'Run!' they take off straight ahead, accordingly to the word, I mean, a yell. They are smart, better than the average baboon, but it helps if they recognize not only the word but the driver's voice, as well. Conversely, if the hips are moved backward, tightening the reins evenly, and the horses hear 'Slow!' or 'Stop!' they will obey again. If the hips are twisted, say, backwards on the right, tightening the right reins and relaxing the left ones, and they hear 'Right!' the bits in their mouths pull their heads to the side and command them to turn right. Conversely, for a left turn. With plenty of extra practice, it is possible, say, to turn and accelerate at the same instant. A firm footing within your personalized foot-straps helps one do this well, but it also means that the average driver, I mean the lazy ones, or those with no talent, cannot do it well and look relaxed in doing it."

"Tell me about the forward foot on the pole, like the monument of my Grandfather shows. He could do it anytime, even in battle, freeing his hands for axe and sword."

"That is the most difficult way to free the hands while driving. It is impossible when dressed in a long tunic. A short kilt is necessary for this position, first of all, so one leg can be flung over the breastwork of the chariot, to plant the forward foot on the pole, wedged between the stiffening braces attached to the pole just there. Now, the breastwork can be squeezed between the thighs, for a firm planting of the driver by the feet and the thighs, which is useful in a hunt or in battle. It is difficult for several additional reasons. The waist must be very flexible and strong to be able to twist the hips sufficiently for the forward-and-backward and turning commands. No wonder that many people who have not seen this great feat accomplished do not believe it can be done, thinking that it is nothing more than an artist's pandering to his king. In fact, I can do it myself, though certainly not as well as the famous warriors of the Great House, according to several scribes we can trust." I felt a flush, an idea, a thump of the heart. I might have an opportunity to return and return, for more and more, to really teach her this and that, but there is also an ominous warning, perhaps from Rehotep chirping in the back of my head, remember the peasant saying, 'the proud jug goes to the well once too often and becomes a dusty scribe's shards.'

She tossed her head, as if to clear a wisp of her hair from her eye. It occurred to me that the three-parted hair was unusual in its low-class origins, but royal finish, one that would take hours to make it look that way. "I will try the simplest method first." The Queen threw her end of the reins toward the basket. "Put the horse ends of the reins on the bit." I just noticed the gold bit in the shape of a stretched-out cheetah and the cheek pieces with falcon motives in the bottom of the basket. While I put the reins on the bit, the

11

Queen wrapped the other ends of the lines around her waist. "Turn around to face away from me, like a harnessed horse would be ready to pull me, and put the bit in your mouth," she said, laughing. "It is new and clean. And drink this wine quickly, so you don't dry out in the long haul. I will give commands to your mouth only by my belly, through the reins, for the test of my doing it properly. But if not well done, you cannot beat me, fast scribe. Get ready!" The goblet was overflowing, and the sweet-and-sharp juice dripped on my hands and I started a mental list of the probable ingredients while she went to the harpist and spoke into his ear, upon which the music became much louder. It was painful to my ears, but probably a good idea, in case unwanted ears were near the walls.

I was facing the large golden statue, seeing only a faint and broken reflection of the Queen and her big eyes and lips and reins in the mirror surfaces of the statue's belly and hips, trying to adjust the position of the heavy bit in my mouth with my tongue alone, when the first jerk snapped my head backward, for the great baboon, she is starting with a straight stop before getting going forward? She has a long way to go to learn the finer points of this, way long, though she has a perfectly wide hip to leverage the reins for the turns, and I only wished I could see her from the back, both of her ball-eyes equally firm, doing her twists and thrusts with the pretend horse, I must teach these special reins to my favorite dancer sometime.

I imagined her belly tightening, the finest tight belly in the Two Lands. She is learning fast, better than any dancer already. The first forward and then the turning commands to my head were gradual and nearly perfect, but soon my jaws hurt in depth, up and down and sideways, like my teeth from hastily eating a big date not long ago, or was it my purposely and stupidly cracking the seed, and then come worse, the experiments on my jaws in my Master's Tooth-Carver Den, he in the red tunic to cleverly hide my blood splatters and giving me a potion of fig-and-mandrake powder in dregs of excellent beer and talking up a long story loudly into my ear to divert my mind and delay my certain vomiting, all one-sided talk, given that I could not fully express myself for several reasons, not the last of it being that he doesn't tolerate that kind of mud-balls language regarding what is a fun experiment for him, on me, nor would the Queen about to carve my teeth tolerate it according to the official rules for supplicants, but what about other kinds of raucous rumors in the palace about the King, some say you can't say his name or a curse kicks in, but hard to resist, he being still too young or forever inexperienced with hedgehogs and such, then what is this taste on the golden bit and dribbling down my gullet, if not the fermenting mandrake fruit fresh from the hand of shining and love-loving Isis, where is the dizzying Queen Ankh now, there she is again everywhere in the statue, hiking up her long tunic to be able to straddle the alabaster chair-back like a real flying chariot's breastwork and squeeze it between her thighs, are they hairless like her toes, for a firm warrior-queen stance, a most lucky breastwork that is, and how rapidly are the fast-learning reins whipping around my ears from behind, it is funny, will I be a toy like her husband Tut's favorite Asiatic wrestler with one-and-a-half ears but not nearly as strong and bragging virile and winning every bout in the league, which way to go next, yes, Ankh laughs, I can see it in the belly of the statue, steer me around the corner, hope to see her behind, both good and plump, very close but never close enough, my head is jerked like the productive bit of a bowstring drill, and clearly … no … something inside my head begins to spin and crash in every direction in the dark … but I can escape from here as always by running alone into the cold desert to chill the fevers, a cheetah pawing the sand and pawing it again, then barely touching it.

2

Hedgehog Nose-to-Nose

"Carver, Count Carver. Yes, you will be."

The whisper, soft as a young ostrich's feathers, barely tickled my ear. Who is it, where am I? Yes, the lavender-scented feather, it must be in the smooth, oiled hand of Ankh, just what I was ready to grab. My leg twitched, and I worried about kicking her, so early in our time together, it could be a disaster. Now the feather went behind my ear, touching skin and hair and suddenly leaping to somewhere farther down, between my thighs.

"Yes, Future-Count of many useful titles, how many do you want, what do you say if it comes to ninety titles or more, honoring only part of your uncountable successes, almost a hundred, like the ancient great Sen's army of titles from Queen Hatsh. But more important now, quickly, let's get on track, make me laugh. Make me laugh! You hear me? Make me laugh! Don't be reluctant, I know you can do it any time you want, word is, you make any servant girl laugh and scream aloud, though I can't do that, or shouldn't, the walls have ears, so be gentle, but I want to laugh a little, and a little again, after years in the royal desert." She giggled, probably overflowing with anticipation.

The feather blocked something in my brain, I tossed my lucky dice to choose a good line and blurted out, "I saw my sweet lover's hedgehog eye-to-eye and nose-to-nose, all night." Immediately, I felt the blood drain from my face for the boldness and crudeness of it, where did I get the nerve to speak to her this way, but maybe she had already heard it from her boasting Asiatic wrestler, Silverbeard, that's where I first got it, in the smelly basket room of the sporting animals. I was praying that Rehotep didn't hear me, or else he would kick me out of his shop and my bed, perhaps forever.

Ankh was slow in her response, but luckily it was a smile turning into a laugh and a suppressed scream, but where is her feather now, down to my toes? No, it's sharper than a feather, it's a straw, and I am in a bed of straws, was it a dream, and Ankh was never here with me, and what is this, with Tut sitting cross-legged by my feet, a straw in each hand. His horse Swift Ray was straining from the stalls behind him to reach and nuzzle him. I inhaled the perfumed air of the stables deeply and forced my eyes to stay open longer, trying to sort out recent events. Indeed, the straw was reality.

What first came into focus was his overbite, rather pronounced from my vantage point of being below him, lips that were reputed to be a characteristic of his ancestors. I tried to rise up on my left elbow that was still sore from a nearly disastrous fall from a careening chariot in an ill-conceived experiment with running on one wheel only, aiming for the ultimate show-off before the Queen. The elbow was stupidly re-injured several times already, like biting a tongue on the same spot, day after day.

"I surmise?" He broke a straw. "I surmise Rehotep kicked you out, for your smelly room, or smelly corner, or something. I hear he can be fussy about little things like that. Lucky. I should pray to Thoth more often. Now we can spend more time in the stables together. Easy, Swift Ray, don't spit on me. What a hot breath. Sweaty breath means a fast horse? Surmise, surmise."

Why did he repeat words, and why did I, sometimes? Did my Master criticize the King for that also? I shifted ever so slightly, but the pain in my elbow made me hiss inward on my teeth.

He scratched his knees and elbows. "Hurting? I wish to hurt like that. Yes, yes. I saw it happen. It was a great stunt. You and I will practice it in secret, as soon as you can walk, then later, for the Queen to see. She will love my doing it. There were many warrior kings in history, pounding whole armies of enemies single-handedly, so it's not a big deal anymore. But a Daredevil King, with a cheetah-like chariot, flying like yours, that's the future, my future, great for tomb art. Right, Carver Boy? Learn to do that art, and I will let you do it for me. Let me win a race, too, against other fast horses, people, women. Right?"

"My Lord."

"My Lord, My Lord. Enough of that. Too much of that, by half. At least privately, you may call me Tut, if Son of the Sun God is too long. Reminds me, what do you think of Aten, my father's god, his only god? Ay and others of high seat hate Aten, because having only one god means less priestly busy work, but, I don't know. I don't know what's wise."

"I think, I think, it's hard to say. Maybe I will ask Rehotep. He knows more." What am I saying? I was sleeping in the stables because Rehotep kicked me out, a setback, but now it brings another kind of opportunity. He said it himself once, a rotten fruit may have a good seed in it.

Tut shook his head. "No. Don't ask him, not about that. There may be trouble. Enough to ask, today, this minute. Enough people know already that my Bastet has a rough tongue and soft lips. You know that even a big cat can be bitten by a small animal. King's luck. Enough of this 'My Lord' talk. Make it less. No matter what, we end up in eternity as a medium nothing. Slightly bitten by life at first, then by Anubis. Reminds me, make me a nice Anubis, no, make it two. Life-size. One a beautiful black, like its own soul, the other gold, not entirely, but good gold skin deep." He rubbed his chin, which seemed a little blistered and dark, probably from the crushed seeds of uli-uli fruit. I remembered my Master making it specially for him from expensive imported seeds, ostensibly for creating patterns of temporary decoration, but mainly to make the King's receding chin and generally soft features appear more prominent.

He scratched something with a straw on the bottom of my foot. In his deep concentration, his upper lip seemed to swell and protrude, and when he stopped, his neck straightened and lengthened, as if expressing pride. "What did I just write here?"

"I can't say. Invisible, for sure."

"Exactly. It is the Great Aten, my father's god. I miss him. But who chose him first? And now it's a crime? Did not have enough time with my father when I could have, then I wasn't allowed, it's bad, no matter which god rules." Where is he going with this strange line of thought? Why is he even talking to me? I suddenly felt sorry for him, and about his father, a weird feeling for somebody in this low position, but again, what about my father, and so many like me?

There was silence, I had to say something. "Who chose whom first? It may be to a king's advantage to choose a good god, but, why should a god care?"

He smiled, but with a tortured twinge. "Unfair to make a young man to choose a god? Listen. What if there is only one god, don't shake, and what if you take away that god? What? Can I?"

"Only, only, I can't say, only a god-king, yes, can think that way, I cannot." I hit my elbow into something, the pain shot to my head.

He made an impatient sweeping motion with his hand. "What if there is one and I want to take away two? Tell me, better yet, show me on your fingers, great scribe of reckoning." He puffed out a laugh, almost choked, but stopped suddenly and glanced behind him. "Enough. I am making a new, slender-stemmed paddle. Forgot to bring it, but one doesn't think of paddles when going to the stables. But then why am I talking paddles now, crazy world. What is the design principle in your shop? If it looks strong enough, it is more than strong enough? I don't envy the form of the Wise Baboon, but his brain, maybe my grandchildren, with effort and luck, brings me to the issue, the real issue. I woke up, woke up, Aten high already, saying, not much time, not much time."

"There is time, Sire. You are young."

"Maybe. Future-Scribe of Ninety-One-Titles, or more. Tell me. A hawk just out of the nest, it's hard. What if someone, maybe many someones, want to clip the wings, not with sharp blades, but with something in the wine, something invisible, shriveling one little feather at a time. And, they changed my name. Can you imagine? From Blah-Blah-Aten to Blah-Blah-Amun, for god's sake. You wouldn't do that to a dog, without asking."

"I can't recall any rumors of that kind, I mean, the clipping of the wings, the wine, or anything."

"What rumors, then? Of more little hawks? All dying?"

"Sort of. There are many people around you."

"Too many. Maybe that's why I like my horses, and your wheels. Fast wheels, by Thoth. You know what? We could start a great cult, like Imhotep, long ago, but still going strong. It could be fun, our cult lasting for thousands of years."

"Only you can afford to think like that."

"Sure. But it could be in your name, well deserved, in due course, of course, Carver as the greatest inventor and physician, eclipsing Imhotep even. But, it would be more likely to come about in my name, with a little management of the cult-starting process."

"You think big, Sire, bigger than anybody I have heard make a note."

"Somebody has to, in this court teeming with small minds. Of course, one has to live long enough for some things to transpire. But, can you trust anybody older? In fact, do we need so many old men in high power? One in particular, I would prefer to see elsewhere, like he would be great dozing off while tending to his goat circling on its tether. Maybe you can help me, eventually, before I am done in by them."

"Trust an older one? Yes. Sometimes, a little. You need one, if only one."

"Sure. But the first one in the cult, the head, that's a difficult position, isn't it? Like the King's midnight duty, three times a month. One has to become famous in the mind of the Queen, first, then in the mind of history. Women are strange."

"I think so. Don't know about queens, though."

"Take my word on this. She loves me now, but, listen, the other day I was reading a story about a great queen, interesting and slow, perhaps only half true."

"I could give you a good one." That was a bit of a stretch, only in hopes of developing this unexpected opportunity, soon realizing that if he takes me up on it, I might have to scrounge hard or even write the piece, but when? Luckily, he didn't follow up on this idea at the moment, and I quickly thanked the Wise One by prayer.

"Women are strange. What do you make of this? One night, Sothis is very bright in the sky, the one I call the Anubis star in the big constellation, with a nice reflection on the water, a good omen for the necessary procreation, loudly announced by all the high priests, and she is all hands on me and says, 'My hedgehog is ready to cry, make it cry,' and I say 'What?' and she says, 'Make it cry again, like once before, a smiling-Isis cry, happy, happy tears, it was so good because our baboons yelled to Sothis together at that instant, a very rare event, then I cried, too, softly, but you didn't hear it, you did not hear it, no, for the shame of Isis-Hathor, or any god or goddess you care about.' You know about this kind of woman talk?"

"A little." That was a lie, but what could I say? "Very little, actually. Maybe the Queen is different, she must be different." I almost offered to investigate the differences with proper experiments, but caught myself in time.

He smacked his lips. "You mean, if I practice with others?"

"Exactly. It might help, or might not. Even a son, not of the Queen, I understand, there are precedents."

"Right. What if a son, any son, will live? Jubilee. What if he is very strong? Surprise and more jubilee. What if he grows up healthy in spite of everything, but crashes? Could ruin many lives, including yours and mine, well before the cult spins in, what with so much malice around, like smoke clinging to the tunic."

"I did say it was risky."

"And all the while, she is clutching and kissing a sizable fertility charm, in both hands. Where does she get these silly objects, and why, anyway? But first things first. Hedgehog business, crying, babies, many of them. But what about me? Enough. I will practice, fast wheels, one-wheeler, show the world, stroke the cult. And you too, with me, we will get fat and old together, you will earn a great tomb, like Imhotep and Sen." He turned and raised his head toward the vehicles parked at the far end of the building, his sloping nose highlighted like a half arrow in the dim light.

"One-wheelers are especially dangerous, see my elbows and knees?"

"I don't care, I must be doing one-wheelers, then the hedgehog things should all fall into place, let them cry to the King. And I want them to hold me, not a fertility doll, with all their arms, many arms. Have you seen the eight-armed creature that was a gift to me? Dead, unfortunately, by the time it arrived, but it gives the idea. Fist-sized body from the sea of the north wind, eight long and funny, funny arms, imagine this animal wrapped around your hedgehog-poker, it's like four consorts at once."

"If you show it to me, Sire, I will try to make an imitation of the creature, for your private use. But no guarantee, it may be difficult, to make it with eight arms."

"I will. But enough time wasted here, a hedgehog is calling, have to go, not really, just thinking aloud, yes, I know that's dangerous in my position. Which should it be today, the Royal Ripe one or your Master's Smoky-Scented Servant with the perfect ball-eyes? A high degree of submission is nice at times. Help me, Wise Baboon!" He rubbed his eye hard and smeared half the thick black liner off the brow. "What's her name, a flower like Saam, or Haam? The best ball-eyes in the whole Two Lands, though a little young yet, so it could get even better. I say, your Master is the best of all my managers within shouting distance, for finding such treasures. Still, where do you find them? A beautiful flower, of course, the more dangerous, as well, one can assume. My mother warned me. Did your mother say things like that, too?"

"I can't remember." Was that a tear on his face? I felt knee-deep in a confusion of crocodiles about him, he needs my help, and for a bonus, see sweet Ankh again and again, my head felt heavier, as on racing into a curve, then immediately lighter, as on leaving the curve on the far side, where is half my silly head, has Seth already taken it into his dark depths?

"Well, enough." He patted his chubby cheeks with the thumb and fingers of one hand, in a quick, nervous, squeezing patter, his father was said to do the same at times, showing who knows what, and he began to hum a primitive tune as he slowly turned away to leave. "My pretty flowers, may Ren bring me your bounty and luck, your excellent fingers to oil and rub my feet, to remove years from my belly and teeth, and to keep my name alive for double eternity."

3

New Wings

Horus was a small dot at dawn in the western sky, but growing as it approached me. It was a spot against the pink upper part of the blue Belt of Isis-Hathor, which was darkest where it met the desert on the western horizon, briefly blending sky and sand. I could marvel at this Belt of the Goddess every day, it was thickest at the middle and pointed at its southern and northern extremes, sort of a bow-shaped half-lentil made of colored air over the whole Two Lands, thinning and sinking into the desert as if beaten down by the rising sun on the east, to reemerge on the eastern horizon at dusk, and growing from daylight into darkness while the Lord of the Horizon went down in the west, repeating the cycle of its destiny day after day, into eternity. I prefer to think of this phenomenon as the Goddess dressing and undressing every day, for the very few who could notice the Belt, though it is there in the sky for everyone, inseparable from the earth like one's shadow from his body, every clear day. Remember the old priest Harekh who said, in answer to my questions, that only one hundred people in the world are given the privilege each day to see the Sacred Belt in the Sky. A new person can see it only if a former seer dies. It's a good feeling, for that new person.

Of course, there is the small matter of possibly getting a belting of a different sort, not directly for watching the Goddess take off her Belt in the west, but for my taking the time from my shop duties early in the morning, especially being so young and new in the job, but the fine wings are worth the risk.

"iii-eeeee" screamed Horus as he dived from the sky on my latest bird-kite. The falcon's approach was perfect, with the sun blinding my kite, if it could see. His beak and talons snapped the thin sticks of the body and the woven wings, scattering my carefully selected feathers to drift randomly in a left-right-left-right dance to the ground – was my kite glue insufficiently cured? My taut string went limp from the kite's broken breast and snaked to earth in the gentle eastern breeze from the river. Was Horus real if he could not tell the kite was a fake bird? Or, was he fully aware of it, and just being jealous of something so beautiful and different in the awakening sky? For now, for whatever his reason, Horus won. Luckily, there is Thoth and plenty of other gods who might be happy to help me succeed with another kite, always better than the previous best, I just have to find the proper sacrifices and the means to pay for them. I threw my fist at Horus, and watched him shake his prey loose and depart.

As I collected the broken and torn pieces and wound up the string, I noticed for the first time a tall stranger standing by his gleaming chariot on a small hill. How did he get there without making noise and a dust cloud? Perhaps Horus is indeed a powerful god, attracting all my attention. I wished to run away, but an invisible fishing line reeled me in. There was no dust on the vehicle, so it must be new, or wiped clean every day. I have never seen a new chariot before. And the two shiny but not sweaty black stallions with their soft pink nostrils, twitching, perhaps unnerved by the screaming Horus, it would be heavenly to touch them and calm them down. I took a step or two to get closer to them, suddenly felt a flush of panic and ran off without looking back. There was no need to look back, since the sound of the wheels and the hoofs was soon all around me, drowning my own hissing breath, when will the whip slash across my back, but there is new hope in cutting sideways to the shortest path over the effluvia of the temple grounds, dying for air, but owning the best reckoning all the way to the carriage shop.

At the shop I hid the kite parts, suppressed my breathing and soon buried my head in my job of chiseling out the through holes in the cracked heavy solid wheel, to accommodate the repair straps of rawhide to sew up the deepest and longest cracks. From what mysterious land did this huge piece of wood come from? The wheel is two cubits across, by Thoth. Harekh had said that there was a land, far from the Lands of the Sand, where there was a vast spread of woods for the pleasure of contemplative minds. Will I ever see that? Not likely, since the priest had also said that what you seek is here, you stylus-licker-wannabe, in this remote place, so I wonder if he is right in everything he says, especially with his rather slow counting on his fingers and persistent dandruff and probably wishing for more baldness for some relief.

The hardest part was to countersink the straps on both sides of the wheel to minimize the abrasion damage it would get when going through brush and construction debris. It was exciting work a few months earlier, coming from the permanently mud-splattered pottery shop of the temple, but now the kite idea was more important to me, except that nobody would give me a brown glass bead for it.

When I first raised my head, I saw the tall stranger at the office end of the shop, talking with the boss. They drifted in my direction while talking, and I became dizzy. What could this all mean? "My Lord," I heard the words of my boss, "a boy's ear is on his back, and he listens only when the rod speaks to him."

I tried to insert a rawhide strap into a hole in the wheel, and felt like a person with his head in the lion's mouth. Will I be sent back to the pottery shop? Not that the carriage shop was devoid of hell, what with the lead apprentice ordering me the first day here to pick up a heavy copper ingot, and it was hot, searing my hands. And, just two days later, when I was still in a black mood, another apprentice was yelling for help at the far end of the shop, but when I ran there at cheetah speed, an invisible thin wire was yanked up and across the isle by the hiding devils, and it snapped my head backward into darkness, to their chorus bellowing "Mudcarver, Mudcarver."

Still, everything had been worse at the pottery shop, perhaps because the work was so much less interesting there. And, that's where the stupid name started. The apprentices sent me with the biggest cart to pick up a load of supplies, which was actually only a handful of wet clay. When I returned, straining at the straps of the two-man cart, with the tiny heap of clay in the center of the platform

- I should have been smart enough to hide it - they were all lined up on both sides of the entrance, cheering and chanting "Mudcarver." I sprung to the clay and hit one of the young monsters in the face with it, all of it perfectly on the nose, I am always proud of my aim, but it was like spitting in the sky and getting a rain of spittle, as they all piled up on me. This was partly lucky, because most of them could not reach me through all the bodies. Still, the bruising was severe, and I might never recover from it completely.

This bruising reminded me of the frequent caning I used to get from Uncle Qedess. Will I now be sent back to him? He was swift with the cane, surpassed the whole town in swiftness, and it was hard to get away from him. He used the cane to fancy himself as in his soldier days, claiming that he was excellent with his arms. He was not my favorite man, but he undeniably had some talents worth observing. He started out with mud he did not own under his fingernails, but he eventually acquired a great field, and a boat of 33 cubits long and a smaller boat to ferry people for a fee during the enriching inundation, but actually he got all of these from his mother, Ibbeb, as rumor had it. She had more wrinkles than a sand dune, and said to me once, "get rich so you can teach him a big lesson." Didn't say how to do that, but she took me far away when the Uncle was ill, to the pottery shop. Thoth bless her memory.

Will they send me back to the pottery shop? Will they tell me anything? The boss shook his head vigorously in response to something the stranger said quietly, most likely about me, but at least he wasn't yelling, which must have been depressing for him, though it was still early in the day. His funny tic under the left eye appeared, and he gestured oddly. Unexpectedly, he turned to nodding agreeably, which could have been the result of the stranger flashing gold, discreetly. I willed my hand to stop shaking and pulled the last loop of rawhide through the pair of suturing holes straddling the crack in the wheel, cut the excess strip off, and wedged the loose end in the hole with a small piece of wood. The rawhide will dry and tighten itself around the crack like a snake on a rat, to last forever.

Afraid to look too often to the side, I started working on another crack in the same wheel, when the stranger moved closer to me. A servant brought for him a bundle of smooth ebony sticks and red leather pieces that suddenly popped out and amazingly became a small chair, like a new gift from Thoth. He sat down without saying a word. The pair of holes in my wheel was ready for the suturing straps, and only the countersinking depressions needed a chiseling touchup. I took a strip of rawhide from the wet pot, and measured its thickness with a stick scale. Four times that thickness was the required depth of the countersinking, so I chiseled and measured, chiseled and measured. I pulled loop after loop through the holes. The last loop was difficult to get in the crowded hole, it needed a touch of oil and a leader string. Finally, it came through like a small fish on a heavy line, plopping out of the water. I trimmed the hide, wedged its end in the hole, another repairing strap to last for a thousand years if not abused by careless workers. I ran a hand over the finished smooth surface of wood and rawhide spanning the crack, my fingertips savoring both materials, but wary of the penetrating eyes of the person of unusual scents sitting on the little red chair. It was difficult to look at anything else. When will I have a chance to make such a beautiful and clever object, and who will buy it? I rolled the wheel into the sunlight to make the straps dry faster, brushed my clothes off, worried for a moment about a dark oily spot over my belly, and came back hesitantly for another task.

"Good," said the stranger to me as he rose, adjusting both shoulder straps of his white tunic, then his headband, while ignoring the shop boss, what's his name, yes, Glodi, who was standing silently a little farther away, outward-turned hands laid on his bent knees, head down, face drained of color, shrunk into a mouse-like posture from his normally bloated self of constant tongue at best and often roaring in the faces of workers for any reason or no reason. I almost smiled at the thought of his likely wishing to spit angrily to the side just now, but afraid at last, this boss of mine for too many months, with awful breath and uncouth habits from hell, erratic in behavior. Still, I was not entirely happy at his discomfort, a new feeling that surprised me. Perhaps it was his deepening wrinkles and spreading facial tics, or my sudden regret for having secretly modified his precious great artificial penis for Afterlife in the Field of Reeds, changing it into a subtle pointed head of Growling Anubis and painting it black.

The stranger motioned to me and I followed him outside. A small linen-like cloud blunted the sun for a moment, and it cooled my face. In passing the wheel that I had just finished, he stopped briefly and ran a hand back and forth over the suture areas, wood and rawhide. He did it slowly, seemingly totally absorbed in the repair area, with fingertips sliding one way, nails the other, like painting with a brush, back and forth. I was petrified, thinking hard about what I could have done better to make the surfaces more perfect, and the memory of one particular slip of the chisel made my throat recall the big sour vomit from a recent food experiment gone wrong, what kind of forbidden berries were they with honey, but the honey not helping enough, my mind turned into a blank stone surface, and my throat more sour.

The stranger patted the wheel's rutted running surface, the last pat the loudest, impatient. "Carver, pack up your bundle. Come. Do you want to drive?"

4

Don't Spit in the Desert

Tut in disguise? I craned my neck from the deep shadow of my hiding spot out into the moonlit courtyard, momentarily forgetting that his personal guard was likely to be scanning the area from a similarly dark corner. Why is he in disguise, and what is he up to? Does the Queen know? His guard must know at least a little, but how to approach him and make him talk without risk to myself? I must find out, I must understand this.

In disguise? My head turned hot and cold as the idea took hold, it was the slightly hesitant step on his left foot that was the clue. It was rumored that his double, while good in facial features like the overbite, was quite forgetful about the details of representative movements of the limbs. I heard and felt a mosquito on my ear, but afraid to slap it and reveal myself, I just shook my head, to no avail. When the distant figure disappeared through the narrow door to the stables, I spun around to run, blinked too long, and hit my forehead into a rough-hewn post. A plummeting star burst into the deepest chamber of my brain, leaving an afterglow as I staggered away. The star was familiar. Adding insult to injury, a chorus of sneering apprentices erupted from the unhappy half of my memory, all around, seemingly every one of my enemies in the Two Lands, hurling at me the name "Mudcarver, Mudcarver."

"Tut in disguise?" Rehotep laughed after I burst into his shop's front room and described my observation, but he also cast a wary glance toward the door. "I told you many times," he said, "to throw away the devil's secrets of that boiled Nubian beer. Come here, young man, it's time to test your breath. All right, it is passable, just between us, but could be better. If you want to get within ten cubits of Queen Ankh once more in your life, as you dream every night under the hot sheet."

"But I never …" I felt the bump pulsing, it must have turned as crimson as the Queen's toenails. How does he know? In a flash, I saw her wiggling her big toes rubbing the thongs of her golden sandals, barely sticking out from under her white tunic, but banish the thought. That long tunic, though, is not good for extreme driving as the warrior kings are depicted, but she wants to do it, so there is an opportunity to get her into something shorter, are her legs really shaved, and all over? Furthermore, there is another related opportunity, start up a school for women drivers, a small and exclusive school for the richest, their hips are wide, ideal for tugging on the reins with good leverage, should I mention this idea to my Master soon, or only after he dies? Stupid.

"Sure," Rehotep continued, perhaps absentmindedly, as he was starting to set up his new bow-drill spark starter that he bragged about for weeks, while working on it in secret, which was his favorite way of working. A lamp was lit already, only one, on account of his eyes being sensitive to artificial light, he had claimed. More likely, he was saving the scented imported oil that he insisted on using. After all, sunlight never bothered his eyes. "Sure. I know about queens and such. Perhaps you can imagine that I was young at one time. Listen. I will give you a new sticky chew-ball to suppress that low-class beer breath. Imported from the north, loaded with fine spices. If you deserve it, later I will give you some others that are brought from even farther north. Why am I doing all this for you? Because I noticed some progress in you. Not enough to impress the average crocodile, but acceptable, when there is a shortage of young talent around. So, if you keep it up, learning the mending of rich bones and the carving and bending of stubborn elm for the secret racing spokes, within a year or two I will have you at my elbow, in disguise of an old maid, of course, when I examine the Queen. For now, watch this." He put fresh friction-resin in one of the starter holes, replaced the worn fire-stick in the spinner shaft and inserted its tip in the hole. He yanked on the bow to spin the drill-shaft and watched intently for sparks to emerge from the board's side slot. After several tries, the little tinder by the open slot caught a succession of sparks and began to smolder. He blew on it with a sustained breath, amazing how long he could blow while his stomach seemed to collapse, touched a wick to the tinder, and uttered a small yell in triumph.

"The King will be pleased, having had trouble with his old sparkers in the dark. This one is small and easy to use, don't you think? Yes, one day you might have to examine a Queen, perhaps without me being there, but don't bet on that. Work for it. In the meantime, it's dangerous for both of us, even for a noble Count, but with an especially gruesome end for you, a red-muddy end to your peasant dreams. But don't shiver prematurely. Before you are ready for the Queen, you may attend sometime when I examine the King. Oh, yes. Was he limping, or hesitant? Was he using a cane?" He stared into a dark corner, not at my wound. Would he notice a baboon's head on my shoulders?

"Just hesitant. No cane, probably." I wished for a cane myself, then for a chair, and darkness. The new light was indeed almost too much.

"Probably? You were staring at the King but not seeing his cane? That will not do here, boy. Not in a million years." Each word hit my aching head, and it took me a while to recover. What is happening to him today? It's different from yesterday. Must be a tooth or his belly. He put the smoking starter set in a copper box and placed a lid on it, but blue-gray wisps were escaping for a while.

I coughed because of the smoke and uncertainty about what's best to say, and how strongly to put it, to the Master. I studied his wrinkles. "Sire, please. The cane might have been invisible to me if it was hidden by him on purpose. I mean, if he was holding it at his far side. And, perhaps it was his favorite, the thin reed cane he cut himself on the river bank. He might prefer the thin one, to make it less visible. He is only seventeen. I would."

He turned with the lamp and looked me in the eye closely. "All right. But what, under Thoth's watch, after so much of my glass beads and purest electrum had been spent on the sacrifices, happened to your head? That reminds me, have you collected the molten materials after the last sacrifice, for reusing them? Did you keep them well separated for easier handling later? Remember, the gods appreciate the superior labor going into the objects more than they need the base materials. Ah, and your head. Were you attacked by spies so near this shop? Carver, always carry your knife, and learn to use your hand mirror cleverly, to see behind you. Here, put this copper scalpel to your head to cool the bump while I wash up to cut out that ugly splinter. Remember to wash your muddy peasant hands every day."

"There was no attack, Sire. I ran into a post, one of the new ones." The chorus began to pound in my head again, but he was silent. Is he going to help me, or does he save the real potent salves for the royal family? I wish I could heal myself, like he has been known to do on occasion, but I feel stupid and more hurting than he is, even when his belly aches so much that he can't hide it.

He gently touched my forehead. "This bump was from a new building post? Those Hittite prisoners are too cheap in the bargain, I have told the King more than once, to no avail. There must be enough of our own peasants who would not sabotage skinning a tree, and do it fast and smooth, for bread alone." Rehotep quietly opened the door to check outside, and closed it carefully. "I did hear something, probably one of Captain Minnakht's men, slipping into the shadows. I tell you, be careful with anybody from Ay's clan. Watch your words. No doubt, they will be talking to you in time, as long as you have a chance to visit the royal chambers, with me or without me. Also remember that Court-Regent Ay may be old, but he has infinite ambitions. Also, he politely listens to my advice about his health, and takes my most expensive salves with no reimbursement. I must say, though, that he knows his wines. If he talks to you behind my back as it is most likely, and gives you some wine to take away, accept it without feeling any obligation, and I will help you taste it.

He returned to examining my head. "Do not worry, I will pull it out in one quick move, it is not as hard as getting a screaming, reluctant demon out of a skull, the biggest job for the healer, as you will find out by your own hands. Note that we should use a large drill bit for live skull bones, at least like a thumbnail, but the handy little bow-drill is not strong enough for that, I mean, to make it fast, and time is of the essence, for a live head. Think about it. You can practice on clean, dried skulls, you can have a cartload of them, of any tribe or prisoners. What do you prefer?"

"Sire, I prefer racing wheels. I want to get high speeds sooner, better cornering. I have an idea for stiffening the rim without adding much weight."

"But riches come from doing sick heads. Sand-dwellers, Asiatics, Nubians, Kushites. I mean, these are for practicing the drilling of them, not for curing them, and the big gold will come later. In any case, always measure the thickness of the skull for practice, not an easy task working inside those shells, and use the thickest heads to set a challenge, and not be unpleasantly surprised when it's too late during a real job, well into the screaming. Stop jerking your head. It will sting only briefly, though if this splinter was a little bigger, it could be a spoke in our next chariot model. Where did these godless carpenters learn their trade? If I say another word to the King, I will surely get yet another big project to manage, all for the same palace food. Of course, much better food than you had at Deir Temple. If you don't stop jerking, the splinter will stay there, for all to see, including the Queen, if you ever get that close to her. Good."

I tried to see what he was doing to my forehead with his sharp-pointed tool, viewing myself in his eyeball, but my whole head was too tiny an image, and anyway, his eyebrows were interesting at this close range, a few turning white at their tips, some from their middle, among the many dark ones, and one, a big-curly, similar to the one that fell to the Queen's foot, but his is all white, funny.

His hands were steady as if bound in dried sinews like the spokes to the hub of a wheel, but soft and soothing, for a man, the same as when he woke me from the nightmare of Uncle Qedess beating me and my mother with a long cane and chasing us all over the village, I lost her when I tried to leap across a wide canal and almost made it, falling back toward the bloated donkey among the rotting lotus leaves, luckily his cane was not that long, but he pulled out his ten-cubit crocodile whip, making me scramble out from the smelly mud, suddenly there is another canal to leap across, barely making it to the far shore, brushing a dead donkey, but his whip is now twenty cubits long, nipping my back and wrapping my ankle, quickly get it off, good, but there is a wider canal and a dead crocodile to leap over, where is the path home, where is my gourd full of clear water, luckily, it was always in my hand, but sadly, cracked in two places, three, four, damn this ability to count. Rehotep's voice was as soothing as his hands, 'Don't cry, little buddy, don't run, you will fall out of the bed again,' and a vague memory arises of even softer fingers brushing my face, briefly brushing, forehead and temples and cheeks, never enough, very strange, how, years later, as little as a fleeting memory of mother's hand on the face makes for a tickling in the crotch, as if the fingers were reins to magical horses, should I ask him about this? He probably knows all about it, but I must ask him at another time, careful about what to say and when.

Without any warning, he hit my forehead backwards with the palm of his hand, there was only a tiny lightning stab in the wound, and he held up the splinter, grinning and pursing his lips like a silly baboon. I breathed with a sigh at this apparently successful event, he saved me again. "Is it all out? Thank you, Sire. It would be good to learn to do that as well. Too bad about the blood getting on your hands."

He pressed the splinter into my palm and laughed. "Don't worry. You will not have to pay for my skill. Others will. Listen. There is profit available without getting messy with blood, too. Take limping. Not just anybody's limping, but a King's, so, he was limping, as you say. Sometimes I think he can control it to a certain extent. It is barely noticeable when the Queen is near him, but he lets down when she is not watching him. It takes an effort, sometimes a huge effort."

Did he prick the skin of my palm with that stupid splinter? I felt something but was afraid to look at that moment. So many wounds, so many illnesses. "Sire, will you heal him? He is so young. Or, can the other physicians do something? He has so many. I hear that the Queen brings them in, even foreigners of pale skin and strange eyes and even stranger bags of medicine. Does it drive him crazy? I wish I could help him, or, her. I heard she wants a healthy king, and sons."

"Indeed, and all that. And no, a million physicians could not help him, certainly not completely. Nor would it be perfect for many of the physicians, to lose such a top patient by curing him. But I warn you. You hear too much, and soon you will talk too much. Remember the ancient travelers' advice. Don't spit in the desert if your water-gourd is dry. I say, scratch your itch with one hand only at a time, stick to the work I give you, and you will live happily. Perhaps you will appreciate it later. Thank Thoth for everything that you have already." He turned away from me and went to his scribe set. He rubbed his bloody hands for a long time in a piece of white linen, threw it in the basket for the washer-man, picked up a medium red stylus, and studied its point.

It just occurred to me that he always wiped his hands before touching papyrus, sometimes repeatedly as if trying to delay the writing. Strangely, once he got going, he seemed to be spending a little more time every day with the writing tablet on his lap. His lips came to life, though silently, like small banners weaving and snapping in the breeze, and his fingers like playing an invisible musical instrument in the air, and finally, when all his toes started to lift and tap his own sandals, to an inner beat, raising tiny puffs of dust, I knew he was ready to put the stylus to the fresh papyrus. Did he also like the smell of it? His nostrils flared as he inhaled deeply, bending to the sheet, repeatedly. Though the smell of new papyrus was pleasant and even exciting to me, I wondered about the material's permanence, and why would anybody prefer papyrus to stone in the eternity business, an enterprise that so many people in the palace were so keen on pursuing? The best guess is laziness, since carving stone takes much more time and effort than scribbling with ink, and it is a dusty job. Clearly, the scribes these days are more interested in quantity than quality, and just hope for the best regarding the endurance of the product. Perhaps, in his case, it was also a matter of physical ability, so one could say that papyrus was invented for old scribes to save their gnarled hands for another day.

Being ignored is not my preference, but there are compensations. I quietly withdrew to a dark corner and stayed to watch him, uninteresting as he was when bent over the tablet, thinking leisurely about what to do with my unexpected freedom. What was Ankh pondering and doing at this time, and what does she want in the future? I should make another fertility charm for her, one bigger and better than the first, and to fit her long fingers to her liking, and what role is there for the long fingernails? I could design a better charm if I had a small jug of beer in this corner, design it for her, while aware of everyone important swirling around in the mist. Ankh is young, and so is Tut, but limping. Ankh is healthy, not counting fertility matters, so will live long. Ay is old, Horem is almost old, Rehotep is slowing down, look at him, self-absorbed, fumbling with the curling sheaf of papyrus. Now, how to reckon my prospects, in this shop, and all around, and not to forget the long fingers and crimson fingernails and excellent ball-eyes, all quietly beckoning, and in the meantime, sniff around, he must have a jug of beer hidden nearby, then my gourd will not be dry, he won't mind, since, after all, it was he who said at Deir Temple to the boy, 'Do you want to drive?'

5

Hedgehog Tickler for the Queen

I tried to get her out of my mind, but the more I tried, the more impossible this simple task seemed to become, like the best clap net still allows some fat birds to escape, with no hope of getting help from my Master, the only one worth asking about personal matters besides Thoth, one of my favorite gods, because I could not ask him without stammering and blushing, and if I did, what is the evidence that he ever had any relevant experiences at my age? Oh, yes, once he said, 'Tie your foreskin against involuntarily putting flesh on your fantasy. It also helps against getting the itchy skin in the worst spot when walking over dusty chaff.' Why? Was he joking or pretending to have insight? And dusty chaff where? I thought I got away from that for good. Do the tying with what? Twine or rawhide? Not rawhide, it tightens upon drying, though not before the bladder calls. Perhaps some kind of a clever clip on the skin, for speed. And what would the wise baboon say? Is there any chance for profit in it? Maybe try it personally, get experienced and finally set up shop, there are millions of young men, each dreaming nightly and ready to try something new and exciting.

Enough of idle stupidities. How was Ankh enjoying her life at this time? Only one thing was certain. She was poised and would not show exuberance, but she was enjoying herself more than mortals could imagine, a life worth sharing, if at all possible, while I wander alone in my dreams, or have to wash the dog piss off the new spokes. Those dogs, they wake from their stupor and make a beeline to the best wheels as soon as they stop rolling. Remember Rehotep's best advice, by his own claim: 'Always carry a little gold so the dogs don't think you are a plain spoke.' As if the likes of me had a little gold to carry around against stray dogs, and if no dogs had ever marked the gold-sheathed royal wheels, and the average mongrel pretends to mark wheels even when there is nothing coming out of him, something worth thinking about.

What would be a good gift to her? Maybe my latest water-wings made of flat bundles of pond irises, to be tied to her arms with my own fingers, and teaching her how to swim with them, with graceful speed, waving at the amazed noble ladies and visiting dignitaries. Waving, like I was taught by my Master to always wave from the chariot at the nameless old man tending his cows at the three-palm split in the desert road, as he sits in the shade and waves at us far in advance of our dust cloud, and long after we are gone. One day I will stop and ask him the names of his cows, and watch the morning-Re-like glow on his face.

I closed my eyes and saw her fingering the sacred hip girdle and double-sacred triangular hedgehog of the small Hathor figurine on her neck, and praying to the big golden statue of the goddess, and playing with her many charms, perhaps secretly and strategically choosing favorites from brimming trunks, a room full of such trunks, surely, from everything one hears, she was dreaming of conceiving a son, a healthy son at last, assuring and strengthening her royal status.

A tickling on my feet caused me to open my eyes. It was Scrawny Boy, his skin of pale gold with streaks of dirt, silent, but looking up with his big brown eyes, unnerving Anubis eyes. He was probably kicked away by Rehotep, and now he was trying his luck with me, not in real love, but with an object of opportunity. It was annoying, just when my thoughts were drifting in an interesting direction. Even more so, it was annoying because it made me quite uncomfortable, perhaps having been a similar barefoot boy not too many years earlier, in memories that should be burned or buried. I looked at his unruly, curly hair, the few tender parts of the scarred body of barely ten years of age, narrow sand-dweller mouth under the long nose, narrow because of irregular and poor meals for ten years, thick lips, the lips of ever-increasing hunger. He was like a keen puppy, equally ready to play and to drop off upon any minute gesture of friendliness, real or imaginary to him, now splayed on the ground and trying to touch my foot at least in a tiny area, preparing for his nap if playing was not imminent. I nudged him away with my foot, gently but firmly, and he sighed happily from the momentarily applied pressure from my warm foot on his naked belly. He closed his eyes, allowing me to pull farther away without making noise, where was I?

The golden Hathors reminded me, and I tried hard to carve the precious memories deep in my mind, each goddess in that room had a smoothly shaped hedgehog, whether remotely hinted at through imaginary thin cloth, or boldly delineated, by its artist creator, raising the fundamental question about the discreet Queen's own, given that royalty, and the rich in general, preferred to be fully shaved and oiled at all times, and to put it bluntly, was Ankh's own exulted hedgehog shaved every day or so? I could just about hear Rehotep growl, 'I warn you,' but forget the old man. The question of the shaving is most intriguing, in fact, it could drive one to turn into a mad baboon with a parched tongue, while the full body shave is highly likely, to the confident reckoning of nine fingers out of ten if the bare armpits of the Queen are reliable indicators, then where did the single curly-curly on her sandal come from, of course, there are other females in the royal household, like unshaved young servants of fair skin and shape, though that remains to be fully investigated, and what should a young man of excellent taste prefer? What about the King? What does He like in the ways of skin and body? Does She do it for His pleasure, and maybe even on Him, as well, if she prefers a hairless man? And is He doing it on Her? That could be delightful, by the sensitive blade of Thoth and grace of Isis, altering nature, working in new arts, especially on the thighs and the rich-skanky hedgehog, the rest is just labor.

If the reserved Queen prefers a hairless man in general, how to find that out, the great secret of the Universe, and grave danger, perhaps to the extent of ninety-five or more fingers out of a hundred, but can't stop now, like the burning forehead can't stop the fever, nor can a king with a poisonous thorn in the flesh kick Anubis away from his own lengthening and darkening shadow.

Thinking too long, waiting too long, it's the coward's way. Another important question is, what to give her next that she would appreciate? What, what, what? Help her to feel the exhilaration of speed, hands desperately grasping to stay afloat on air, hair blowing wildly in the wind made by horses would be fantastic, but not private enough, not something she can hold and caress for many a day. I could create a better shaver, maybe? Can't ask anybody for advice, it might be best to make an excellent blade and try it on myself first. It could have some extra benefits, like letting out the excess heat from my brain and crotch. What to give her to make her cool hedgehog tremble? Yes, yes, another charm, a most worthy recurring thought, since she loves and needs charms. I should make another fertility charm for her, one bigger and better.

She loves all things foreign, of course, but, like all women, in the bottom of her heart she probably most appreciates the earthy local gods with their recognizable parts and uses. Our Ptah-priest says this all the time. She could certainly never have too much of Hathor, Bes, Ta-wer, especially in an excellent-equipped charm and spirit, it is good to see this fabulous charm in the mind's eye, make it from the finest of materials that don't have to be expensive, and imagine how to give it to her and what to say for best effect, that's the hard part. Except that Rehotep should not see this thing, he is too old for adventure at this level.

Yes. To make it a practical soul-and-hedgehog-tickler, Hathor should be the centerpiece. Let's see... half a cubit tall, two fingers thick, with a prominent head enhanced with a headband and cow ears just big enough to do some extra tickling in every sense of the word, but rounded and smooth little ears so as not to cut the sensitive royal skin. At Hathor' feet, there should be, like tiny children at their king father's feet, a pair of balls in the shape of fat little gods, certainly the dwarf Bes is one, or his female version Bestet, for a queenly good joke, but in either case for emphasizing music and joy and dance and offering fertility, good birth and a healthy infant.

The second ball, of course, should be a fat little Ta-wer, the image of a pregnant Great Water Beast, she will also appreciate that, and she will get all the charm's jokes with all the serious underpinnings regarding the royal hedgehog and everything beyond. But wait, two balls is too simple, any peasant has that, let's go a step further, make it three, but what? Think about that, as long as it takes.

There, it's done in a blink of the mind's eye. The next question, what material to use? All in one, like wood or stone or clay, or only the half-cubit-tall Hathor object being firm and the attendant balls slightly loose, realism of one kind or another, and the third ball, coming unexpectedly like a lightning in the parched desert, an even more excellent ball, should be the fertility fruit, the shiny-hairy, reddish punikha-alma, loaded with a multitude of healthy seeds, more than enough for the keenest of queens. There, the royal Deep-Tickler, the first of its kind, soon to be ready to wake up in the most private world, the assuredly eternal world of the fully shaved and scented Queen with urgent needs, from the fine hands of her humble servant.

6

Count Ay's Wines

The messenger was waiting, tapping the threshold with his light spear, growing impatient. I did not want to go, but had to, and Rehotep was far away that day, perhaps for several days, so I could not ask for advice, let alone protection. It occurred to me that the timing of this messenger's coming was chosen precisely for the reason that my Master was away. I thought about feigning illness and thus avoid going, but could not think clearly beyond that step. I thought a quick silent prayer but forgot to dedicate it, and nodded to the messenger in confusion. The soft words from his burly face did not inspire confidence. "Count Ay, Priest and Prince of Amun wishes to see you, at this hour." How many times did he say this, if sometimes garbling the name? Clearly, he was not chosen for the task with the same care as the Count may select a scribe to adorn his tomb.

A hairy brown spider started to climb his spear and I hoped it would reach his hand before I had to respond properly. No luck, the spider turned back down and was soon crushed under the tapping shaft. Unexpectedly, the image of Uncle Qedess emerged from the depths of my mind, and an urge to run twitched my thighs. I asked for time to change my tunic to a cleaner one, just to delay the inevitable and allow me to think why this complication was happening to me and what to do, but nothing came up. Soon I was carefully stepping over the smashed spider for better luck, and marching behind the fellow who was smelling of burnt sacrifices, but which tribe? Funny to think that not long ago I was suspicious of cleansing powders pushed into my hands, and now, if I were a King or Count, I would change these people's habits.

The messenger passed me to another man just outside Ay's quarters. There was a rapid succession of transfers, perhaps meant to help me lose count, each transfer with a small but noticeable improvement in superficial qualities of the individuals. The last one searched me and took away my whittling knife, which upset me because it was one of my few treasures from my younger years, and I was seldom without it. At the next door was Captain Minakh, who had dark oily hair and was clean-shaven, and dressed in a short white tunic with a touch of red on the bottom edge. He also searched me, with unusually long and strong fingers, much too closely.

We passed a servant who was greasing the hinges of an enormous, thick door. It creaked just a little as it was opened for us, eliciting a kick from Minakh who grunted from the effort. The room inside was bathed in a glint of gold, lit by several fret lamps, with the kind of interlacing foreign decoration, rectangular in form, that I heard came from a land of innumerable islands far in the north, across a very large sea, perhaps wider than the length of the river, hard as it is to even contemplate. Rehotep had claimed that people from that land were from the farthest with a desire to steal our secrets of the King's new racing chariots, the ones with cheetah-like agility. They came as merchants, like so many others, and wanted to spy and steal like the rest.

There was nobody else in the room, and the two of us stood side by side, silently. Which one of us was supposed to break the silence, and if it was for me to say something, what? I stayed quiet, figuring that he had more experience with situations of this kind, and took in the room to pass the time, wishing only for a handful of roasted pumpkin seeds to busy my mouth and mind. Many bouquets of flowers in bensu-vases by the walls. A large relief showing Ay standing on his chariot, horses surging, reins on his waist, he is aiming an arrow at a double sheet of copper target with five arrows already halfway through, but one of them without feathers. The smells were dominated by the lamps, burning aromatic gum-resin mixed with fat. At first it was pleasant, but later it turned too rich, and I coughed, nervously. There was food on several small, veneered, inlaid tables: honey in jars, fruit in baskets, bread rolls. My mouth began to water, and I became self-conscious of my repeated swallowing. To the vultures with him! In a flash of anger, I stepped to a table and rolled the fruits in my fingers, choosing a fig, without looking at the man.

The wine jars were unusual. Two-handled fat jars with conical lids, standing on wide conical bases. There were also tall and thin, one-handled foreign amphoras, Mitanni maybe, on thin-legged bronze tripods, reaching upward like egrets struggling to swallow fish. Several round-bottom wine cups were lying on their sides, and a large one with a lion's head was standing on its sand basin next to an armchair of elaborate decoration with battles and hunting scenes. Was that a Wishing Cup beholding felicity? A traveling bard sang about such a cup of a great warrior king not long before. My head slowly turned to study everything in the room, while munching on the fig, and spitting the stem to the side.

A cat behind me attracted my attention. I heard it before I saw it, large and fearsome with gray speckled fur, walking on crusty paws or stiff claws on the thin floorboards, that's how I could hear it from a distance. Village people would have hunted it down with clubs and a pack of dogs. Another noise made me turn again, and saw the man sitting on the chair.

"Do not be shy, boy. I mean, enjoy the fig." He handed me my knife, after studying its simple figures and patting it appreciatively. His ashen round face made a distorted little smile as he motioned to Minakh to leave. The door made another creaking sound in closing, and I heard the Captain's kick on the servant before the door shut. Ay reached for a bread and flicked off a bread beetle before offering half of it to me, along with a piece of ox tongue. He picked up a dom-palm fruit and thoughtfully brushed the excess sweet crust from it with his kerchief of fluffy byssus. He wiped his lips with the fabric and raised his eyes upward. There were no wrinkles on his face, only a few on his neck, which he occasionally rolled between his fingers, perhaps a minor form of scratching.

"Wizard boy, welcome," he said as he offered me a cup. "What is your pleasure? You name it. How about a sample from Iaty, or by the famous Penun from Tiaru, or by the more famous Ramosa from Qaret? Or the very best of pomegranate wines by Rer from the House of Aten on the Western River? Try every one and then decide which two to blend for the best of all worlds. That's my secret, always blend the best two of your own palate, so even the aftertaste lingers well, but please don't tell anyone." He poured and poured again, putting his own cup on the sand basin to free his hands and pour for me. He licked a running drop off my cup before handing it to me. He closed his eyes briefly and turned his head slightly upward, pursing his mouth, savoring the single drop.

He dabbed both of his lips from corner to corner, using tiny, fussy touches with the kerchief, talking through it. "Tell me, please, a little of what you know, which I hear is like a pyramid under construction. Tell me, young man, about your understanding of medicine, which is of special interest to men of my age. His Highness, for example, is he getting cured as we all hope? Sometimes I worry, seeing his neck stiffening and his step growing heavier by the day, so it seems, or is it just my imagination, and yet his driving is becoming wilder every day on the new flying chariots, shaking his bones and brains to pieces. He sure likes his fast horses and wheels, sneaking into the stables at night in disguise to hug Horuswings and Swallowwings. Do you know about all these things?"

"No, Sire. Not all. I like to sleep."

"That's good, very good. I also liked to sleep a lot when I was your age, so it could be a good sign of your prospects. Indeed, perhaps you know less than all, but you could find out more. It could become of great value for you, I think. Just for curiosity. His affliction, the strange and stiff neck, for example, what is that? No injury that I know of, and he does confide in me, of course, every day. He does tend to be shy. Does this particular condition have a name by your Master?"

I hesitated. I felt a great reluctance about opening up, but also knew that faking reluctance at this moment had multiple advantages for me. I blessed Thoth for allowing me to feel comfortable with my silence at this special moment.

43

"Go on. We haven't got all night for this chat, unfortunately. But do taste the wine, and tell me if it is good enough to take home with you and get fuddled at your leisure, or wait for yet another taste right here." He rolled his cup between his palms and looked at me smiling, as if this wine was the most important thing in the world.

I took a deep breath and spoke slowly, to allow me to think of the weight of every word. "He does have a name for it, Sire. Klepel." It was a distortion of the real word, but close enough to work with Ay and to cover my tracks toward Rehotep, perhaps the only man of insight on the disease. I also worried about my Master right now. Will he return, will he be healthy? Ay had so many people in his employ, all over the Two Lands. Did the Count arrange this trip for my Master? "A spine thing, but rare, Sire. I am not sure." I took a draw on the wine to allow me to think further, but also because it tasted good. What was the name of this and its maker? Deserves royal patronage.

Ay waved his hand broadly and spilled a little from his cup. He licked his wet fingers, repeatedly. "Oh, yes. I have seen it a few times over the decades. It is worrisome. But some things in nature are not only worrisome, they may even be necessary. What if, what if, here, have more from this jug now. You see, if I were King, I would certainly choose a young man of multiple skills to be at my side all the time, let him learn and rise ever more, no limit to the sky, is there? Or, to the number and quality of eager young women, especially when carefully selected for a purpose, a strategic purpose. My own fine daughters, for example, any one of them would make a Queen of Gold. We would be frequently enjoying a cup of Amun's best wine together, and plan and sip and plan more for a fine eternity. So... What if the King, far from having the crusty vigor of an old locust, had an accident, extremely unfortunate as it may be for some of us, but he is almost asking for it, and a nasty fall could happen any day, or even an experienced scalpel during a simple internal leeching could slip wrong, not exactly wrong but slightly undesired, or a medicine mistake arising, the medicine of course is always better than the flow of blood in the open. No, no blood. A good general prefers wine to blood, and needs only plenty of time to win battles. Properly blended fine wines, each being good in its own right but achieving incomparable greatness when cleverly blended. Yes, I can see a young, future-fat-scribe, are you practicing your stylus-licking enough? See this seal ring, for example, wizard man? Two fine scarabs, delicately wrought, holding the sun disk. It can be yours before long. In the meantime, I will safeguard it for you, so you can dream about it. You do like to dream, I assume, as you came very far in a short time from your muddy-dusty village. And the best of all dreams, have you seen my youngest, about your age. Sweet, like the blending of two great wines. Here, the pomegranate, up to the cup's wide belly and top it off with the sweet Qaret from Ramosa's House of Aten, let's drink to health and prosperity by Aten or Amun, who cares, it will put the Sun-god in your veins. And there should be many another high time, after the princess purred into your ear, and passed her own private Sun-god from her lips to the fat young scribe's bellybutton and the rest, the first tickles of feeling divine. What do you say, Future-King's-Scribe, do you wish to wait with your ascent until you can't smell a hedgehog?" The empty cup slipped from his hand and shattered.

"No, Sire. Yes, Sire. What if, what if, what if, I can."

"Good."

"I can glue it back together, it will be like new."

"Excellent. It will be part of your heritage. That's enough for now. Health! Prosperity! Prosperity forever! Prosperity now and upon our return to this Good World from the Field of Reeds!"

7

Wailing at My Secret Wedding

Ay put his left hand on his ample stomach, a large gold ring snake-tightening into the fat of his middle finger, how much longer before I will be asked to cut it off, and he motioned the wailers into a circle. One of my earliest memories is of wanting to run away from the sounds produced by such odd women. I wonder who established the custom of dropping a cat at their feet and stepping on its tail, for beginning the ceremonies, and now my stomach was starting to churn. Still, the paint on their drawn faces was a happy red and yellow, and their initial whispering voices an uncertain mixture of funeral and wedding. I looked around for a gap in the rows of people, who were all these strangers with their cruel smiles, but Ay's palm turned up and his fingertips curled upward, the voices broke into a loud wail, and his youngest daughter stepped forward from a dark corner into the bright circle. She tried both to smile and hide her jumble of teeth, and I was expecting the result to be the laugh of a hyena. She was richly dressed in what, an imitation of the Queen's latest style of spirals and tiny pyramid shapes, or was it actually from the royal wardrobe, and the blue pearl on her neck, where do they find that, and her competitive perfume mingling with the wailers' earthy odors...

Ay handed me a cup and made me drink the wine, it was probably the same he gave the women around me, the women with the twisted-smiling red and yellow faces and sour voices, perhaps spiked with Asiatic powders... please Ptah and Wise Baboon, find me a gap, where is Rehotep when he is really needed, what did Ay say about the marriage qualities of all his daughters, and that some should fit me nicely, any quality is a nice gift from the gods except her laugh, help me, Ptah, no, not that way...

"It's time to show your pleasure!" He yelled and shoved me into the first wailer's arms, she was wrinkled but squeezed me tight and ground me like a cow's jaws grinding thorny fronds of bracken and handed me over to the next, and more, their arms stretched out like starved monkeys grabbing for a fruit, it's funny how the squeezing is on the chest but the head hurts most, remind myself later to ask him about the name of this wine and avoid it if I want to live, but there are many other noble daughters waiting yet, there must be at least a tiny advantage in hitching up soon, let's see, the royal dilemma, how do you get to the apex of a pyramid when Queen Ankh is at the biggest cornerstone... especially when all these women are laughing like drunk hyenas in the moonlight and wailing as if Sobek grabbed their husbands by the crotch, as he is well known to do but never seen, since he prefers the dark waters, and drags the victims deeper than dreams... and Ay poking me in the ribs, "What is this reluctance? Do you want it or not? Yes? Yes?"

Horrors... it would be best to get lost in the desert on purpose, but my name is not yet carved anywhere big... and my new bride is blessed by the High Priest Ay himself... full of advantages for a young man of various talents but no means, as he boasted for weeks. First of all, a pedigree, essentially of royalty, close to the Queen in quality, should be Queen herself within some easy years, and certainly will be, if you praise Amun correctly. Descended from people of blue pearls on the neck, shimmering and reflecting on the sweaty brown skin, who themselves have descended from the earliest... what... people who don't slurp like cattle, and very healthy, look at the teeth, and strong as an ox and plump in the right places, perfect for childbearing, again and again if necessary, but not nearly as obstinate, though prefers not to do laundry, not that she would ever have to shake rags in the river. Might even be willing to learn to write, perhaps of interest to you, not that she would ever have to do your menial work. And, when she is deeply bathed, a beauty, in a way, many a man might say, even several foreign princes who came and looked, here and there. Look at those hands... excellent childbearing stock, and properly educated for all the useful preliminaries with small fingers that make you seem even bigger, and get at least one boy, the more the better because they drop like flies, and don't forget that she has already inherited many valuables, and will inherit some more, hopefully from other members of the family, fairly divided, except the indivisible numbers, which are innumerable as far as the eye can see, aided by sweet wine and a fine new name or even a dozen for you in eternity... please, please, my personal Ptah and my Wisest Baboon... let me find a gap, a tiny gap among the wailing crowd, forget the famous qualities and the blue pearl on the perfume-dripping skin that will attract wasps...

I feel a little dizzy, the wailers' smells are mingling with the blue perfume, they are throwing handfuls of pomegranate seeds on us for good luck, but the ducks going after them get under foot, where is Rehotep when he is needed, his last advice for trouble was to shout my own name and wait for an echo, but there is no such thing on dunes, but I hear footsteps, so it's not a dream, I need to get my feet in cool water soon, does Tut know about this, let alone approve it, and what about Ankh, no time to think, another wailer grabs me and lets Sobek loose in my stomach, chewing its way out, but the next... ah, Happy Haam, the two paints on her face are crying and laughing, and her excellent fingers are playing an inviting tune on my hips, she will dance for me for a blue pearl...

8

Tut's Rearview Mirror

"Have you been to the nightmare room already?" asked the apprentice Sheshon, son of the royal Second Barber. He thought of himself higher than second in everything, which was laughable. Too bad... it is hard to find a friend, a male friend. But he may be useful later. "It's the most secret room here. It's especially bad when you are still high from a long night of drinking. Maybe the Master's recent problems with skin rashes are a result of something strange happening there. Avoid that door, boy."

I thought that he was exaggerating, but I was curious, so I gathered information. Everybody knew a little about that room, but nobody seemed to know a lot, discounting most of the boasting. There were sheets of fenge and mika hanging on the walls, some said, causing the room to appear larger than it was. They also talked about foils of gold, copper, silver, electrum, and shiny flat pieces of bronze, granite, and obsidian. There were basins of water, oils, and fruit juices, and large lentil shapes made of glass of all kinds of colors, with lamp holders on the side. Most scary, in a special locked case, were several shiny whole fingernails of a princess, now dead, whose true name was not obtainable. Some of the nails were natural light pink, some silvery, some crimson, but all polished, they said. Were all these facts?

The inevitable happened. One day I got inside that room after minimal effort with the lock, but suddenly found myself facing Rehotep, who emerged from a dark corner. I tensed to run, but he smiled. "You are rather nosy, but stay. Are you ready to face the devil? Well, not the real one but a distant and harmless cousin of his." He motioned for me to follow him.

"Carver, relax, you are fairly safe next to me. Besides, there is no devil in any of the mirrors. My aim here is to help the King, and you can help me. Just remember that he grew up with mirrors all around him, and you did not. Come, we will start with a basin of water. Don't close your eyes. Trust me. You know I have spent years experimenting with all these, and still have the same face, believe me." He stamped his foot and created a small ripple.

"If that is really my person," I said. Images of village people welled up in my memory. The red-nosed Areshep, he was a famous vintner, he woke up one day after a long night of wine mixing and tasting, looked in his expensive mirror and found that he had grown horns. And the neighbor Pawah, whose daughter turned ugly when she saw herself in oil.

"Trust me. The devil has little interest in people like you, because of no prospect of profit. Anyway, these things may help you see the King more often, and better yet, the Queen. If you can keep a secret, I will tell you a thing or two. It helped me to get close to her mother, Queen Nef … ah, come and look into this foil of pure electrum."

I swallowed a laugh. "I meant to ask you for some time, Sire, if you forgive me. What do you mean by pure electrum? It's an arbitrary alloy of different metals, depending on the maker. You call it pure? What exact proportions of gold and silver do you have in this?"

He smiled and his head nodded in a tiny, repetitious and bouncy way, like a fast wheel running over small stones. "Good. Questions lead to answers and to new questions. Let me know when you run out of questions, like about pure women." He polished the sheet of electrum with a fistful of linen. "Listen, don't be afraid, like your village people tend to be, people who wake up to find, only in mirrors, of course, that they had all grown horns during the tiring nights of festivals, drinking serpent's blood, crying from song and inhaling stupid fumes. As they certainly would deserve, and that may yet happen if they keep it up."

"But the horns, Sire, I have seen those myself in a mirror once, and they were moving on a dog's head, as if waving. People were screaming, even the melon merchant, who reminded everyone that it was the anniversary of the death of Osiris, god of the local mil-fed serpents underground, and of the dying everywhere."

Rehotep grabbed me by the shoulders. "Stop babbling. Listen. The demons hurt only the stupid. You make them work for you. Like this mirror rod." His hand brushed a small box and opened its veneered lid, which creaked on its dry hinges. "Scares away some, doesn't it? Learn when to grease and when not to grease things. Now, about this bronze cubit-rod, touch it only when necessary. It is protected here from air and water and sand by electrum of royal quality. Not pure, just royal. It should be in Amun's Great Temple, but I am a better owner of it than the lazy priests would be, and the King lets me have my way sometimes. You might be in charge of maintaining this rod in its perfect state when I am gone, so keep it safer than a royal tomb."

He closed the box abruptly. "Where was I? The King, what about him, yes, he believes that I can help him with his strength, maybe, see, when he turned seventeen, his belly expanded a little as it should, and he also firmed up in his mind. Siring children, in spite of the busy tongues, well, it was good for his confidence, not having heard any of the rumors about the happenings or non-happenings in the royal bedroom. On the other hand, Anubis normally prefers to take infants, and for heir-wishers this is especially hard. Still, his voice has become deeper, king-like, which is not always good, what with Ay's spies lurking everywhere. For us, there are expanding prospects because he dreams big, and he could back them up with his treasury, and that is useful, because I have already spent my family fortune on ideas, and we need to get things done better and faster. A sore point with Ay, who wouldn't give beans for the fastest chariots, but he worries only about the size of his inheritance from Tut, and how soon he will get it. The strangest thing for a rich old man. You will notice this, too, when you get to know him."

What did all these meandering thoughts have to do with me? How am I to do things better and faster in his projects, and how fast was I getting a step closer to the Queen? Her image flashed across my eyes, causing a bold madness to spring from my mouth. "Sire, if I may? Our racing chariots seem as fast as the swallows. In a top burst, we can sprint at thirty cubits in an easy heartbeat. What else is possible? How? Adding horses would only slow the team down, since no other stallions are faster than the two fastest ones in the Two Lands. Sire, I sometimes I have doubts about my further value to you."

His face turned purple as he stepped closer, making my hands rise for protection. "What's the matter? You want to give up now?"

"Sire, this work, this great work, I don't know what to say, but the Great Barbershop … Sire, please understand me."

"Yes. Sure I do. Does it have anything to do with an opening there for an apprentice of your age? Who has been talking to you? I will kill him, that dirty dog. Now I know why I never trusted the barber's son in my shop, and now I see he is your best friend. Yes, indeed, of course. I can guess why you are interested in that stupid position, it's your steamy hedgehog dreams, admit it, you wish to shave a prince, and glimpse a princess here and there, and advance in the glorious job of scraping royal skin. And I invested so heavily in you."

"Sire, please, please." Drops of sweat rolled down my face.

His lips curled down in a bitter smile. "Carver, I feel like telling you to get out of here, right now, and out of my sight, forever. But I have a better idea, because I always have a better idea, and because I know you also have better ideas, better than average, except when you are more eager to copulate than a donkey... luckily, you are restrained from that entertainment by your purse. Therefore, you will always want a bigger purse, and thus I should be able to convince you to stay. Listen. What is better than being a fat barber and shaving the King or even the Queen? Think about that for a moment, while I catch a pesky flea."

I studied the nails on my toes. Strange thing, my left big toe was longer than the right one, but the smaller nails were more alike, in pairs. The nails needed trimming, all of them. How could I ignore them so long? Luckily, the Queen is not about to see them. I heard a tiny cracking sound, probably my Master popping a flea between his thumbnails, a useless but fun skill that he learned from a Sand-dweller. Should I say a word about the failure of the powder made of dried fleas or using oriole fat on the skin against fleas? Just the same as the fat of cats smeared on the floor at traffic points doesn't deter the mice from trafficking. If anything, sprinkling fresh, sharp natron water should be the best to keep both of these pests away.

"Sire, it is best to be the King because he gets shaved by the barber."

He laughed. "Furthermore, a King can choose a Queen, and sometimes a Queen may choose a King, a matter of possible interest to you. Indeed. Now we can make progress at a new level. I shall try to tolerate your impertinent behavior, and in turn you do a little work for me, like it or not. Now, the matter of faster wheels... Exceeding thirty cubits in a heartbeat is impossible? Strange to hear that from the kite-flier. Anyway, what's next with the kites? Make one to evade the diving Horus. To impress royalty, learn to control it from your hips, like the best drivers do with horses. I bet it can be done. Fly two at a time to dizzy Horus to distraction. Fly three at a time? I don't mind your playing with these, but we also have to do mundane work. Like finding a tough glue. Remember, when the chariot has only three strong elements, the wood and the rawhide and the glue, each one has to be Thoth's best gift to man. Unfortunately, there is too much bogus glue around, keeping several testers busy, as you know well enough. The King will be furious if he crashes because of the glue, or anything. So far, he trusts me and will trust you." Rehotep picked up a crooked measuring stick, studied it for a moment, then broke it in two. "How did this inaccurate ancient piece get in here? Burn it. Do I have to tell everybody again not to use green wood for measuring bars?"

"There are many such bad scaling sticks around, Sire. I am guilty of using one, on occasion. Is a bad one worse than none?"

"It depends on what you are doing. For important works, always come back to the metal one for comparison. I will give you the key to get to it. Use it often for the wheels. They could kill a driver if they are made poorly." He slapped his left ear hard, as if giving notice of changing the subject. "Why do nine out of ten mosquitoes attack my left ear and not the right? And my hearing."

I suppressed a laugh ... maybe his slapping hurt his left ear more than the other? I had tried that myself and remembered the long ringing in the ears after the hardest hits. Or, was it caused by the ivory ear-pick he liked to use for digging at the deep itch? It was a gift from the King, after having used it for a full moon, as desired for the greatest value, he had said. I recalled the clever experiments that he had done on himself, with pebbles dropped on various blocks of materials for making distinct and repeatable sounds and using an earplug to check each ear separately. He had claimed that dwarf-figs were the best plugs of a hundred things that were tried, with the elongated seed of a date a close second, both much better than a solid gold plug.

"Sire, I worry about the King and his wild driving, regardless how well the machines are made. His klepel-whatever affliction."

He followed a big green fly for a moment, while I hesitated. There was always a bug or something to busy his eyes when he was pondering something. "Klepelfele. I am glad you have trouble remembering the word. Yes, there is an extra danger to him from that, but not as much as from sweet-talking Ay's ambitions. However, we can help reduce the danger to him from other people in many ways. Let's talk about these mirrors that we need to choose from. I promise there will be no real demons here. The general science," he picked out three shiny bronzes, each the size of a hand wide open, softly blew on them one after the other, not for dusting but to put vapor on them, and polished them with a fine linen.

"For now, consider three kinds of mirrors. Flat, or almost flat, with imperfections more common than in measuring sticks, is the basic kind of see-face. It's a good challenge to make these better, so think about it. Poor people, especially, have difficulty identifying themselves, I mean, distinguishing themselves from others, even in these basic mirrors. Cats and dogs and simple monkeys never can. I am yet to try a clever baboon. Even rich people, including royalty, who grow up with these kinds of mirrors, often remain haunted by what they see in it, or what they hope to see but cannot find. I admit something myself, Carver. I cannot look at myself even in a flat mirror with indifference, and perhaps nobody would or should. These flat ones are prized by some of the anxious rich people who are afraid of assassins. Ay, for one, knows about some of these objects, and he is pestering me for many large fenge sheets, which would cost half his treasure, to line the walls of his porticos and help him avoid a dagger in the back.

"The other mirrors are curved, the two lentil kinds, just for a good name. Lentil as we look at it from the outside of the bean, and lentil as if we were looking at the bean's skin from the inside of the bean, if you can imagine that. They are all interesting, but the lentil ones are the real demon-kinds. Wait, you barber-spirit, don't run, I saw your eyes flicking and the legs twitching. Demons... what most people think, which is not for you. Demons are only for priests, so that they have something big to talk about. Not long ago, the three high priests of Amun declared that lentil mirrors have magic powers under the control of sorcerers, and they condemned anyone gazing into shiny lentil shapes, or showing demons in any curved mirrors, swords, ivory handles, spheres, and even polished fingernails."

His eyes began to sparkle, and he lowered his voice. "Look here. The demon in the outside lentil is smaller than the real one, and his world is bigger than in the flat one, and there are other demons around and behind him, fuzzy in their hazy-dusty landscape. Look at these reduced and blurred demons moving abruptly, sometimes with little horns flapping like ears, as if their large space was concentrated in this hand-sized object to torture you. All right, squeeze your fists and stiffen your neck, but stare at the stupid demons, they cannot bite. Then, the opposite effect with the inside lentil. The demon here is bloated, look at his huge nose and lips and bushy eyebrows, but his world has shrunk. Smile and see what he does. Now turn away and come back to it and do the same thing, repeatedly. It is exactly as you will, predictably. Well, not exactly, but it is under your control to some extent. But don't tell anybody, except the King, if you have a chance."

"Is the King concerned?"

"He is not afraid of flat ones, although it's a woman's thing mainly, but I am not sure of the lentils. Most certainly, the high priests murmur into his ear every day, to maintain their sway. He will soon see that the magic lentils can work for him, for fun, and perhaps to save his life, like with the golden sun disk on the pole of his chariot in a fine lentil shape, so he can see people and horses in his rear dust, without forcing him to turn his head."

"But the priests?"

"It will be almost like a flat disk, just barely lentil-shaped, on the Horus stand on the pole. Eventually, he will not be afraid to drive with it, priests murmuring or not. Here, have a fig and watch yourself as you chew, you beer-fed young demon of frightening hairs and fangs. Do you see a barber behind you who is hoping to shave you?"

Perhaps some of this is good, but he is also weird, I worry about some of it sticking to me like dark pitch to a boat, he talks too much, teaches too much, rambles on, but what can I say? "Sire, I can't figure the barber in the see-face."

"You will, I bet. How much are you willing to risk?" He scratched his bony throat, his neck stretching and head rising like a cat's, and fixed his eyes again on me. "One more thing, a little advice, expel the stinks of your body before a big night in the cool breeze by rubbing yourself to a redness with a roasted mixture of equal portions of ostrich egg, tamarisk gallnut, double portion of dung beetle, and tortoise shell." He dismissed me abruptly and began softly singing a new version of his favorite, "The ibis gorges on the snake and the red fish leaps off my fingers."

9

Smash the Whole Bag

Why is it so dark in here? Why, because I am afraid. Darkness, and silence. Because I am afraid to turn up my most ingenious tomb-lamp to shine on the wicked mirrors. How did I get in here, and how long ago? And why was it so easy to slip in, through all the locks and doors? Makes my spine shiver, as it was with those scratchy scorpions running down from the neck to the buttocks. Sheeh. What's worse, darkness with silence or with banging noises? Sudden noise, no, sudden silence, that is. Another word on my tongue, what happened to it? Like smoke from the nose, singed brain, gone forever, get a grip, swear to Ptah.

Could turn up the lamp, maybe I should, just a little.

"You can't do that!" Is that Rehotep's voice? Must be through the wall.

"Yes, I can." I must assert myself, one time out of ten, like Ptah. Good enough for a god, good enough for me.

I reached for a glint from an object, but it was too far, my shoulder felt a sharp pain, like an arrow or a hornet or an asp, no, it was the busted shoulder, busted from a stupid bet, to grab a toy hedgehog through the swishing spokes of a wheel on the test stand, but the preceding test was a success.

Why am I here, stupid? Not to grab a glint from a wicked object, but to smash it, once and for all. Yes, smash them, but how. Poke around, somewhere here was a bag, there, a huge leather bag, toss them all in, let them glint inside, let them glint and flash but just to one another, not to me. Good. They are like living creatures in the bag, but getting subdued, I hope from their own fears, first, give them a drink, double-boiled Nubian red, then they will not feel any pain, yes, it's coming, but I need a club, a big club stronger than glass and shiny metal, where did I put it?

"You can't do that!"

"Yes, I can, yes."

Tie the mouth of the bag with wet rawhide, it will tighten further when it dries, enough to hold Sobek and all his teeth, they are shiny and curved like fingernails, the priests say no gazing into them, then thrash it down and left and right, let them scream, but muffled, broken glass makes such strange little squeaks inside the thick leather.

Listen carefully to the squealing devil glass and mika and feng, tongue-twisters in the muffled leather, they will never see the beer-puckered moon again, like mad baboons with their tiny hedgehogs on fire, hey, that's an idea for bad fun worthy of a Sand-dweller genius, but what is their crime and why is this urge to see her face in broken glass, soon, another night.

She said she was going on a long river cruise, with him, but would prefer my papyrus boat, tight and scratchy, and creaky noisy, shhhh, they will hear.

Does beer burn silently or cracking in the brain?

Will she come back, or is she looking for a new frog charm elsewhere?

Smash the jug, too, harder, again.

10

Rats and Frogs

It was still dark when Rehotep shook me out of my stupor. "Roll out, Carver! It's time to settle the bet."

His hand was cold, and I jerked mine away, hitting my elbow into the wall. "The bet? The last bet? On the Queen's what?"

"Wake up! The last bet, on the rats, the King, too, wants to know this, and asked about it last night, more than once, because he has bet with Ankh on this, so one of them will win. Let's go. The bakers have fired up the great oven." My lower arm was aching from the elbow, with sensations of repeated pricks in it, as if gripped by the seven-cubit crocodile that I killed the day before and celebrated with too much vigor. I had trouble putting my toes on the thongs, so decided to go barefoot. His hands waved impatiently. "I am curious, of course, about the final answer to the question," he said as we started walking, "but hate to do this. Burnt hair is awful, even in tiny amounts. No wonder the King declined my invitation to attend the experiment, but I suspect she will watch it from a distance downwind or upwind, depending on luck. The only real winners will be the lovers of roasted rats." A servant girl in a doorway held a basket of fruits, and offered them to him, but her bent head allowed her to look past my Master and deep into my eyes. She was a little too young for me, with hips not wide enough and ready to drive horses yet, if she had been of a higher class, but her eyes and feet were nice, and thus her shop swiftly registered in my memory.

The great oven was rippling the layers of hot air all around it, but mostly at the top, like tiny waves on a sand beach. Rehotep got too close in his hurry, so he retreated a few steps. He studied the oven for a moment, then looked at me. "You bet that less than half of them would find the opening and come out alive. I say the opposite. Most of them will get out. Here are the ten subjects, all from the Great House, equal in size and health and appetite, look at the empty food tray in each cage. The happy creatures had a feast last night." An ash-covered apprentice baker was throwing more wood under the oven, which was pouring heat out of its big opening. It felt good in the chill of the morning, but only at a distance of ten or twelve cubits. "You toss them in, one at a time."

"Me, Sire? Why not tell the boy to do it? He works here, and is an expert with ovens and such."

"You would trust him to do it uniformly, with each rat landing on the same spot far back on the brick platform? They must have an equal chance of getting out or perishing. This lame boy can't even put two logs on the fire to please the eye. You are the best shot with the rag-ball for miles around, as you brag much too often. Not fair to throw them too hard, either, to damage them prematurely."

I was now fully awake, and had to control my urge to scream. There was no point in arguing further, but it was a most unpleasant task, let alone the multiple dangers. My options were limited. I thought in vain about the King's hunting gloves of fine red leather with new appreciation, although in this case a double layer of those thin gloves would be desirable, but here it was only rags for me, at best. My mind was racing, a mixture of unrelated feelings, one of shear panic from last year, from my first crocodile encounter, then a tinge of pleasure lately, the pleasure of sensing something different about to happen, good or bad, and all these made me light-headed.

"The King is waiting to hear from you. And, as luck would have it, that wrap contains Ankh, standing and waiting silently. Go ahead."

I cast a quick glance in her direction, and scanned the pile of fresh loaves of bread on a shelf and deeply inhaled their life-giving scent. A well-worn and scorched bread-shovel popped into my sight,

I tore a loaf of bread in half and dug out its soft belly, eating it hastily. Still chewing and savoring the sweetening bread, I used a rag for a glove, picked up a rat, and stuffed it in the bread shell, not entirely easily, loosely sealing it with the rag. From the corner of my eye, I tried to catch my Master's face, hoping to see surprise and curiosity at least, if not immediate approval, but he seemed emotionless. But Ankh smiled, yes, yes. The package was easily slid into the oven from the shovel, the rag part near and facing the far wall, as it would be done uniformly in each subsequent test.

I counted evenly, one-finger, two-finger … at seven, the rat burst out from the tight ball, leapt over it, and made a straight run at a blurred cheetah-speed to the center of the oven's opening, then down and out and away between my legs. I scooped out the bread and the rag from the oven to save time for the next tests, although after every three I made a new shell, mainly to eat more of the royal bread. The results were more or less the same, with the burst counts ranging from four to ten, but with each animal running straight to the center of the opening, and gone into the dark in a blink. I imagined them all lined up at the edge of the crocodile pool, drinking lustily. Should I say anything about the few rat droppings in the oven and the potential of them being baked into the crust of the next load of breads? The King was known to enjoy fresh brown crusts enhanced with ash and tiny particles of charcoal. I jotted down the rats' escape times to do something with them later, and looked up in triumph to meet Ankh's eyes, but she was gone, for Seth's double curses on those stupid numbers.

"I win," said Rehotep, grinning broadly, "but will not collect on it this time." I wondered if he had done this experiment himself, if differently in detail, a long time ago. He twisted his nose by moving his upper lip sideways, although the lingering smell of the escaped hot rats was not had. "Let's go and fill ourselves with the sunrise and clean mist on the river. Re will be the perfect god for me this morning, I can feel it in my bones already. Bring my jug of purified water … never drink from the life-giving river if you want to live long." He took a golden-brown loaf and nodded toward another one for me to take.

Rehotep reclined on a mat of reeds in our old boat and told me to paddle softly and not often, just to avoid drifting into a nest here and there. Geese flew overhead, in a pair of straight lines that matched my pointing pair of fingers most widely separated. I always checked this against the sky, and it was always the same angle, even if the legs of the lines were never the same in length. They were honking garrulously ... did I detect a certain rise and fall in the group's sound? Maybe they were dead musicians' spirits teasing us with new melodies. Did some fish swim in a similar fashion? Keep looking. A large frog plopped into the water from one end of a floating tree, while on the other end a pair of ducks just looked at one another in surprise, too lazy to move.

Re's long narrow fingers pierced through the willows like golden spears. Rehotep rolled his back left and right on the reeds, making a crunching sound. He grunted in pleasure or pain, hard to tell. Klepel in his neck, too? Will this happen to all of us? Small fish swam across under the boat, their tails going left and right. Why not up and down? A heron stood knee-deep in the water, slowly stretching his neck farther up and back, beak pointed like a lance for the shortest strike, then he relaxed. I put the paddle out above the water and watched the reflections of the drops running off its pointed, slightly frayed tip, hitting the mirror, rippling its surface. Little circle demons leapt out one by one from the center and grew and ran away and died and were reborn from the center. A bank of thin mist rolled in, struggling with the rising sun.

Rehotep also watched the circles, and also a snake as it was inching to the only spot of sunlight available, on a low branch. "We should come here more often. Look at these wheels without spokes, these circles. Do you ever wonder how the spoked wheel was invented? Certainly not by carving out a solid wheel, as many people believe. The grains of some spokes would be lined up to be strong, while the other spokes would be terribly weak, so, overall, no good. Let's reenact a better development, as the god Thoth might have helped somebody much before us. Start by cutting a bunch of willow twigs, Carver, and make a small hoop. You have twine?" He handed me his newest treasure, I have seen it just once before, a small knife with an ivory handle and a silvery iron blade. I touched the sharp edge cautiously, and it sent shivers through my spine. What will happen to copper and bronze, and to us? Or to wood? I carefully shaved off a hair from my leg and studied the spot on the skin, and then steered our craft under a willow tree.

Making a hoop was nothing new to me, so I could work fast. It was less than a cubit across, smooth yellow-green and good to the touch, like a freshly-bathed rich girl, and I twirled it on my finger. "There," said Rehotep, "you are ready to reinvent the spoked wheel, from a hoop like you have, it's child's play, certainly for Thoth's clever boys, stiffening the hoop with straight sticks, attaching a piece of hollow bone at the center for your finger, easier twirling, faster and faster on the finger-axle, then let it go to sleep."

He took off his sandals and rubbed their soles together in short bursts. Frogs answered from the shallows, and he laughed. "That will make the spies' work a bit more challenging, and that willow, it reminds me of a poem." He was distracted by a pair of black-and-white storks that landed in shallow mud and began to dance around and flap wings and rattle beaks, thrusting toward one another and breaking away, with the nearby frogs suddenly quiet. He cleared his throat repeatedly. "You can learn much from the animals, Carver, and should. It is very clear, sometimes. I mean, toward women. A young man, especially, yes. But it's complicated. Some like this, some like that. I mean, the women, especially the young ones, and even more the experienced ones. I mean, with men. See, I was young once, do you understand, and had to learn on my own, like when to use poetry and when to avoid it. Because, she might love your poem, but turn to another man. I mean, it would not be the first time in the history of womankind. Also, even more difficult, you have to think about when to bathe often and when to rub elbows with the oily wrestlers in their den before seeing her. It can be easy or hard, depending. Look at those clumsy birds, Carver. A mystery, how they learn so much from the dull clatter of their parents. No scribes among them. And where they go across the great northern sea for half a year, and why, young and old."

His distress was amusing at first, then I got an urge to rescue him. "Sire. What was that willow poem?" His knuckles relaxed, he sighed and closed his eyes. His head tipped back, and his low voice blended into the humming of reeds and rushes and the call of birds, and a frog starting up again.

"Fragrant flower, sweet saam in your hair,
Let's recline under the willow's breezy curtains.
Touch the blossom with our lips.
Lay incense on the flame
To remove years from our bellies.
Open your heart to your lover
Who braved the trembling of earth's bones
And risked the sniffing crocodiles
Laying in the shallows."

Where did he get this? It was new to me. Is he half asleep? I twirled the hoop, making a tiny swishing sound. Rehotep shook, raised forward and stared at me as if not recognizing me. A pair of orange-breasted ducks cupped their wings and spread their toes for splashing down nearby, almost wingtip-to-wingtip, but the male just ahead of the female. He ignored the ducks, touched his eyes, which first followed my hoop, but then they skipped around without a focus, slower and slower. His head fell back against the reed mat, and he sighed with little purrs, with an occasional whisper, shorter and shorter fragments of his poem.

He kicked his sandals around as he stretched and twitched. A frog on a leaf froze as we glided near it. I counted its toes … can they count on their toes? Did the child Ankh ever go with friends to collect frogs on the moonlit shore? Perhaps it's never too late to experience, and she would like that after the flood begins to recede. I will bring the bucket to the willow and my newest tomb-robber's lamp, preferring no moon. I must hurry to finish that lamp.

11

Sips of Bowmen's Red

The moon-shadow of the acacia tree nodded and brushed the floor of my small room with sleepy-eyed leaves. I liked this kindred-spirited tree, with leaves closing every night, and lazily opening again with the rising sun. A shielded night-scarab, sounding like a frayed zither, buzzed in and out the window and finally into a wall, cracked, and fell into silence. I started counting … how long before it starts up again to keep me awake? It can't be dead, on account of its hard shell, or can it? I wished for the night breeze to come up sooner and stronger to brush the mosquitoes off my skin, white clothes are best to ward them off, and the sun's heat, to be able to see and smash them, but then the blood shows on the tunic in big splotches, like now the moon bobbed up on the celestial Winding Water, too bright to allow sleep, in collusion with the scarab, but where is that insect now? My counting seemed full of gaps like an old donkey's jaw, better to start over. I reached for the three-hin jug of Bowmen's Red on the floor, or is it a two-hin jug by now, on the way to be a one-hin, then half a hin. Luckily, another jug sits tight on a dark shelf, puffed up as the sacred cobra Wadjit, containing the premium Ibhat brew from the Master's cool cellar, waiting patiently for its turn, but no, a good brew is rather impatient, like a horny Sand-dweller. Still, who is the boss in this room … maybe I will save that jug for another night.

The snake ... not the dusty dead ones in the village, the big ones slashed into pieces by peasants and the little ones beaten by boys, but the jug-shaped serpent poised to spit fire at the King's enemies, or at least a gold strap to cool the divine forehead, a great invention, another royal advantage along with the pygmy fan-bearers stirring the hot air. The cobra ornament for cooling the head, with a stone amulet in the intricate shape of a scorpion on the neck to ward off the serpent's stings, now that's science, something Rehotep the master chameleon himself would be proud of, he should be told about this discovery of the cooling head ornament, but not too fast, first I must recommend it to the Queen for favors, for joining our vital and feverish ka's in time, patiently waiting by necessity, but gradually losing patience, like the best brew will not wait forever. I hope to see her when the big goddess Nut is done with the night, the blood-splattered small goddesses having butchered all the Sun God's enemies, with iron knives that only gods can afford, the blades sharpened on my bow-spun honing wheel wetted with expert spit from the red brew, and the dismembered bodies of these daily reborn enemies thrown into the deepest ravines, so the morning god Khepri can rise again, but wait, if I can't count straight and steady.

The wooden plug made my fingers sticky, best not to replace it, although the jug-handle was sticky, too, and the whole thing, and what a disaster if it suddenly turns into the long-sought perfect glue. Anyway, the plug rolled away on the dark floor, where is the cat-god, what's his name, to chase it and retrieve it? The brew is bitter and sweet on the tongue, how do they make it both? The day before, or was it two, it was dominated by the bitter part, probably from a worker's yellow leak, how many fingers' worth of proportion out of a hundred, and is it superb brew art or revenge for getting placed on a low rung at birth? Maybe the brewery crew, just these poor devils, should be given better food and drink regularly, so we can get a better taste. I take a big bite of the lotos-bread-stick, the best of the far-traveling foreign recipes, but don't give this to the devil's crew, they will never get done, this is for the upper one half finger of the population. The slow chewing of any lotos food is one of the most impossible things to obey in the Two Lands, it is just against human nature and taste-buds, but it is firmly recommended by Sobek and others who know the effect, but also remember that the monster Sobek can thwack you with his tail, doesn't even know how to give a tittle.

After tossing and turning like a foul bean in the fat Nubian, I got up, opened the aiming door of the tomb-robber's lamp wide, and searched for something, not sure what. I stepped on the lost plug and rolled and hit my head on the wall like a night-scarab, but the wall was close and the lamp didn't break, only the flame quivered and died. I crawled back to the jug to recover. Restarting my aimless search and soon moving outside for better light, I found a slave girl's tunic on a clothes line and placed it to block the cool burning face of Khons in the sky. The coarse fabric, made by the nimble fingers of child workers of Hedhotep, cut the light down by eight fingers' worth out of ten, some scribes of numbers say that's the same as four out of five, but how can it be both, for Thoth's blessing, but the remaining whatever finger's fraction of the total was just enough to let through a mocking demon's distorted faint smile. The moist fabric will dry soon, what will that do to the moonlight sneaking through it? Stubbornly, instead of simply adding my tunic to the screen, I searched for another slave's garment, in vain.

The bittersweet suds earlier prickled my tongue, a hundred baby asps, but now it was getting numb to the thousand little teeth. With a full crocodile yawn, limbs becoming heavier than a water beast's tail in warm mud, yet with eyes more awake than at dusk, I stared at the chopped-up light coming through the slowly rippling double layers of the tunic, what is it now, for Renet's gifts of fertility and fortune, brown thighs in the dim light, wide hips swaying to a distant flute, two dancing legs meeting at the pink-blue lotus cup up front, tantalizingly twisting and traveling to the Two-Mounds place, hiding the moon here and there, then again back to the darkening Wishing Cup, begging for attention, the lotus-sniffing brew-snake of wrestlers' lore.

What kind of chameleon cloth of Tait's shop is that, mocking me, Tait is a true deity, never finished with anything, there, green stripes appear at the bottom of the tunic for richness, but the material is only half as thick as the slave's, it allows even the Dog Star to arise in the tunic, hovering near the lotus cup. The brown thighs shimmer in the devilish light, the hips swaying to a distant flute, but Tait suddenly has another creation, a goddess cloth flashing on the line, thinner than any and banishing the other two by its brilliance.

The wrestlers would be astonished, since they cannot imagine this tunic of Ankh, let alone the Queen herself blossoming in it, their brains are banged up beyond help, so I must tell them about this sight of the lotus tunic in the bright night, rush to them, but no, she likes them too much as it is, so it's better to kill them all, including their muscles and scars. No, they can't imagine Ankh with her fleshy lips and big sapphire eyes in this light, like the unattainable Zymema flower blooming once in a thousand years, yet they talk about her as if she was just any female, they are ready for a final dog-walk, as soon as I have the weapons and power, or let them bash quarry stone to dust, and may Osiris refuse to give cooling water to them. Better yet, force them to write and cry with the chalk on the slate.

What does she like in these sweaty creatures? Why not the scribe, excellent with the fingers and the chalk? Women are strange, perhaps falling for their hap-hap whistling in the raucous din that exceeds temple music. They roar at any stupid joke but not because the tunic ripples and reveals an elusive edge of undergarment on the lotus skin, the long neck barely covered in gold and glass strings, the crimson-tipped toes teasing the thongs, wishing for Tait to make thinner goddess-cloth.

Does she whoop at the prick-bets of the Sand-farers? They should be castrated for stealing my two model wheels, for betting on who can first spin it on his prick, then who will spin it longest with plenty of lubricating spit, the water-clock dripping pit-pit-pit for the measurement, and others cheering and offering chicken fat and olive oil and fig juice and steaming urine to make the spin last longer, then the boasting winner making a grand bet for spinning both wheels at once.

If she likes these games, I have to try it and win.

One more sip before it tastes bitter, and wait for the tunic to fall to the ground or come up, all the way, but which is fastest, and how many ways are there for the cloth-tube to slip on or off, pray for better sights of transparent tunics and count all the possible combinations, the basic one is overhead on with overhead off, then underfoot on with underfoot off, overhead on with underfoot off, underfoot on with overhead what, confusion so soon, and wishing to get one more drop from the jug, all gone, never mind, the full one beckons from the shelf but teasing and receding to the Ibhat Brewery, I must go there but there is a new bearing problem, since there is always a bearing problem, but what makes my chariot roll so heavily on smooth ground, I should set the dry vessel down to help the horses, but where is the floor, it must be near because the night-scarab hits it again, revived, like the coming sunrise and chiseling and sawing in the shop, the pounding of the head, my scarab is buzzing on papyrus wings into the stone floor, falling into the silence of cracked wheels and chalks, and I have to get my own stallions and fly faster than any King ever before, to impress her behind the acacia trees.

12

The King's Stables

At dusk the plastered walls of the Palace of the Dazzling Aten were starting to turn gray. I was sitting cross-legged on the warm court-yard siding made of pounded river mud, under a small window of the Pi-Amun Stables, with nothing better to do, since Rehotep was traveling over the rough Secondary Horus Road to the cooler uplands of the Kush, ostensibly searching for a reliable source of uniformly tough, spoke-quality elm, and also hoping for new discoveries of minerals and gold. A fly buzzed the big veins on my ankles, indecisive about which foot to try first, but I let it, rather thinking of the King on his most recent staged hunt by the pomegranate orchards, where he mostly sat on his camp-throne, agitated just a little when he was plucking his bow-string. Maybe it was an unusually hot day, but anyway the King was sitting on his chair, pointing out a fly to his fan-bearer who was struggling with a bundle of ostrich feathers. There were several flies, which made it easy for the King to point one out, but frustrating for the little fellow. The King sat quietly, obviously not in the mood to talk. I wondered if some of the older men around him compared this scene with those of the giant warrior kings in the great hunt or battle. He sat and waited, and pointed to another fly. When the game appeared, he waited for a nod from Ay, and shot, with his thin arrows missing every one of the old rabbits, which were then rerouted and batted closer to him by the ground-keepers. That was a lot of action compared to what my spot by the stables offered. I had an image of a young goddess float around, even a fine servant girl or two, for amusement. My swallow got the pesky fly, and I waved to him, it's good to be friends with the earth-god Geb, it's like having a secret army.

Dull thuds came from the Pool of Tranquility and Purity, from the two water-pigs bumping one-another, rocking the lotus leaves with rings of waves. A guard stopped and allowed his dour baboon to drink from the pool, before continuing on his rounds. I normally avoid looking into the closely spaced severe eyes of this creature, since that slow-healing baboon bite on my thigh, a stinging memory of a mistaken attempt at friendship. The skin was festering until the Old Man of the village decided that only the hair of the same animal could cure the wound. It took me days of stalking the beast, trying in vain to catch him napping, trying in vain to have a soft heart, before I got a good tuft of hair from his dead body, which did help me recover quickly. In spite of that incident, I have good relations with some baboons, the holy ones, which is only wise of any young man of ambition.

The swallows were making their last swoops of the day in and out the window, in and out their mud-straw nests under the eaves, carrying fat flies from the stalls. The nests were more tightly built than the town full of people, yet there was food for all the swifts. Inside the stables, the chickens were scratching for seeds in the horse-droppings, then settling down on their roosting beams. The horses were munching and lashing their rumps with well-brushed tails. I inhaled the smells of the well-groomed horses and fresh straw and oats, though the generously applied day-perfume of the stallions was mostly worn off. Just as well. I thought the excessive perfuming of the nobility's horses was ridiculous, and wondered what the horses felt about it. On the other hand, I recalled that the Queen certainly used expensive perfume to good effect.

A black rat was outlined against the dark-blue sky, as it descended from a scaled palm, his limp tail leading the nose. It stopped, and I noticed the sacred hedgehogs passing under the tree. The furry-bellied, short-quilled adult Hemekh was twitching its nose, perhaps annoyed by the horse-perfumes wafting out of the stables. Every seven counts, as I reckoned out of boredom, it was snappily rotating its big, fox-like ears, to check every direction. All along, it was softly clucking to encourage the two drifting youngsters toward the pool. Word was that the medium-quilled Parakh was the King's favorite, and the longer-quilled Hetikha was the Queen's. I wondered why the wrestlers liked to joke about her little animal, and why they drew crude hedgehog symbols of various sizes, each an egg-shape with short lines pointing outward all around, on the walls of their den. Does the Queen know about this? Perhaps she would more appreciate a little golden figure of the animal... The hedgehogs went to the pool, faced down a small crocodile resting its jaws on the warm stone edge, and drank from the pool nearby.

The last stable-boy came out, hung his whiskbroom on a peg, nodded to me and went to his bunkhouse. A bat passed me. Perhaps the one I found in the folds of the awning I opened in the morning, clinging upside down to the canvas, shaking, clear drops of urine rolling down his body and off his pointed black nose. Circling, he thanked me for refolding the awning after that early daylight scare.

A figure appeared in the distance, as cautious as the rat on the tree, spending much time behind the posts, probably one of Ay's lurking men, or Horem's. The control-crocodiles of Seth, what are they after? Different personalities, yet they are similar in their hunger for more power. I crouched and slipped into the stables when the man was hidden for a moment. Clucking to calm the chickens, I hid near them in an empty stall. Darkness floated up, and the noises diminished. A few stars appeared through the windows, but smaller than those painted around Nut on the walls and ceilings of big tombs.

When I became stiff and even tired of the good scents, I stirred to leave, but a shadow appeared in the doorway. The figure then opened the door of a tomb-robber's lamp, casting a narrow beam of light. He was stepping slowly, tentatively. A horse snorted, then another. The visitor crept closer, doing silly clucking for the chickens and snorting for the horses, almost in a whisper, but enough for the creatures... and sometimes I could hear the slight tapping of a cane.

The light was faintly reflected from the stalls and horses, and my heart leapt, it was surely that lamp in his hand, the lamp I carved from kalkh for a month, on and off. He stopped and widened the beam a little.

I remember Rehotep's hooting laughter, when the first model of the lamp was done. Nobody can say which one of us invented it, because we both did, kicking ideas around like a rag ball, more ideas coming out like puffs of sand from the ball spinning high in the air, but who had the first spark of the big idea, perhaps he did, I hate to admit it, because it all started with the King asking him for an unusually fine but small lamp for the royal bedroom. Surely my Master had the idea for the sliding copper door to make a light beam in one direction only, or close it up for privacy, and with a cloth hood for an even more perfect temporary hiding of it all because the flame inside the kalkh shines through the stone which is beautiful in the great temples and bedrooms, but I said to add a sliding horizontal copper tray for the light itself, push it in or pull it out a bit, to change the width of the beam at will, and he took it.

He laughed when the first working model was in his hands, tenderly stroking it, a hard belly laugh that echoed on, almost choking him, as he tried to speak and gasp for air, "You and I, Lampcarver, we could be rich, not that we are starving, but still, guess what, where is the most gold in the Two Lands? Not in our locked bronze boxes, but in the tombs of the nobility. No, don't worry, I am not suggesting that you go for it, certainly not directly, because it could become gruesome gold in your hands, but there are clever men breathing torch fumes in tunnels who don't mind the risk and love the excitement, and no, I am not suggesting either to give them the lamp for a cut in the enormous profits, like two fingers' worth out of ten would be about right, but it may be the best practical joke on both sides of the river, just to contemplate it, of course, think of saving the magnificent treasures from oblivion, for the pleasure of wide-eyed future generations, but even more interesting, think of what you could offer to a pretty young goddess for an immediate smile. Yes, yes, or get an eternal smile from a mature goddess of plump lips, excellent fingers and cuddly hedgehog."

My heart pounded in my throat, yes, it is the King swinging the lamp and tapping the cane and shuffling in the straw. I looked toward the dark door in the distance for his mute bodyguard, at least one should be hovering nearby, but nothing else stirred. But why, for the sake of Seth and Sobek, is he in my clothes, if I can believe my eyes? It was mine, except for the Horus pectoral flashing occasionally through a gap in the tunic, flashing gold and brilliant dark blue glass platelets. Also, he has a gold ring on the right hand, either for an emergency, or just too tight to remove over a bony joint. Yes, it's mainly my clothes, but I did not notice the disappearance of any pieces, or did his tailors copy mine? I could not think of an incident, except, once fitting the King's ceremonial tunics on my wooden models, to provide figures for the painters and poets and sculptors, without tiring the King. It was a simple but pleasant job, touching the finest fabrics in the world. I hoped for a similar task with the Queen's finest, up and down and inside and out, with fingers and nose, but not to hurry with the carving and the final smoothing along the grains.

He stopped at the stall of his current favorite, the black Sun-Swallow, the tallest of them all, muscular withers reaching to his own shoulders. He put some dry dates between the trembling lips of the eager animal, and stroked the pink nostrils, which seemed to glow like hot coals in the lamplight. I inched closer to see better, carefully sliding among rather than crunching down on the straw lying everywhere. He embraced the head reaching out and bending down over the stall gate, but suddenly he dropped the door and hood on the lamp, deepening the darkness. There were murmurs, a feint neighing, and the tail slapping the sides of the stall. Could it be that the King is crying? Sun-Swallow is heaving huge sighs? Next it was the sound of the horse sucking on dates or fingers.

His light went up again, and he started stretching his neck upward and back and left and right a little, several times. There was a small pop, just a little louder than if he crunched a brittle flea between his thumbnails, thanks to my hearing that rivals a blind baboon's, and he froze for a moment as if hit by a viper, while my heart pounded upward in my dry throat, it's a good thing I did not have to say a word, then he started out shuffling toward the adjacent chariot barn, using the cane only to swipe down the numerous cobwebs at the stall gates. It was known that he hated the webs, because he gave repeated orders for cleaning them out, but the spiders were always moving back behind the stable boys, like hyenas chased away and again trailing a caravan.

Inside the barn, he opened the lamp wider, its door fully up and the tray halfway out as I knew precisely how it worked, making a dazzling view of the first chariot, the Rolling-Sun. The King cast only a glance at the plush vehicle, hit the gold breastwork and the propped-up fancy yoke with his stick while going around it, walking faster than he normally would, over to the bare-bones vehicle, the Whistling-Wind, the pride of my hands' work, also Rehotep's pride, and the envy of the best drivers. He studied the elaborate sun disk on the head of the brightly painted wooden hawk sitting on the pole, and carefully replaced it with a smooth-disk mirror from a plain, locked box. He looked into it for a while, making faces and twisted fingers, moving back and forth from the magic lentil, just like I had done many times. He hooked a corner of his mouth with his pointing finger and pulled it far to the side, making the image extremely grotesque. He was rather quick and clever with his pointed tongue, slashing it around like a small sword. The Queen would most likely not be amused by this kind of behavior, especially if word got out.

He began stroking the pole, as if it were his lion cub, even scratching the yoke like the animal's ears. He plucked the acceleration brace in front of the chariot body, and put a hand in the socket where top drivers wedge their forward foot while squeezing the breastwork between the thighs, for a firm stance, allowing the reins to be tied on the waist, freeing the hands for fighting or hunting. I was happy with my work on this clever foot-socket on the pole, but was also depressed that Rehotep, while liking my contributions, yes, he is tight-lipped in such matters, especially face-to-face with me. I have to sneak around in the dark to hear him say a good word about me to others. Unfortunately, he is also tight-fisted in rewards, beyond reason, and getting worse as he is getting older.

Tut climbed on board, threw his shoulders back and stretched his neck as if looking far ahead, and proceeded in a pretend drive of the hardest kind. I moved a few steps closer, ignoring the risk to myself, to catch him if he falters. He tied the reins on his waist, and with effort placed the left leg over the breastwork, wedging the left foot in the foot-socket on top of the pole, and the right foot behind, in its own strap on the floorboard. He stiffened into a fine warrior stance, almost like the stone carvings show his great ancestors, and uttered a small yell of triumph. He retightened the reins to eliminate the slack, and began to work the imaginary horses, with gentle command words and the whole set of basic waist movements: lean forward to loosen the reins and accelerate, lean backward to tighten the reins and slow down, twist the hips left or right to turn the horses left or right. I could judge from my experience that he had talent as an advanced driver, or else, he had practiced these complex but effective movements much more than anybody could have realized. Perhaps he used the set of reins he had asked for, a few months earlier, in his own quarters, where the imaginary horses would run just the same, except for not having the actual vehicle, of course, he could have used a large armchair to stand on, and a stool of the right height to put his forward foot on, and squeeze the back of the chair between his thighs, all right, much can be done with little equipment if nobody is watching. In fact, why does he have to sneak into this place for an imaginary practice run? Nevertheless, it is better to think of Ankh straddling a chair's back as if it were a chariot's breastwork, tunic hiked high, or no tunic at all, and twisting her wide Hathor-hips in learning how to command the stallions, who would respond with eagerness.

The floorboard popped under Tut's flexing foot, bringing me back to reality. Why is he engaging in this effort, with plenty of dangers, even in this pretend situation? Ay would disapprove of it, and Horem would disapprove of it, since both big men have more to lose than gain if their puppet King is injured, or even worse, dies, although, he is apparently becoming less of a puppet these days. Rehotep would also disapprove of it, and the Queen would. Yes, yes, that's is the idea, by Seth and Thoth, he is doing it for no other reason than to impress her with his wild driving, trying to imitate the most famous King Thutmose of legends. He needs the wild showing because he has no war booty to give her, no Kadesh battle over the Mitannis on the poets' tongues, no 333 Syrian princes on their knees at Megiddo, no islands to offer for a cool summer retreat. What is best to do? Tell somebody? No. This secret could be useful in other ways. It should be best for me to practice quietly and learn to perform better than anybody else. But stop dreaming, this is not enough, the Queen will not notice a young man just because he can make a fast wheel, or drive well, even if he can do it better than the King. So, which great warrior king would I wish to emulate, to get her smile and favors?

Thoth and Horus, help, please help! And they do, as always, when the need is great. Yes, I can make a great stunt hawk, better than the last one, then soon make even more than one, fly them at once, she will be delighted and astonished and smiling with pleasure and granting me all kinds of favors. For good luck, I will cross my toes on both feet at once, like the lucky baboon. Then, when Rehotep eventually loses most of his teeth, which apprentice besides me would be able to take his place in the palace? There are many of my peers who are good at one thing or another, but nobody else has a chance to become great beyond words, to match the Master, let alone exceed him in anything. Certainly, none, since the only other boy who had a fair amount of overall ability has disappeared without a trace recently. A pity, everybody said. No, it will not be too long in coming, considering the number of hairs that fall out from his head every day, or else start growing inward and reemerge from his ears, a sure sign of old age. And he knows it, too, and fights it, judging by the amount of time he spends with the mirror and tweezers poking in his ears, like a baboon staring in the mirror, the same mirror that all the cats ignore, as I have noticed in an idle moment. Will that happen to most of us? I will use pitch on the tweezers to make it easier and catch all the inner hairs, though pitch is tricky, like my perfect fly trap with pitch and honey and secret ingredients, but what will the swallows eat if I catch all the flies, or what if a swallow takes a sticky fly from the edge of the trap and finds his beak shut? Hopefully, it will bother him only momentarily, or else he will come to me and I will clean him up. Sorry, friend. Silly me.

In the meantime, the big question is how to fly more than one hawk at once without other people's help? Of course, they have to be made first, but that's the easy part, though requires excellent fingers. Each hawk needs two lines for good control, like a horse, and that is fine with two hands available. The key is then to control two lines individually with one hand, like tying one line to the thumb and the other to the little finger, or, better yet, put the two lines on a short stick, say a half a cubit long, to be held by one hand. With two sticks like that, that makes for two hawks flying at once, but independently of one another. Great, great! There is more along these discoveries by the well-rested mind fancying itself as being born on Hawk Mountain, by tying the third hawk's two lines to the sides of the hip, like the reins of the King's horses are tied to his waist, using the magic in the belly that came from swallowing the knowledge of every god. And there is no reason to stop here, because there could be a fourth hawk guided by the head's movements, a fifth by two knees, a sixth by two feet, a seventh by two shoulders, they all at once tearing free from the fetters of the earth, carrying my name high for the things done that never were before, but no, it's too greedy for now, to control three hawks at once is a big enough challenge and most impressive, it's better to do three very well than four or more birds clumsily, crashing some, causing wicked laughter by my peers. Rehotep will love it too, hopefully forget his criticism of my wasting time in making hawks, and reward it in his own way, a double benefit. For a thousand years or a million, it will be a most difficult feat to be matched by the best hawk-flyers everywhere.

During these wanderings of my mind, the King practiced with the reins a lot, at first somewhat painfully, judged by his jerky jaw movements and occasionally squeezed eyelids, but gradually loosening up and enjoying it. He finally stopped and scratched his ear, was it tickling wax or ear hairs from premature old age, he got off the chariot, and, what on earth, he raised the axle on the left side and blocked it up to tilt the floorboard sharply. Luckily, the vehicle weighs very little, even for him, but still, what? He is about to practice a one-wheeler? Does he know what he is doing? Has he practiced this on his big chair? He took out the yoke pin, allowing him to twist the yoke back to the horizontal position in its lashing, essential to let the horses run properly during the one-wheeler act. Yes, he knows the tricks that allow this most difficult stunt maneuver on earth. He climbed back on the chariot, jammed his feet in the restraining sockets, this time held the reins in his hands as necessary, and began practicing the body swings necessary to master the one-wheeler. The lashings of the chariot, and especially of the supporting wheel, creaked as he tried to raise the axle off its block by lurching his body to the right. Maybe one time in ten or so, he managed to pull the axle up a finger-width above the block, a good effort, but the axle always fell back to the block quickly and a bit noisily, a small imperfection in his method. He was breathing hard, but his face glowed as never before as he wiped it on his tunic. What will the Queen think and say of the streaks on his cheeks, and will rains darken the sky, and will the earth's bones quiver and snap?

The King dropped the reins and swung his arms back as if ready to leap off the platform, but stopped in mid-motion and climbed down slowly. I sighed with relief. He patted the thin racing tire of elm on the well-exercised right wheel, returned the yoke and the pin to their proper places, and finally removed the axle from the block. He picked up the light chariot by the middle of the axle, using two hands where I would have used just one, raised the axle to a height of a cubit, and dropped the vehicle, which made a groaning sound, the same as after a brief flight off a big bump at high speed. He picked at the lashings of the two-piece composite spokes in the hubs and of the rim joints, and seemed satisfied that there was no loosening of the hide straps at any of the joints. Once more, he gently patted the tires, but mostly while staring ahead over the yoke and the imaginary horses. He uttered sharp commands to these horses to accelerate, then softer words for them to slow down and stop. He praised them profusely and individually, picked up his lamp, turned it down, and reached for his cane. There was a limp in his shuffle as he left.

13

Broken Feathers

The papyrus feathers felt good to my fingertips, like the touch of fresh linen on the Queen's new servant girl, holding excitement and mystery, but still quite different from the real hawk wings, one from an old bird I found dead, just before the dogs did, and the other of a young one gotten by myself with great effort but mostly a lucky arrow. The real feathers were splayed out by the side, a beautiful set of gray and brown and blue colors, for a constant reminder of my difficult task. I was deeply absorbed in mulling over some of the mysteries of gods' wheels and wings, especially these latest wings, starting from a state of hopelessness, getting to hopeful, and at last standing at the threshold of perfection and fame, but still not able to enter the temple full of sunlight. There arose a whisper from deep in my head, and whose voice is it, must be Rehotep's, "There is always a path for the Little Nobody to arrive at the Golden Temple before the Big Somebody lazily shuffles in. And, don't strive just to finish second in a temple race." But these words represented his benign philosophy, rarely voiced, not his normal work orders. At this moment of some erratic leaps of my mind it struck me that my proudest achievements were from my own doing, from my penchant to do the odd exciting thing, the irrational thing he often derides, forgetting his own occasional musings about how the kingfisher flashes out of nowhere with a silvery catch, or how the Six-Day Race can be won by a first-time driver on the poorest of soft wheels, against all odds, but of course six is a sacred number. In a blink, a palm-roach ran over my largest feather... not as good as a scarab, but still a good sign.

The latest papyrus feathers were good, perhaps very good, but can any blooming baboon tell me if the remaining differences from the real ones were great enough to worry about, or if, by Thoth's infinite grace, they might even be more excellent. I was imagining myself standing tall before the great god, awaiting an encouraging whisper in the depth of my head, then anoint myself with scents fit for the gods and seize the flower of the royal ornament, gladdening the heart of the Finest Hedgehog in the sweet breath of the north breeze, and enjoying the sound of the Queen's water clock as it merges into the sound of mine, to borrow a few words from the Poet-of-Amun.

The whisper came up as prayed for, but rapidly increasing to a wind, a shout, a storm, a gale, a lightning crack in front of me, smashing the real hawk and the papyrus one alike into smithereens. I screamed, as the cane barely missed my fingers, those excellent fingers that had just caressed the new wings that only the god Thoth could fully appreciate, and my head turned dizzy as if blood was suddenly drained from it.

"Follow me," hissed Rehotep, his face hard-lined like Hawk Peak in the Barrens Howl, raked by the claws of Horus himself. He led me to a far corner, sat down and let me stand in front of him, wobbly on the knees, as a gambler seeing his last throw fall off the table. His eyes, just yesterday twinkling, were now piercing, like heavy practice arrows going through several copper ingots. What's happened to him? Hopefully, just a bad meal. He keeps buying new spices from shady, transient Asiatics, and now I have to pay the price.

"I may have to let you go," he said with a calmness, which made the words even worse.

"Sire." I tried to say something, anything. Would you like a bowl of your favorite fruit? Oh, Thoth, what's his favorite fruit, and also forgive my proud face one day, and my feeble faith the other.

"Among other things, yesterday you renamed my dog. My dog! Next you might rename a god. Go back to your village where nobody cares about your manners. Go there and invent rat traps for a living. Rename my dog, what's his name? But the list goes on. Next. It is useless to look for better wings for your own pleasure when the King calls for better wheels to roll more smoothly in ruts and bounce softer on rocks. How can you forget that our new wheel is already more clever than all of the great monuments put together? They are just piles of lifeless stones, but the wheel rolls fast and carries more weight than its own. Next. It is even more useless for you to dream of a certain demi-goddess' honey-bitsha. A word to the wise: when you climb a very high mountain, the closer to the sun, the colder it gets. But how would you know that, Mudcarver?"

"Sire? Please." I rubbed my eyes to stop them from clouding over, only to give rise to dancing spots of light, like dust motes in the light beam of a tomb-robbers' lamp. "Please. I know little."

"Ah, as I expected. You betray your muddy roots. Perhaps I shouldn't tell you, but it means, to the select few, what your people call, crudely, a hedgehog. I mean, of a woman." He coughed, and again, looking to the side. He studied his cane and found one of the small papyrus feathers from the busted wings sticking to it. He brushed it off and watched it drift and settle on his foot. The spirit of my old hawk, surprising his big toe, but he kicked it off. His sandal made a brushing sound against the ground and flew off, farther than the feather. He pretended it was intentional, by clapping his hands. "Of course, if you have an itch, scratch it. Of course, it's safer to scratch a servant's hedgehog than a royal honey-bitsha. But forget what I said. Now get out of my sight and don't come back until tomorrow. Right after sunrise."

I bowed slowly and deeply, uncertain if any words were proper or necessary. With hesitation, I picked up the delicate piece and turned toward the exit. Hot air was swirling around my head, but my thoughts struggled to reach higher than the air, into a cool stillness. My fingers felt the tear in the little feather and the prospect of repairing or replacing it momentarily distracted me. Wings, wings, my Horus wings, surely I shall return to the task, but not straightaway, and not barefoot. No, it cannot be done barefoot, especially not when the Queen is looking. In the meantime, have I already earned a small chamber in the bowels of Oblivion Mountain? Never again to see her finely trimmed and painted feet, the most delicate feet, surely indicative of her apt and keen mind as well, as her priestly scribe said.

From around the corner, strains of scratchy music ruined the air. Most certainly from the blind musician who was allowed to sit in front of the whip-maker's shop, as if to signify the low status of its products. The saddest music in the world, each note starting out smooth and warm and pleasant but curling up into a wobbly, tiny scream, like my life at times. Was it a strange poison in my blood that made me imagine any music that way? There was a vague pain wandering through my chest, belly, and head. Why can't I have real conversations with Rehotep or with any of the apprentices? Where should I eat my supper? At times it was nice to eat alone, as if all the food in the world was mine, not having to look over my shoulder, or hurry like a scrawny dog, but other times it was best with friends. Better yet, be fed by the smooth fingers of the chubby dancer who had asked me about using one of my new glues for the big glass bead in her belly button, to avoid chronic redness, let alone losing the precious bead to a customer. Properly preparing the skin with my own fingers seemed to be the best procedure, and soon. Still, I worried about being too successful and not being needed again. Of course, there are others, plump breasts adorned in flowers, dancing on soft feet and hinting of mysterious nude encounters, one in every corner-house, time will pass, no more dreaming of snake potion, dizzy-breathing, I will lie alone, tired of smelly women, beer slowly coming up through the reed, Thoth's special cool beer from the secret cellar, slowly seeping into the mouth, slurped along the two sides of the tongue, to the highest slurping-feeling, better than the goddess' imaginary honey-bitsha might be, slurping the brew to the back sides of the tongue.

"Come back!" His voice was like a magical spear, curving around the corner of the alley, kicking a couple of servants out of its way, bouncing off a hot pile of crusty breads carried on the head by a vendor, and slowing to a surprisingly gentle touch on my ear. I had to strain to get it, although I must have half expected it, if uncertain about its implications for me, just when I was recovering from the pain he caused and started to settle on some pleasant diversion, while trying to yank the pole of my life in a different direction. I returned, but at a snail's pace, hoping for a sandstorm to come up and save me, or something.

He was seemingly preoccupied with the crude sign of a hedgehog he drew in the dust with his cane. Was that a fleeting smile? He knows how to torture somebody without using any sharp instruments. I could hear from another corner, or was it only my imagination, the painfully slow drops of a tired water clock.

"You see, Mudcarver, there could be a big problem for me, if the Overseer of Royal Latrines finds out about these papyrus wings of yours. How come we have so much papyrus that we can waste it on silly wings, while he has to scrounge for scraps? You know, you can play with the wings when you wish, but he has to get his quota of scraps every day, no exception. More after big feasts. Are you going to tell him to provide leaves and straw to his boss as in ancient times? And the same to the fine women? Think about these delicate issues."

"Yes, Sire." I stared at the papyrus feather in my hand.

"Now, since you always have time to waste, start inventing a new sign, the honey-bitsha version of this plain hedgehog. That would be a worthwhile achievement, something to carve in rock with pride. Of course, I have some ideas, but I will leave that glory to the young." He poked the hairy little circle in the dust with his cane before turning away abruptly, possibly to hide another smile.

14

General Horem

A messenger woke me from a great depth where the Crocodile-Headed Amet was holding my feet. He was a Maranu Brave, clean and neatly dressed in white linen. I struggled to arrange my tunic, while he was adjusting his black-striped headdress, looking into my larger-than-average personal mirror on the wall. My priceless mirror, he had the nerve.

Why do so many messengers come to get me, always too early or too late in the day, and why is there no conversation with any of them? He motioned and I followed him across the courtyard, becoming a little more clear-headed while looking at the stars, realizing that it was almost dawn, in the seventh day of the promisingly rich New Flood Year, because the Dog Star Sopet was sitting brightly over the horizon. The heavy door of libani cedar opened smoothly in its fortress-like frame, on its ebony hinges, to the porticos of General Horem's quarters. Ebony, Ethiopian treasures. I had seen his doorway only from a distance before, not able to discern any details. I had stayed away from it, not because of lacking curiosity, but for not wanting to arouse suspicions regarding my ambitions and strategies at court, or about the General's fine young women. I had enough silly dreams for the moment.

Inside, a nearly finished small obelisk, with tools and sheaves of electrum scattered on the ground, showed the creator-god Ptah of Memphis blessing the General after his first Kush campaign, presenting him with the golden shebu collar of honor. Leopard words were leaping down from the god's lips: "The soldier laughs with the bull and the crocodile, the soldier weeps not at death." Just beyond the monument I caught a glimpse of a room full of palm-leaf baskets holding papyrus rolls, the biggest House of Life I had ever seen outside of the Great Perfect Temple of Amun at Karnak. The baskets were lined up on shelves like rowers bulging with muscles on the royal Sun-barge.

I was expecting to be transferred to another attendant soon, but the original messenger handled it all. He pushed a brightly painted door open and motioned to me to enter while he turned away and left. The room was simply furnished and decorated. In fact, it looked more like a shop than a rich man's house, with benches and tools. A large piece of stone showed the early cuts by a sculptor's hand. I smelled some animal's presence.

"Don't be surprised, young man," said a smooth, deep voice. The man came in through a side door, letting more light in from the rising sun. He was holding on leashes a large dog and a cheetah, similar in size and shape, except for the heads and colors. "And don't be afraid, either. They are perfectly disciplined, better than any servant. How do you like these safsaf willow leashes? I am sure you are the best person to appreciate such a refinement in animal control. A little more than a leather leash would provide. Here, with the willows, you can pull as with leather, but also push a little or even encourage them sideways, which includes up or down. Every direction imaginable is at your fingertips. Want to try it? All right, if not, maybe later?" He smiled and pursed his open lips as he slightly wiggled the willows with one hand so that first the animals separated from one another and then came together, almost to touch their cheeks. The cheetah's nose flared with each breath, bending the whiskers up and down, and the General's broad nostrils flared likewise, as if they were searching the air for elusive scents.

"Sire, I can't think."

"You will. Relax, you are among friends, even these two beasts, if I tell them, and I already did. Now, why are you here? I will cut straight to it. I know about you, just little things, of course. You have ideas. That invention, for example, to teach a fellow apprentice how to swim, suspending him by a rope from a pole, the rope being attached to his balance point at the waist, that's rather good, thinking of the problems of the current. I should have every soldier learn it that way, improving the whole Army. Or use it to tease crocodiles with criminals. It seems to me that we should talk a lot, for years." The General raised his high forehead even higher. His broad shoulders protruded from the leopard straps of his tunic. "Talk about Akhmin, first, where we both have roots. Do you know about your roots? Not that we want to spend our lives in the sleepy town, but there are good memories from there, right? My first knife, which I had to make of desert obsidian, being poor, and my first chiseled figure, my first reed pen, my first god, my first goddess." He put a hand on the sculpture emerging from the stone and stroked it gently. "Just like this, my greatest Ptah, as it will become soon, coming to almost-life out of the stone, to help me in the coming years. It is a good relationship between the two of us. Is he your god, too?"

"Sire." How could I tell him that I liked Ptah just fine, but preferred Thoth.

"Sure. It can be hard to say the right thing about gods, at any age. But, remember that Ptah is the oldest and created the sun Aten from pure thought, and Horus is his heart, and Thoth, I assume your favorite, by knowing my friend Rehotep well enough, is Ptah's tongue. Surely, your tongue will be as good as your hands are now. We will talk more about gods some other time. They have lots of patience, we could learn from them, especially if you know how to make them from pure thought." He opened two folding stools onto their bovine-shaped legs and motioned to me to sit down. The legs of his stool were made of ivory, mine of acacia. He dangled a hand below the leopard-skin cover and stroked the ivory. "Good to touch. Suppose I give you all the ivory you want, and big enough pieces, would you make a set of wheel spokes out of it for me? Very strong material. I pay well for a commissioned project like that. You are shaking your head?"

"Sire, please, if you wish to hear some technical detail and ..." My stool creaked on its ebony hinges. I looked around for some grease.

"Of course, I wish to hear it, all. I may have heard part of it before, but there is often something new from your shop. Continue."

"Sire, there are many things. Ivory is too hard to carve and glue to last for the long time. It cannot be bent into the necessary shape of two fingers spread wide apart, like a flock of geese flying, for six of those to be tied together to form the wheel. Also, ivory is heavier than wood in the same size, by two fingers out of ten in the water test, and the ivory wheel would also have a greater rotational heaviness, altogether bad for the horses to pull. It would be difficult to find a replacement for elm, which we can bend or grow into the ideal goose-flock shape, to make up a wheel of six composite spokes, which is important for secret reasons of flexibility, and strength at the hub." Suddenly I caught myself, being much too revealing.

"Two fingers out of ten, you say?" His eyes were widening.

"It is the same as one finger out of five, Sire. That is a lucky coincidence because three out of ten would be harder to simplify. I am sorry."

"All right. Talk about speed. How fast can you go? Can your wheels beat my Che-Che? I want to see this race, and so will the King and the Queen. Can you set it up? It should be a short race, so we can see it entirely from beginning to end, for assurance of no cheating. We can have Che-Che a little hungry, and let her go for a controlled prey a short distance away. The horses will be the two best of the King's Thousand Swift Horses. Of course, this project can simmer on the flame's edge for a long time, because there are more important things to do first. And, to learn. How do you make those spread-finger spokes? Here, take this small gift. I made the obsidian blade myself when I was young. I like the color of yellow sand, with swirls of black. It has an uneven edge, by its very nature, but sharp. Making it was a great joy, I am sure you appreciate it better than anybody else can, the carving of a carving tool, so to speak. So, how about the making of those spokes? It seems impossibly difficult even to me, who is excellent with the fingers. The steaming of the elm is easy enough, but the copper strap clamped on the stretch-side of the piece before the bending, I have seen it done, and... It feels strange not to know something in a shop. Not a simple shop, to be sure, but still a shop."

"I am your humble servant, Sire, but I am not allowed to say it all. I am sorry, and am prepared to die."

"Don't be afraid, you will live a good and long life. There are many other things we need to talk about. For example, my Army always needs improvements, and I hope you will help me... For example, I saw your new hawk that you control in flight. Imagine what such a little god could do to the enemy in a battle, striking them with terror from the sky. Think about even more than one hawk at a time, think big, and think of much gold."

He saw it? For Seth's curses, the precautions were not enough. "Sire, anybody can make such a hawk, although of lesser quality, but controlling it is my secret, and battles are bad."

"I understand. I am the survivor of battles and kings, yes, you live longer if you stay away from them. Still, think about the idea, and let me know when you will try something along those lines, literally. In the meantime, Ptah is generous in many ways, which leads me to the next proposition. I will tell you a secret, but lean closer. I am here and I am what I am because of good luck in becoming, at your age, a military scribe. Of course, I also had my sharp knife to carve part of my luck, but so do you. In the long journey to the Far Western Horizon, the scribe needs to plan about how he travels and with whom, to arrive properly dressed and well fed."

"Sire, it is difficult for me."

"I admire loyalty more than anything in people, and I will not press you in any way. Furthermore, I admire your Master, who is a friend among a very few friends. You should not abandon him, let alone betray him. But, he is beginning to have some pain in the mouth, which even the best healer cannot heal, and that is a sign from the Lord of the Extreme West. Perhaps he is not confiding everything in you, a matter of pride even in a non-soldier. You should understand that he and I are very similarly inclined in much of our thinking. For example, we both have utmost pleasure in the scrolls of a good House of Life, or in venturing beyond counting on our fingers. The big difference is that he can heal and I can kill. That is fine and makes the world safer for both of us. Where do you fit in all this? That is entirely up to you." He stood up and touched my hand and shoulder. "You have the bone architecture of a future

Great Scribe. One day you will be proud of your own words in stone, like I am of my carved New Stela, and I can help you when you are ready. In the meantime, you can help me a little here and there, without any undue pressure, of course. I have patience, exceeding the patience of Sobek, when he is quietly submerged in the river, with only the eyes following the sun. One more thing, all the good in the world will happen faster and better with a fine young woman in your house, so, when you come back after a deep bath, you will see my best daughters and hear their happy songs."

"But, I do not have a house, and can't see how and when."

"You will get one, it should be a very fine house, before or after getting the wife. We will see." He turned and nudged his animals out of the room. On the way through the courtyard I kicked a few pebbles, watching them careen and come to rest in the dust. Should I collect pebbles?

15

Quill-Lick

Horus shrieked his sky-godly name call after he attached the safsaf willow line to the heavy gold shebu collar of honor on my neck. I put spit on my skin where the collar was scratchy.

He motioned widely with his pointing wing. "Have you been to the latrine recently? You have to be as light as possible. Can you reckon how much lighter you could be? You are not the first to calculate anything, but the best. How much lighter are you when you are emptied? Of course, the more beer you drink, the more you empty before the flight, I have done that calculation already, but always check others' reckoning, so, you are showing me one finger's worth out of a hundred? Good. Superficially, that's not much of a difference, but even the big carrier hawk appreciates it.

"Carver, put that earthen jug down, it is many times heavier than air, even half empty. You cannot wing it safely with a dizzy head, you village dolt. I will smash that jug. For Ptah's sake, you may need to go to the latrine once more before you are ready. For safety, do you want a lentil mirror in front of your nose, and feel like a king? A King with a beautiful Queen at his pleasure? You will need a lot of mirrors, and big ones, to save your scribe-skin from the Akhmin Gang's daughters, watch out, said your Master, because they hunger for young men. Take your sandals off, they are heavier than air, and you will need to steer with your sensitive feet, lacking a proper tail.

Pretentious foot-covers." He picked up a stalk of tickle-nose and began to scratch the sole of my feet while starting to let out the coiled safsaf line. "Stretch out your excellent arms and move them as if to make waves, but like birds do, invisible waves, with sustainable effort, not like the flight of turtles."

I felt a tug on my collar upward, and it happened. Horus let out the line, all sixty-seven cubits of it, rounded to the nearest sacred number, and that allowed me to rise and travel forward, as well. I yelled with excitement, but Horus, behind me in the distance, motioned for silence. He guided me, and it was so warm and smooth high in the air that I did not care where we were going. I was feeling light, and I marveled how he steered me with one line to my collar.

It was the smells that revealed our destination in the darkness. It was the smell of oils and sweat, and also of food and wine, of surprisingly high quality for the infamous den, Gods-Avert-Their-Eyes. There was also a mixture of perfume scents, rather strange for this place. Horus guided me to a safe, dark upper corner in the den, a place I have to remember if I wish to come back later, by any other route, like squeezing in through a ventilation passage, right behind me. The wrestlers were all there, close below me, in high spirits, but there were no women present as I first assumed from the perfumes. I scanned the agitated faces, and assured myself that nobody has noticed me, while checking my escape route with a hand probing in the narrow tunnel. Where is Ankh? Another time I watched these crude men, she was among them, playing with them for hours.

The leader, Basted, strangely named so because he was not the cat-goddess, although he was strong and agile, stood up and roared a long one to call for silence. "The worst loser will now get the lowest prize, the bare hedgehog, go, and do it quickly, we are ready to move on." The loser wrestler grinned, took a long drink from his round-bottomed cup, got up and went to the wall, which had several carvings of fist-sized egg shapes, each with a set of outward-drawn short quills.

Basted smeared pitch with a knife in the middle of a hedgehog sign on the wall, and he yelled, "Hetikha-kiss," what, that's the Queen's favorite little animal, and a chant went up, accompanied by their drumming with every implement in the den, "Het-lick, Het-lick, Het-lick." Soon the chant broke down and everybody started yelling randomly, "Short tongue, loser," "Ouch," "Sandy-tongued loser," "Only the quills, loser," "Not the sweet taste, idiot," "Practice your tongue on the quills, loser," "Stuck to the pitch already?" "Limp tongue, loser," "Quill-licker, quill-licker."

"Enough of your pleasure, loser," shouted Basted. "Get away from that work of art, and now comes the winner's choice." He went to the wall and wiped the biggest sign with an undergarment of fine linen drenched in perfume, where did I last see that delicate cloth of tiny weave, the strong scent was of sweet sage and pomegranate flower, driving the noise ever higher. He got on his knees and put his hands on the quills, throwing his head back and roaring and grunting. The chant and drumming echoed ever more, "Het-lick, Het-lick, Het-lick, Nose-to-nose, Rough-tongue, Stone-licker."

What does Ankh like about these filthy athletes? I leaned out to see his tongue better, and lost my balance. Horus must have been inattentive to me just then, or the collar line broke by willow fatigue caused by the long flight, and I fell into the chaotic pit. After a moment of sudden silence, all eyes and hands fell on me at once, and I shrieked like a rabbit torn alive by hyenas, feeling the knobby fists and grappling fingers of the drunken wrestlers.

"Stop," yelled Basted, blinking fast, probably from the perfume getting in his eyes, "there is a better punishment for the silly Carver-scribe, so hold him tight. Bring out the Akhmin noble wenches of the long-wilted lotus hearts, and let them pluck this intruding rooster." He spat on the wall and waved, and dancers appeared, Muu dancers, softly wailing to the harps. They swirled slowly in their long tunics, slowly because of the tight cloth, closer and closer, slapping their thighs and bellies. The oldest one flashed a thin smile at me with her dark teeth, and leaned closer to breathe hot vapors into my ear. "Young Master, future keeper of the happy treasure, rejoice forever, since my father Ay hid my hedgehog from the hungry foxes, we can prove it later if you want, to save it for your pleasure, in the great house that will be yours tomorrow."

She sucked a deep breath out of my ear, ready to continue, but was pushed aside by another dancer, pushed into the groping hands of the wrestlers who began a chant, "Ruffle the quills, ruffle her quills."

The new dancer in front pounced upon my ear with agile baboon lips to shield it from the noise. "Let's have you, young military scribe, work with fresh quills, and let you earn the great house of my father Horem in a day or two."

How many houses will be there? She raked my buttocks with her sharp nails, it's a mixture of pain and pleasure, but she was punched from behind and knocked aside by another Muu, while the chant resumed, "Pluck the quills, pluck her quills." The new dancer up front kicked off her golden slippers, slapped her heavy thighs together to the chant's rhythm and clucked with her flaming tongue into my ear. "Crawl into my experienced duck downs in the great house of my father Pentu, inherit his Royal Scribe tablet and First Physician bag at the first opportunity, the first who can approach the person of the King and caress the Queen legally."

She was yanked away by a wrestler on each ankle, and I prepared for new lips in my ear, but there was a jerk on my collar, where was my protecting Horus all this time that I needed him, and I was soon far from the Averts-Den, first climbing to the clouds, learning that not all flights are smooth like hawks soaring with hardly a wing-flap, then plunging into reeds and mud and linen, choking and wet, remembering something about sweaty wrestlers and dancers of perfumed flesh, but a memory only one finger's worth out of a thousand times a thousand.

16

Prick-Fish

S tars were my only light as I struggled with the lock on the heavy door. The goddess Nut was teasing me with her constellations, just when I could not linger on them. Tomorrow, yes, they will be the same, they will wait for me, easier to study than crocodiles courting in the mud, or eagles mating in the air, or frogs teaching their tadpoles. Like a young girl, doing her face in the same colors every evening for her lover, though they both change from day to day. Now, I must work in the starlight, from the fires of big caravans that sleep in daytime. Where are they, and are they burning dry dung, and why, just to allow me to see this door at night?

I resisted the temptation to open my hooded light ever so slightly to see better into the huge but torturous keyhole. The rich have fat bellies and heavy doors. I stopped and listened, as it is best to do periodically at this time and place, and meanwhile studied the gnaw marks on the bottom of the door and its frame, the crazy hedgehogs, why do they go for the plywood? Or, why do they want to get in here? Must be the animal glue used to put together the plies, because they prefer the six-ply pieces to the ones with fewer plies. Could be an interesting project on the telltale experiments for a hungry little fellow, and proclaim the results on the rock wall of my tomb, many decades hence. A great obelisk with plenty of electrum would be even better for the health of my lasting spirit. Rehotep would be especially proud of me, and my Queen at the time and future readers a million years later especially astonished, a bonus for the thoughtful scribe-king.

I tried another key, and another. Like a dog that gets excited by hedgehogs and toads and any similar-sized pebble at dusk. My first dog, Red Fox, is probably barking, wherever, at imaginary rocks and toads.

There was a noise, and I had to freeze. It was the guard at the expected time, tripping on the well-placed branch as expected, releasing a scared bird from the bush and consequently the guard's worst curses against several lowly gods. I was sorry for the man, but he had the best possible job in the palace for somebody with such a foul language. This was not my favorite time of the night to be out on foot, either, preferring dusk or dawn for any serious activity. Onward … the guard was gone, most certainly for the rest of the night, for this area. And, he hasn't even faced a real ghost yet, let alone two or three at once. These guards are easy to spook. Luckily, Pentu is too tightfisted, like every rich man, to have more guards, or to train the few to perfection. I will do better, when my time comes.

There were only a few more keys remaining in my right-side pouch. There are so many doors that are hard to open, and many creak even in the palace, as if chicken fat or heavy oil was prohibitively expensive, but ultimately they all open to the right key and ears and fingers. Finally, the seventh key, a perfect number, as expected, began to yield the lock. But, why could I not pick the seventh first, and succeed right away? I notched the working key's handle for future reference, before putting it in the left pouch, and oiling the hinges with a feather at the tight spots, and gently pushing the door open, half a cubit wide, for a tight squeeze through, while exhaling deeply to flatten myself. The door closed silently … how could this fine oil bring some gold for me? I should try to sell it to Pentu himself, first.

My light set at half brightness was adequate for the space and the objects in it, with tolerable smoke emitted. In fact, the smoke of fragrant oil was good to suppress the smells, which alone made me happy to not work here, not to be a fish-carver here, although the prettiest ones employed by Pentu do merit a glance even from a wheel-maker or a military scribe. My light beam scanned the room full of surgical tools and supplies on crowded shelves. I let the light linger on a beautiful new bowstring drill, probably imported from the north. I resisted the urge for taking it. The light fell on a shelf full of mummies, supposedly of the sacred and rare Oxinkha, the sharp-nosed fish, also known as the sting-fish, also known as the little-lightning-fish, also known as the phallus-fish, so named by the waab priests. Next to the mummies was a red granite statue of the red-haired Seth, appropriate because of the devilish curing powers assigned to the fish by the physician-priests.

I passed a cool stone vessel emitting a fruity smell into the reeking air, like a small island in a vast sea. It was chunks of ripe yellow melon, and it tasted good during the short break that Nut allowed me, winking through a small window in the ceiling. I had to force myself to take very little, to arouse no suspicion of anything amiss, later. I am not a thief. Anyway, the melon would be overripe by the next day, so I took two more chunks.

I began my search for the live Oxinkha rumored to be in the forbidden room. These sting-fish are known to impart unpleasant jolts to the person who touches them at the wrong part of their skin. Not deadly, unless from fright. Enough to be cautious, though it's nothing compared to real sky-bangs, which are extremely rare, perhaps once in a hundred years. Of course, there are stories of them, some too fantastic to believe, like the huge fire-snake preferring to lick bronze swords strapped to the waist, and charring the whole rain-soaked soldier in the process, while nearby others with wooden spears laid down on the ground escaped. Surrender to the Amun-fire must be the healthy choice. What is certain at this point is that the melon is peaking in perfection, and will be declining rapidly by daylight. I noticed a crock of ground nutmeg next to the melon, and dipped a piece in it, momentarily forgetting my dislike for the spice. It was a mistake, the nutmeg made me cough, and pure chunks of melon were needed to wash it down.

There was a stone tub, the size of a child's coffin, on a heavy table, and wooden sticks and copper rods and gloves covered with magic symbols. My mind was racing about the dangers lurking in this tub, and the opportunities … how could the fish cure a pain in the mouth, or any other affliction, without burning the skin, let alone melting a bronze sword by the fire-snake? Perhaps this strange shop is the work of desperate old physician-priests grabbing at every unusual weed or toad or fish or scorpion to cure their aches. I lifted the lid of the tub, scraping the heavy stone on stone. I stopped to listen, then leaned closer, cautiously. The eyes of the phallus-head-fish reflected in the light of my lamp, yellow with flashes of red, like a small monster protruding from the dark recesses of the tub. It opened its small round mouth rapidly, as if gasping for air. Monster or not, I felt sorry for it, and searched for food. Nothing around the tub was obviously prepared and waiting for the fish. I tried a small chunk of melon, no interest. A sprinkle of nutmeg, the fish took a piece floating on the surface, but spit it out, a comrade at heart. I put on the gloves. Oxinkha seemed to make a sound, but it came out growling from elsewhere, maybe from behind the table.

"Sneaky fish, another fish?" The voice was from the floor, behind the table.

"No." While fumbling with the light, I glanced at the doorway, how many leaps to it?

"Yes, you, who? Have another drink, stupid fish."

"I am not."

"Yes, show your face, now!"

Was it Pentu? That grinding gizzard throat. I shifted my feet and the light to see, yes, rising up on his elbow, huffing from a small effort. Not threatening, so far. But I will not put the light on my own face. "I mean, Sire, sorry."

"Sorry? No need. Aha, your voice, that fine voice. Did the fish recognize it, too? Hungry. Give him melon in beer, and to me, too."

"No, Sire, there is no beer here."

"No? That light is drunk. But it's the finest lamp ever, and I will buy one, though short on gold, but have glass beads and a daughter or two. Find that beer. You gave all the beer to the fish? I am thirsty. Dry and thirsty, and tight, it's yours, for a ladle of beer, here." He tore at his heavy glass shebu collar, which glinted in a dark blue color. "Hurry!"

What to do? Give him a drink, any drink, but carefully. He had no weapon on him, but the large ring on each hand was worrisome, because of his huge size. His size was legendary, if exaggerated. Two events sprung to my mind, most unwelcome at this moment. First, when he crashed through the bottom of his chariot. That was properly strengthened, and then he stepped up another day, bringing his two stallions to their knees, the science is clear, since the floorboard is supported by the axle at the rear and by the pole resting on the horses' yoke, so his weight is partially on the animals. Still, it is possible that the horses were just weak.

"The ladle." The fish may have heard and recognized his voice, not surprising if it was that sacred, because it made a splash as it turned around in the narrow space, spraying me with smelly water. I found the ladle and gave Pentu a drink from the tub, was it full of bubbles stirred up by the tail? I resisted the temptation of trying it myself.

He slurped it up too fast, and belched. "The best brew, right? This is what we will serve at your big wedding, right? You have a future, Carver. With a little luck, a little time, maybe become the Second Physician Who Approaches the Person of the King, I say. Or, even higher. You need more ambition, all the way. Give me more." He poured it over his face while gulping it down.

"Future? When, Sire?" It was stupid to ask, but too late to stop.

"When? After the wedding. Let's see, which remaining daughter is best, most promising as your future Queen?"

"Queen?"

"They all have some royal quality, useful to a young king-to-be, yes. More ladle, hurry! How to choose the best, why, you can look at them closely, with your bright light in the dark, on top of it, the melon contest, to reveal their heir-delivery prospects."

"Heir? To me?"

"I, I, the First Physician, will certify the winner. All from this groin, hard as a rock, all healthy females, but different. The melons will tell who is the best for you, while you watch. My great discovery. Who can eat the most melons in an hour? They all stand in the river to loosen their bladders, nonstop, nobody squirming. The winner is sure to have the best flushed crotch for making heirs. You will see, Son."

He wiped his face and licked his hand. "I encourage you to experiment with your body like that, but mostly with other people's bodies. There is value in that. It would be especially valuable if we could find new cures for the King. In addition, he should stop driving his chariots, and stop dreaming of racing and the like. He is too daring, and you could help, but worst comes to worst, you will step up, after he is dead, all the way, and you should be hot on making your viable heirs, since you need many, just in case, and my daughter, winner of the melons, will help you. Well connected, we will all win."

"Sire, please, I don't know, I cannot, my Master …"

"He? Soon he will need more cures himself, if I am not mistaken about his mouth, and I am never mistaken about tongues and lips. Reminds me, the groom has a bolstering, too, the fish brushing your prick to make it excellent, not today, it needs to get fat, then he will be ready, with the daughters lined up to judge when you're prickled enough, you will tell me how it feels, let's experiment forever, what is this, warm beer on my legs, where was it when I needed it, but it's good to stand in the river and let it all go, tell the fish to practice on prisoners, it can be yours, everything, the melon and the ripe daughter." He rolled over, groaning and cracking, and I backed away, undecided about my shaky light beam, shuffling faster and faster toward the door.

17

Hedgehog on a Donkey Ride

Ay squinted downward from the setting sun, and into the golden bowl, while the wailers pretended to suffer in silence, shifting their weights randomly in the beginning, then increasingly in unison, a slow wave of nudging shoulders and hips propagating down the lineup circling us. Where is Happy Haam under the two-faced paints, maybe I can find her by her swirling long fingers, shiny nails.

Ay squeezed his eyelids shut, and his thin lips trembled. Blue Pearl is dead. Was she killed? Who killed her, and why?

Ay's eyes catch a flock of rekhyets sweeping overhead, strangely banding together and going higher and higher and farther out over the desert, where they can't possibly have any business going, but just about when they became indistinct flecks they turned and came back toward their grove. "Rekhyts," said Tut a few days earlier, having observed a similar strange flight when he tried to be alone in the dunes, just for a short while, to see creatures without people. He says it differently, like nobody else, but he can. "Halfway between dawn and noon, or a bit closer to noon, who knows, why and why they fly that way, never mind. Two dozen, exactly. Rekhyts." He talks that way. And often counts, though might dislike it. "How can you learn not to count?"

She is gone. Why? It is sad and not so sad. She was plain in rich clothes, too plain for a desired royal role, like those birds, but had good hips and hands and heart. Maybe the hips were too wide, in somebody else's path.

Ay motions to the priests and wailers, and a melodious hum arises. He reaches into the bowl and raises a handful of fly wings, taken from desiccated insects when the wings fall off by their own weight. Not a job for anyone who can reckon numbers. He casts the wings into the breeze, sings a quiet line, and tries to shake off the last wings that cling to his skin but not to his rings.

A sunbeam glints off the silent tears next to his nostrils. He joins the wailers for one shift of pitch, and tightens his lips.

Why, why, and what next?

What was before? She had excellent hips, and there was that first-ever-last-ever ride during those months of secrecy, after the secret wedding, why all that, only Ay knows. We go for a ride under the peeking half moon, with Blue Pearl clutching a jug of Ay's sweetest wine, starting out on two donkeys, our hands reaching out, pulling the animals closer. She says, giggling, tossing her brushed hair and breezy linen, "Why go on two donkeys when one is enough for two?" Sure, why not, a grand experiment, soon it's her bare hedgehog on the bare donkey, a most sturdy creature, and in nine breaths of inhaling the stars the hedgehog cries, "Please, Isis, please, Hathor, yes, Carver, enough, strong Carver, let's slide off and make it a long night, the sand is better than gold, but one day, soon, teach me how to drive like a warrior Queen, no hands on the reins." Why, good, but is it all safe, every young woman in sight wants to drive fast, with hands on my hips, hoping to fall off into soft sand together, laughing and crying all the way.

Chaotic sounds, the wailing momentarily subsides, is that Ankh's sweet voice rising from them? "Carver? What's her name, Blue Pearl, yes. Give this to her, Carver, this blue-green excellent wine, a little more green than blue, just right, make her relax fully when the tiny crocodile kicks to get out, in the hot and sweaty hour of the night, make it a cool night for her... she should finish the last drop." A week later, again a cup for her, in another hot night. Ankh knows her wines.

Ay squinted hard and shook another wing off, still not the last, back into the bowl. The wailers raised their fake pain, how many wings would fill that bowl, a final stupid question, but learn to reckon more, Rehotep always suggests.

The wailers began to hurt my ears, how can I plug them fast, if nobody is watching?

18

Fly, Chariot!

Rehotep was agitated and that tightened my stomach. Was it his age? How will I handle him this time? What does he want, just when I should spend more time on my new poem for Ankh, instead of doing ever more clever axles and spokes in this dingy shop, and how to make the words clear to her but not to others? Her voice last time was sad and tired, though she would deny it. Perhaps fretting about the husband who is watching from a height, like a hawk, thinking up curses. Come, fly with me on my fast wheels, sweet lotus, you always liked my reckless speed, but where to go and stay alive? Sweet saam, that's better for her hair, to go with the eyes.

"Where did you put the Amem-Five split axle model that you carved? Just when I am ready to work with it again, it's gone. I can't get a minimum of order maintained in this godforsaken shop. I should let all of you go back to your dust-heaps, so I can live in orderly peace. Let the King fashion his own wheels and axles." Rehotep was soon red in the face as he went from the shelves of the currently used models to the bin of discarded ones, where he tossed objects from one heap to another. "Perhaps the spies have it by now, or the sweeper took it home to his boys, or broke it and burned it to hide his crime. I have seen it all before."

"No, Sire. None of these happened, because I hid it from all other eyes. There, in the crocodile mummy's belly, through the bottom slit.

Some time ago, if you please recall, you suggested that I find a good place for these. I also made huge changes in it since you last saw it." He kicked the bin, went to the mummy and pulled the hand-sized piece out of its belly. The model consisted mainly of a lengthwise split round stick, which was tied together near its ends so that it looked almost like the original stick. The devil made me to talk big. "Let's see, Sire, how fast you can figure out all the changes in this little stick. Should be easy for you... although, understanding the secrets in this piece may be hard. I will start the water clock on fast counting." I took a deep breath, ready to run if he flings something at me.

"Wait. Give me time to get ready." He dusted his tunic. I knew he wanted to talk, ranging over many things, depending on how much time he needed to think about my crazy challenge. "Yes, I like the mummy, it might deter some of the inexperienced spies. And models are great fun, I feel it, you oiled the mating surfaces before tying them together, they move a little. Is your bragging about the slight scissoring of the stick? Hurry, I have an unpleasant appointment with Pentu, possibly about his new fish, do you know anything of it?"

"No, Sire, rest your mind, I do not have his fish. Anyway, this split stick is more profitable. If the scissoring is up and down, the strength of the split-and-bound stick is the same as the stick's strength was before it was split."

"That could be fun to prove. How did you reckon?"

"As you taught me … in simple bending, like using a log to cross a stream. A stone in the middle of the model to weigh it down, a scale to measure the amount of bending. The deflection is the same for the two sticks, split and not split, but only if the scissoring is up and down. If we make an axle like that, properly oiled and bound together, one wheel to each half piece, the scissoring will allow each wheel to bounce up and down, quite independently of what the other wheel is doing. On the other hand, if the split face is turned so that the scissoring is toward the horizon, the split stick is acting weaker, using the same stone for weight, than the original piece."

"All right, but why make it weaker?"

"Weaker, Sire, but not worthless. That weaker axle would make the ride softer, in a given vehicle. The ride that you feel is easily changed, simply by turning the split direction of the axle by a quarter circle, and adjusting the lashings to the desired tightness. In short, we make a stiff axle for stunts and racing, and a soft one, quickly rearranged, for travel on rough roads. Even the spies could not see the difference, let alone understand the science of bending sticks."

Rehotep suppressed a smile. "The stunts, that reminds me, the King is pushing for a private showing. When will you be ready with the flying version of Amun's Wind? I only worry that he will want to fly, too." He offered me a fig.

"Sire, the ramps for flying are ready, but you give me a lot of diverse projects, if you allow me to say it. I lengthened the axle so that the wheels can roll up the two identical ramps while the two horses run safely through, between the ramps. I tried it myself, as you said not to allow other people to watch me fly the chariot." I didn't say that I was trying to find a way to show my new skills to the Queen, and only to the Queen.

"What kind of ramps did you try?"

"So far, only the straight ramp, heavy, solid wood, both dug in to stay in place when the wheels hit them hard, but perhaps an upward-curving ramp, smoothly curving up from the horizontal in the beginning, is the best. The straight one works, though, if a bit bumpy. That one was set at a twenty-finger slope."

"What?"

"Very good, Sire."

"What is very good about my not understanding your stupid numbers?"

"Sire, these stupid numbers are to confuse the spies, and make us holy priests, in a way. Your own words. So, let me call the vertical line, with respect to the horizontal line, ninety fingers. Just using my fingers effectively, because it is quite handy for dividing a circle evenly, and consistently clearly, like sixty fingers between spokes in our six-spoke wheels, and four sets of ninety fingers for the four-spoke wheel."

"Too many fingers, Carver."

"Here, Sire, please look at this adjustable tool, a takeoff on the builders' triangular plumb-line and leveling tool, for converting fingers to slopes. Not perfect yet, needs refinement, but that is also good for befuddling the eyes of every spy."

"We were talking about flying."

"Sire, do you want to try it yourself? Start with a low ramp. Another good way of controlling your flight is with the speed. Of course, the bump on the ramp is rough on any old teeth … as for me, if you care to hear it, they are scary, but, like a child again, did your father pick you up by the ankles and spun you around, faster and faster, up and down in the circle, nose scraping sand once. It's similar here, full speed, using the sharp whip, but the stallions love to run like this anyway, I can feel it, thirty cubits of ground in a heartbeat, the horses' sweat hitting my dusty face, then the wheels rise on the ramps, they kick me toward the sky, I feel talons pressing down on my head, through the buckling knees and to the toes digging into the matting, then the talons suddenly grasp my scalp and pull it up, my body is stretched through the knees and toes, the feet leave the matting, I am a hawk for two counts, but I lose count, it is crazy that I can't reckon to three. Then I plummet back to the track, a great jolt to my neck and back and knees, but the wheels hold, and everything holds, I must learn to flex the knees like a leaping cat. I want to do it again, and measure the distance, farther and farther. My flight is like jumping from a tree into the river, but floating upward first."

Rehotep waved his hand to cut me short. "You flew higher than the chariot? Are you recounting one of your silly dreams? And you have no witnesses other than the horses. How do you explain these two different kinds of flying, occurring at the same time and place? It's the chariot that puts you up in the air, yet you go even higher than the chariot. Maybe I should try the same drinks before driving."

"Sire, please. I drink nothing before dangerous experiments of this kind. Not even water. Afterwards, that's different, if the experiments succeed, or if they fail miserably. So far, it has been three fingers' worth of success and seven fingers for the failures, and I would like a better proportion of successes, but I have to live with what Thoth grants me. All others should be happy with one success in ten tries, you said recently? Perhaps I can show you my separate flights right here." He raised a hand, then dropped it, looking resigned or annoyed.

I went to Amun's Wind and patted the matting of the floor frame for reassurance that nothing was loose. I slightly raised each wheel at a time and rotated it until the tire touched the ground at a point equally distant from the nearest two spokes. In this position the rim was the most flexible, not having a spoke there to add stiffening. When both wheels were set in their most flexible positions, I put a locking rod through the wheels and the body frame. I had a fleeting thought that good and bad sometimes are entwined by a special will of Thoth. The same flexibility of the rim between the spokes, the bending of the rim that causes the wheel's own bone-jarring motion even on a smooth road, that same flexibility allows me to fly higher from the ramps if I hit them just right, but how can I put it in a few words to an impatient man?

"Watch my hair, Sire, and yell if my head comes too close to the ceiling."

"What? No way."

"You will see." I checked to make sure that the wheels were indeed locked to prevent rolling, and stepped up on the matting. Carefully trying to stay in the center of the thong floor, where it yielded most, I began to bounce up, slightly at first, then higher and higher, catching the beat of an inner music. The matting and wheels and axle and pole all creaked and groaned to the same beat, emitting an increasingly loud heaving sigh from the effort of putting me in the air.

My hair alternately whipped my neck and tickled my ears. "Carver, the ceiling!" he yelled just as I felt my flying hair brush the beam above me, I let out a yelp, it was high enough to go, and I gradually let myself down with decreasing bounces.

"I bet you can't kiss the beam," he said. "Too bad my knees would crack early in the game. Now a test, what makes it go? Limit the bragging."

"Sire, the big bouncing is mainly from the taut matting and the floor-frame that holds the matting, and the frame is acting like a springy bow, bending and twisting. The pole also bends like a bow, boosting the bounce. A little more push is added to my flight from the flexing of the wheels' rims, and perhaps also a tiny amount from the bending of the axle. Many springs, big and small, and I can adjust all of them, some easily, some not so easily. It is a matter of time and funding from you. Try it, perhaps just a little, avoid kissing the ceiling or the ground, to get the sense of floating in the air, a pleasant feeling." I uttered a small laugh and said, "Then you will fund it more generously, as it deserves."

"Some other day, but it should be before the King sees it, let alone when it becomes a popular entertainment among the nobility. In the meantime, just hearing your description of these devilish flying experiences makes my bladder heavy and anxious. Some other time."

He turned and suddenly left me alone. My thoughts shifted to a full jug of tongue-prickling beer and I began to wonder if Ankh might enjoy such a stationary ride, and more so, what her long hair and tunic and breasts and buttocks might do when the flying talons pull on them upward and downward and upward, and more so, how she would shriek each time near the ceiling, it could be as much fun watching her as doing it myself, and better yet, doing it together, soon.

19

Pass the Time, No Hands

Through the open door, I heard a bucket of water being dumped in the shop's latrine. Waiting for Rehotep, I put a beer-soaked and roasted pumpkin seed between my teeth, and licked the spicy shell with anticipation. He returned and sat down, tilting his head, like an excessively trained dog waiting for a word.

I was ready to make a wisecrack about one of his failed improvements on the latrine, to compete with his scatological jokes, but caught myself in time. Why is it that our failures in minor inventions are so bitter? But there was a more important issue for us. "I am sorry, Sire, the King has seen it, and likes to watch it, and is excited about doing it himself. He wants to show it to the Queen as soon as possible." How much should I tell him? My mind wandered off, imagine the Queen happily screaming during my bounce-flight, as I am about to slam my head into the ceiling, or if she is watching the King, do it less perfectly, that means two different paths for my future. What should I wear for the event, and what kind of oil should I put on my muscles? I need to talk to a wrestler. Never mind, she is likely to miss it even if I plan it carefully, she has no sense of time, in spite of having sensitive fingers and other refined senses. How could I plant the seeds of time in her mind, and would she appreciate my help?

"Awake!" Rehotep knew when I was drifting away. "What has he done? I told you not to allow him to do risky driving."

I pushed the seed with my tongue to the side of my mouth, into temporary storage. "Please, allow me. He has not done it yet, though I could not stop him if he felt ready." Rehotep was either losing interest or just going back for his cane that fell on the floor. My tongue retrieved the seed, it's an uncommon skill to use only the lips and tongue and teeth to hold and split the seeds edgewise and extract the meat and spit out the shell. The vendor called his latest concoction of spicy seeds Tut's-Pass-the-Time, but I wonder if the King would approve of this. I swished the seed around in my mouth, but as I was becoming confident, the seed turned reluctant, I got annoyed, and smashed it on its flat side, in primitive form.

"Stop that rude chewing," he barked, and stomped with the cane. "And those shells under foot all over the place, it drives me crazy."

"Sire, you taught me how to do it, and, yes, it's relevant to the King's driving safely, in fact, useful for all of us." This was not entirely true, but I just hit upon a good idea involving the seeds, to calm down his anger. "To prevent a roll-over."

"You are dreaming, or lying, or both. What does your stupid seed have to do with the problems of fast driving?" He sipped water, as if to think in silence, clearly coming out of his angry corner, either because of his curiosity, or sensing a chance to corner me, a pleasure for him.

"Not just any seed, but nice, big, flat pumpkin seeds. Here, take one, but don't chew it apart yet."

"You are delaying and delaying this, Carver, while you are glancing around, to see which way to run."

"Speed is involved in the problem, but the solution needs slow thinking, and, in this case, delayed chewing. So, hold either end of the seed between your teeth, but not to crush it. Hold it like a cat carries a kitten by the neck. Now, pinch the other end of the seed with your fingers."

"You devil, now I can't talk," he squeezed out the words around the seed, but also struggled to suppress a smile.

"That's true, too. How do you like it? More importantly, if you gently try to twist the seed with your fingers, your teeth resist it, and keep the seed horizontal, and this shows the essentials for preventing a roll-over of a chariot, with a properly shaped pole, flat at the tail end, nested in the axle socket, like the seed between your teeth, in real life the flat pole tail is kept horizontal by the yoke at the other end of the pole, and, as long as the horses are running evenly and not falling down, the axle will be kept close to the horizontal even if it bounces up and down, and even during small flights over rocks and ramps. Isn't this the most stupendous invention? A simple device to prevent a rollover. Too bad we have to keep it a secret."

"Stop bragging. The flat pole tail was not your idea."

"Sure. Like the seed between your teeth, but I find further uses for it, all the way to a seed-eating contest between you and Tut, not to mention Ankh, she might be quick with the tongue, turning the seed this way or that, between the teeth."

"Stop dreaming about her. But turning the seed reminds me of the more difficult problem, and the great danger, of the sideways wheelie, running on one wheel, which you plan to do, much against my advice. Of course, when you dream of oiling yourself for showing off before the Queen." He was unexpectedly struggling with the seed in his mouth, perhaps a sign of his age.

"Indeed, that is a tough problem, with several possible solutions, none of them refined yet. Do you want to hear these now? All right. There are three kinds of stability, as you know, and they come into play in doing stunts at high speed." I picked up a small red stone sphere of the meta-kha board game. "Look, when the ball is on flat ground, I can push it a little, and it will stop. This is indifferent stability, as you called it. Now, if I put the ball in this empty bowl, too bad the fruit is all gone, and push the ball sideways, it will quickly return to the bottom of the bowl. You called this perfect, or constrained, stability. The horses holding the chariot stable through the yoke and flat pole tail is an interesting case of this. After a chariot wheel hits a rock and lifts into the air, the tilted chariot comes back down. This works if the bounced wheel does not fly too high.

"For the most fun, there is precarious stability, like my balancing the stone ball on the top of my head. If I push it sideways a little, it will stop there, almost like having indifferent stability. However, this is deceiving, because with a slightly bigger push the ball will fall off my head. This is also the special case of the sideways one-wheeler. At the sweet spot of the axle pointing into the air after coming off the ramp, which means an angle of about forty fingers, it is as stable as the strongest wrestler holding a crocodile's jaws wide open. He can either gently let it close down, or it will be against his will and he loses his hands in a blink."

"Wait, Carver, wait."

"I know, this example is not perfect. In the one-wheeler, it's actually much simpler, because the axle will either snap back toward the ground safely, or it will keep rolling over, with the rider and all."

"That's how you wish to die, or kill the King?"

"I will not. There are several options to make it safe. The simplest, perhaps, is to learn how to manage the precarious situation by shifting your weight from foot to foot. Every driver has to do this kind of balancing on the road, anyway. Another is to have a mechanical stop on the pole to limit the high angle of the tilted axle, just at the sweet spot for that particular vehicle. Sire, may I say something bold?"

"Bold?" He cackled and sucked his lips as if he was savoring the word on his tongue, or was it the seed in the way? "A bold word from you? I can hardly wait."

"In short, the flat pole-tail socket is our greatest achievement, greater than all the pyramids together."

"Maybe."

"It is great because it does different things very well, but even more so, because it can do them at the same instant, that's the key. Subtle and stupendous, I would say. Perhaps you have not fully appreciated that, yourself."

"Common for people with a less than full hair. So, tell me more."

"The pole-tail socket does two things at once. First, it allows the pole to slide a little, back and forth, smoothing the horses' jerky motion. Second, it prevents rollovers, as long as the horses are running normally. Both of these can be demonstrated simultaneously with the seed, if you barely hold it between your teeth, slide it in and out, like madly mating baboons, while twisting it slightly. It is clever in the extreme, Sire, more than any part of a pyramid, but for the one-wheeler stunt I need to improve on this socket, or eliminate the

113

socket and use straps to limit the twist of the pole. My guardian Wise Baboon willing, I can do it, and will carve the acknowledging words in my tomb, hopefully near the King's and Queen's. My problem might be to put down these designs in words, so I get full credit, yet obscuring them from our enemies and competitors."

"Full credit and more, is what you want. Luckily, you can still fall off, even if the chariot comes back to earth, right side up. Enough talk, give me more seeds."

We sat down to chew and spit, chew and spit, with little noise, using our hands only to load our mouths, glancing at one another's lips, lost in savoring the spices and the curves of the shells with our tongues.

What about the Queen? Could she see too much and too soon of the tilted one-wheeler? How much oil should I put on my muscles and at what time of the day are the light and the shadows best and … when was the last time the King traveled leaving her at home, when it happens next, I should immediately show her everything, and she could try the bounce if nobody is looking, the pull of the sky and the earth is good for the skin and soft flesh, offer to hold her hand if she is afraid of the ceiling, and barely brush the beam with our long hairs together, but what if the straps of the floorboard can't bounce two bodies to the ceiling and they break in the heaving, a certain multiple disaster at once, let alone the shame, and never be able to see her again. I must practice it a lot more, first alone but with double the weight, and what about my hair, it should be shorter and less unruly, and what kind of ointments to use to match the royal qualities, but long enough hair to sense the ceiling at near contact with it, and what will happen if everything works out as in the best sweet dream, see-through tunic and all, and Tut is on a long trip, and never returns.

20

Racing Tut on Sobeks

Tut unbuckled his electrum-and-glass-braided whip from his cobra belt and uncoiled its hundred-cubit length. He stroked the reed handle that he had carefully measured to fit his palm. The King stood tall and strong, biceps bulging like an asp with a rat in the belly, and I understood by reading his lips that he was ready.

He swung his left foot onto the imaginary pole and squeezed the breastwork between his columnar thighs and grinned, a boy at last having turned into a warrior-king. He cracked his sparkling whip and yelled a command seven times, upon which the first monstrous Sobek entered the empty arena, periodically rising high on its tail. Each additional crack of the whip forced another Sobek out from the pits, and soon they were evenly lined up along the circular track, raising their heads and snapping at the whip in vain. Will I ever get enough credit for creating this fine racing track, the first of its kind?

The snaking whip and the commotion around the track made me dizzy, but I could see the small feathers making the cracking sound. First he floated the line's tip forward, then jerked it back, making a small boom, like a tiny lightning, that also loosened a few feathers and dust in a puff, all of them drifting down.

Now the King made two cracks in quick succession, the first done amazingly behind his own head, not even seeing it, floating the line backward and snapping it forward, then floating it forward all the way so that the tip was inside the first crocodile's teeth when the snap was made, ready for the same action with the next Sobek, like a steady drumming, then the creatures took off. The first one ran up the pair of ramps I had set at forty fingers, and it flew high into the air, came down splashing on its stomach and sliding some dozen cubits on the muddy track. It continued toward the next set of ramps, while the second monster approached the first ramps, with the others getting ready to go. Soon they were all going up ramps, flying and splashing down and running again. Then the King stopped them with a triple crack of the whip and turned to me.

"They are ready for the riders. Bring them all out, naked, and order them to mount their beasts, or you put them on if they refuse. Once they are on, they will love the rough ride on the bumpy hides. Here's my decree. Ay's daughter shall go first, then Horem's, then Pentu's, then Rehotep's, then Minakh's, then Heket's, then Sothis', then Maya's, then Ay's second, then Meret's." He looked down at a bug biting his thigh, and attacked it with spit-drenched fingernails for simultaneous killing and soothing. "That will teach all their fathers to take me seriously. Right?"

Their richly oiled skins were like bronze of various ages, from yellow to brown-green, their lips and fingernails and toenails all crimson. Each had the reins wrapped properly around the waist, able to control the direction and speed of the mount. Their hips were adequately wide for the task, if not as perfect as the Queen's, as I had proved to the King, by measuring them with my hands. They filled the track like a string of pearls on the Queen's neck, and some of them started giggling, soon screeching, but why do they enjoy riding like this, even when screaming, I always wonder.

"Enough of this slow shuffling and small flights," shouted the King, snapping several bare bottoms to a mixture of cries, and directing the procession off the track. "Off, off! Keep only the two fastest Sobeks, we will have a real race, but lengthen the track, with two straight sides. Get the judges, the experienced daughters. The first race shall be a short one to get the blood flowing in pure acceleration from start to finish. Line up side by side! Go!"

He and I blasted off and covered the marked distance in a blink. He looked around triumphantly. "Who was the winner? What, the judges say we were dead even? Not a single finger of a difference, not even edgewise, over the whole distance?"

My bottom was hurting from the rough ride, but the King shouted again. "The next race shall be more difficult, seven times around the Shenu track, to demonstrate straightaway speed and cornering ability. Line up side by side, no cheating, Carver! Go!

It was over in seven blinks, and he looked around while raising his arms. "Was I the winner, of course? What, again, the judges are dead on their hedgehogs, they say there was no winner? Then we have to run this again, but wait, only after I lighten my bladder for helping my Sobek with the weight." He stormed off for the royal latrine, and while he was gone, I cheated by emptying mine on the spot, certain that my tired and muddy Sobek could not care less. I patted the big creature, getting used to it and losing my fears, and gaining confidence and new skills, but not sure whether winning or losing this race was the best for my future, thinking of everything, and of the Queen.

The King's fancy bucket made a clatter from the distance, no doubt a half-trained baboon was banging it around and damaging its precious decoration, I was annoyed because it meant more work for me, and he was soon back next to me and climbing on his mount, refusing help from the filthy Sobek-grooms. "Line up side by side, no quick and clever movements are allowed this time, Trickcarver! Ready? Go!"

It was all a blur to me, until coasting to a stop. He stood up on his mount, and said, more quietly than before, "Who is the winner? They can't say? These judges are incompetent, I see their confusion in their faces." He broke his reed whip on his knee and tossed it among the women.

His brown eyes narrowed and darkened with determination, perhaps anger, and he shouted more loudly, and not with a chunk of honey-reed in his mouth, for all the judges to hear him, "The greatest race shall be the left-sider, Sobek will love it. Set up the ramps, just one for each of us, just for starting us sideways up in the air. We will see who can stay running on one wheel the longest in time and distance, and ahead of the other. Ready with the ramps?" He ran his hand over his own ramp, testing it for a smooth surface and firmness in the ground, checking the angle of the rise, and figuring his approach to it from the takeoff direction. His squinting distorted his features into a half-snout-Anubis smirk. I shook my head to clear it of all the previous blurs, fixing my eyes on the track ahead to avoid dizziness. "Line up quickly, snouts abreast, no reckoning is allowed on the inside of your palm, Cheatscriber! Finish the last scratching of your belly. I am a fair King in every race, even when I am destined to win. Get ready! Go!"

We thundered toward the ramps together, and I felt just the right amount of tension in my body, a light touch on the reins, and confidence in all my reckoning that was backed up by a thousand secret tests. As the ramp began to lift the right side of my mount, I felt the momentarily increased heaviness of my body, especially on the right foot, in the right hip, in the right eye, followed by the expected lightness and brief suspension in the air. The balancing touches from my excellent waist to the reins and with my feet firmly planted on the rough hide made it almost easy like walking across a stream on a chariot pole, there was plenty of time to reckon the future, the air was pleasant and warm, and then it turned into a cool breeze from the north, I needed no hands on the reins, and it became clear that a dead even race with Tut was the best for my future.

The King slid off his sprawled Sobek and looked around, speechless for a moment. He fingered his tussled hair, licked his dry lips and shook his head and sore legs. "Another good race ending in a small difference between the two best drivers in the Two Lands, according to the judges, who should be boiled in last year's beer. Since I am the King, and Rampcarver is older than I am, we shall declare him the winner. I am the King, magnanimous. Will be great on fast wheels, in good time, beyond words. But it is warm here from the silly race, give me a hin-cup, make it two-hin, of cold pomegranate wine, no water, and bring me the Queen, naked!"

21

Carver's Pastime

I was getting restless in my hiding spot in the musty chariot barn, and wondered if I had enough of fine pumpkin seeds to pass the time during a long wait. The sand-dweller variety was plentiful, while the god-pleaser was difficult to get at any price, but I managed to get a fair amount of it. I savored my paying for the spicy, plump seeds, joining the baker girl for the cracking of a sample seed by the two of us. The memory of her salty lips and tongue made me think of other ways of managing the seeds with her, to keep her interest up. Balancing a seed on a nipple? Not a big challenge, apparently, this was not my day for coming up with great ideas. But keep thinking, suggest to her, perhaps, some sensitive hiding places, since she seems to like the ideas that I claimed to get from the Virile Baboon, one of my increasingly productive spiritual patrons.

What about the Queen, and how to refine my approach to her? Forget the screeching, hair-raising driving for a while, that could come later. How about a new ring, a fine little fertility ring for her long finger? Miraculously, as if it was an answer to my prayers, my hand found a straw, and I tried to bend it into a small ring, but it broke. Not my day. I found another piece and licked it and sucked saliva in and out to soften it, but it was useless, other than passing more time while laying in wait, crouching on the frayed floor of the ancient chariot in the midst of the heap among the other discarded objects, damaged wheels and poles and axles. It was a good spot for waiting and thinking, but not the most comfortable, nothing like a papyrus boat among the murmuring rushes, though the junk pile was safe from crocodiles. The thought made me smile, because Rehotep once suggested to me that I should be wearing his new papyrus life-floater on a boat, showing how to put it on like a bow over one shoulder and under the other arm, as if the crocodiles would respect it.

It was the best spot for waiting, although it was my third night in a row, and nothing yet. My hand played on the worn thongs, able to feel the circular area where the driver stood most of the time, at the middle of the right half of the floor. The other half was also worn, to a lesser extent, because a second rider was less frequently standing on this vehicle. Will Tut come at last, and will he be attired in one of my older short tunics this time? I worried. What if he manages to kill himself in my clothes, as Rehotep also worries sometimes, and the necropolis low-lifers hurry about their putrid duties in poor light, and unceremoniously dump his body in the river to fatten Sobek? How could I prove I am alive? Perhaps that would be a chance to spend a little time with Ankh alone, a chance to show her something, give her something. I must hurry to think of a fine gift, inexpensive.

I tried to think of the stars' arrangement at this hour. My mind's eye jumped to the best place for thinking, my one-person papyrus boat that was recently recovered from thieves and repositioned in a better hiding place, and the reflection of the stars on the water, which will never be the same, like the river itself. The thieves are yet to be punished with a cruel hand, or at least indirectly with a curse, which I should learn before advancing to a higher position at the court. But how to sort out the stars, and would the Queen like a new experience, like watching the sky change ever so slowly from my boat? Or change fast, if she prefers, I will think of something.

I imagine the King will come, even at the late hour, but why is he delayed? The feast was too long, there was too much stupid wrestling and wine and beer, but the rich have no sense of the slow-moving stars, nor of reed boats and floor thongs worn thin by gripping feet. If the King does come, he will turn on his lamp bright and set his dripping clock, but not yet. First he should check every life-floating item, from the pole to the axle to the matting, and retighten every thong to bounce his weight toward the ceiling. He might start on his all fours, to save his legs and back and aching neck, no, no, it is better standing upright, for saving his neck, and throw away the cane, it's no use on the matting.

Now I regret coming to this stinking place. It would be better to watch the bright Sothis from my silent boat, the temporary double Sothis of sky, with its reflection on the river, pray for a lightning-fast star doubling itself by reflection for good luck, for long-dripping hours of the night, even if the King goes to the barn and is gritting his teeth in trying to reach the ceiling with his flying hair.

In the meantime, my plans begin to multiply like drunken locusts, it's a stupid old saying but where did it come from? Yes, what is the best plan for pleasing pretty Ankh with a new taste of seed roasted to perfection to crack easily with the teeth, I will teach her quickly but not too fast, and extract the tingling spicy meat with deep-reaching tongues, especially if the beginning hide-and-seek is played well, hide a seed in the mouth, or in the folds of the skin, or between the toes, or in the hedgehog quills, make it a handful in the quills, and sharpen the superior taste with a cool beer of my own made just for her, my ideas are all lined up like dry logs to put under the oven, only a good name is needed for a new beer, how about the Brew-for-Utmost-Fertility, she is brilliant and will get the idea, and another name needed is for the gods' seed, like Carver's-Best-Pastime, but no, what if the King gets on with it too and plays with the same excellent seeds and brew with her, perhaps well before me, the King is always first, even if not healthy, it's a hateful thought, so how can I prevent this before the Fertility Brew goes flat?

22

Queen Ball-Eye Rolling in the Air

The Celestial Winding Waters are more pleasant than the barns, especially in the rising glow of Re over the hazy eastern hills, the best time of the day, which will be hot. The quiet little branch of the river is beginning to stir with the chirping of birds and muskrats brushing through reeds, strangely reminding me of wheels making noises in the sleepy-sticky bearings at the start of a trip, as if responding to one another and to the horses' yawning and sluggish pulling, sounds of excitement mixed with reluctance in the face of the coming day. But who knows, the groan of a bearing may be music to its mate on the same axle, like the harsh clattering sounds of a courting crane, spindly legs bending but always snapping back safe and straight in the feverish dance, crest feathers ablaze from the spicy meats of a hundred fertility frogs and snakes. I must write these down for Ankh, and offer her a chance to see these sacred rites at the best moment with her own almond eyes, and start to remove years from our bodies, but who said that silly thing?

"Your skin is blessed by Isis and Re," she would say, and touch it with long, excellent fingers, hopefully she doesn't mind touching goose bumps, and a new fragrance is arising from her, a dizzying scent.

The rushes and willows make thin spokes of the sun touch the water here and a lotus there, as if the moving yellow-green spots were the innards of a slumbering, giant water clock. My papyrus seat makes a chafing sound as I shift to follow a scarab-shaped spot of light approach a floating and dozing ruddy duck, climbs up on the bird's near side, glints off the emerald feathers, and leaps at the other side back to the water, all in a blink of Re. My boat drifts and turns away from the duck, but I leave the paddle resting. I wonder if the feather of the paddle feels the warmth of the sun like the duck does.

An immature dua-rekhyt with yellow and black spots on its back and wings hangs on a vertical stalk nearby, looking at me curiously from its sideways position, I have never seen that before, perhaps nobody has, so I must brag to Rehotep about it. Only its head with a hint of a crest is rocking slightly, back and forth to some inner beat, and I wonder if it's not hurting from the pulling on its upper leg by its own weight, nor by the compression on its lower leg at the same time, from the same weight. Which god sent this curious bird to me, and what could it mean for my future? I must learn how to read the future better, like aiming an arrow ahead of a flying duck.

The bird has spent a long time in that difficult position and should be hurting in the legs by now, I know, having tried the same kind of sideways hanging by my hands on a thin vertical scaffolding pole, attempting to impress my friends, and even more the lush-lipped girl in the window, looking at me in her rich hand-mirror. How does the rekhyt push away from the stalk to start flying from this impossible, awkward position, without falling downward, perhaps into a lurking crocodile's jaws, before gaining enough height for safety? By the time the next flood is over, the rekhyt's crest will be long and curvy-pointed, and it will be working the muddy fields and not my brains, but where is the girl with that mirror now, and what is her name?

"She is just another girl, so ignore her and the others," the Queen said once, "if you want more than just another girl."

A flash of light comes alive, it's a ball-eye-net-stitcher landing on my bare knee, a drab creature, exhausted from its first brief flight in the cool of the morning, having misjudged the temperature, or too hungry to wait for the sun to get higher and dry its damp wings, or simply sent by its god with a message for me. How did it sense the sideways breeze and know the small point of warm spot for landing, and aim correctly for the knee in a blink? It is itching my skin, though not biting, they never bite people, and I am about to scare it away, when I notice several things on its wings that are strangely new to me. The net of its veins, is it carrying blood like ours? I could squeeze a live one ever so slightly to check for a pulse in the extremely thin wings, but not today. Another good question is, how would I measure the thickness if I wanted to? Stack up ten or twenty and measure them together, of course, and then do the reckoning easily, but what should I call such a small thickness of one wing, and why is the hind-wing narrower than the forewing?

Another curious thing is the, what to call it, the dark balancing weight near the front tip of each wing of every kind of ball-eye insect, is that a pool of blood in the wing? Must be, because a tiny parasite gnat is chewing on it, while the host is resting on my knee. No, it's not a balancing weight, but a place of offering of blood to the gnat-god, perhaps cleverly offering dark tired blood. It is maddening not to know it for sure, though noticing such a thing is more important than immediately understanding it, says Rehotep. That's why he, on occasion, uses a ball-eye to test a bright-eyed peasant boy. "First, how many legs does it have, just from memory, and quickly, since you have seen a million? Have you measured one on your finger, any part of the body or wings? Next, tell me whether its eyes are touching one another in the middle of the head." Then he pulls a well-preserved ball-eye out. "Tell me everything curious you see in this creature's wings." The top prize, entry into his famous shop, goes to the rare boy who notices the small dark pool of blood in the leading edge of the wing, though he is not sure it is blood.

He can be weird and unfathomable. Therefore, I am not about to show him my newest pride anytime soon, because it is a total failure so far, my own big ball-eye flier, much bigger than any alive, exactly a cubit in wingspread, but too thick of papyrus and heavy of stupid sticks. Perhaps if I glue together a lot of real wings, with the tiniest dabs of glue, but Rehotep would kill me if he ever found out, as he surely would. Instead, I should make much thinner papyrus sheets, though it has no good use for anything else but silly wings.

Better yet, do nothing, leave the feather of my paddle dry, let Re take my thin thought-offering, and let him transform this and give it as fleet-footed golden rays to the shivering insect. Fleet-footed, true, but how fast, indeed, are those rays? Never mind, Rehotep has already spent years on that, and says it cannot be reckoned perfectly, ever, with the average King's average treasury. Maybe a different King with a bigger treasure, but it's hopeless, the same as with Ankh, who is not an average Queen.

Never mind. Recline in the warm cradle of the papyrus boat, watch the dua-rekhyt, where did it go, watch the ball-eye gather heat with its body lined up for all the sunlight available to it, the opposite of when it's too hot and it aligns itself to make the smallest possible shadow, how does it know and sort out all these big or little things of heat and cool in the same day? There is more to watch on the river than in a troupe of crimson-and-blue-painted pygmy dancers, my insect is whirring its wings, is it to shake off the obnoxious gnat, or to warm the stiff muscles, making ready to fly and eat a plump bug for strength and clasp a female to mate in the air like a tumbling wheel, a blur to watch. They mate only for a double blink of the human eye, triple at most, much too short, but suddenly there is a flash of color, could it be a Drab Ball-Eye and a Queen Ball-Eye rolling together in the air like a golden hoop?

23

Reckoned Arrow

Immature rekhyts light on a branch of a fallen tree, arranging themselves noisily, as if I was not there. I dip my paddle in the water, but I am undecided which way to turn. Where did the mating insects go, and has Ankh ever seen such tumbling in the air?

"Here's a jar of lavender ointment for you, you alone, it came with the north breeze," she would say in her warm, quiet voice, but tinged with command, something I should learn. "Better than your natron soap to get rid of the shop stains and scribing odors. I want to learn it, too, but with inks of better scent. Can you do it?"

"Yes, Your Highness."

"Ankh, if you wish, and you may. And you can speak louder, no one else is here." She smoothes the tunic over her ball-eyes, though it was not wrinkled. Many young women have this curious habit, the hand checking the hair or the tunic, sometimes nonstop. "What shall you teach me today? The reins without hands on them, all is done and good, and my stallions can't learn any more. The two kites flying together like geese? I like them twisting and turning, silently, fast and slow and fast, together or apart, way up."

"Well, I am not entirely ready with them, but will try harder."

"Don't wait too long! The sky will not stop for you to get on it, leisurely."

"Yes, Your ... Ankh."

"You can step closer, I am not afraid of your white teeth, in fact, I want to look at them, they seem as perfect as the Tooth Baboon's pride." Fine, fine, but how close should I step, and what is best to say or not to say at this time? Oh, no. Where did she go, did she fly away again?

There is a noise by the side of my boat, and a disturbance on the water, a crocodile? I jerk around and raise the paddle in defense, hopeless as it may be compared to a good spear and Rehotep's powerful liquid against the monsters, where did I put it, but wait, it's a human head breaking the surface, strong shoulders emerge, then two hands grab the side of the boat, not a good purchase on the thick bundle of papyrus siding. General Horem? Why, in the name of Amun-Re, I almost smacked him dead.

Aided by a huge thrusting kick, he pulls himself over the side and into the boat, quickly correcting for the sudden tipping motion and shaking water all over me. He swishes the water off his rippled skin on the breast and belly, more carefully over a rough red patch at his navel. "A perfect day," he says, smiling. He turns toward the shore, whistles in bursts and waves his two soldiers away. They were not noticeable among the bushes until now. He makes a broad hand signal to make them move away. Their glinting weapons disappear.

He pulls his iron dagger out from his sash belt and moves closer to me, towering over me. "Don't be afraid, Carver, this is to protect the metal from rusting, as you should know." He repeatedly wipes the blade on my tunic, making me cringe, then holds it up to Re with both hands, as in an offering. The reflected light spot sweeps over the rekhyts on the branch, a fine aim if he willed it. He pulls his des-knife of flint from the other side of his belt and dries it the same way, also holding it up to the sun. "This one does not need the drying, a great advantage, but Re likes to shine off from both, against the dark depths. Seen any crocodiles here today? You don't have a big enough knife on you for a monster, but your three-layer bow is a marvel."

"No, Sire, I am no match for a crocodile. I am not a soldier. I rely on knowing where they are."

He laughed. "The best way. But I did it once. Maybe it was sick or full and lazy. Still, a victory is a victory. And it's good to have two blessed knives at all times."

"What about the new repelling liquid, Sire? Our experiments show it might work."

"Let others use it. I prefer good knives and my destiny and fate. A superior destiny is the best protection for a man. But quick eyes and hands are part of it. Even while bent over your papyrus, right?"

"Sire, I am learning to write while looking aside, I am not sure why, but the result looks like a drunken scribe's work, punishable. Good scribing and carving require the eyes all the time."

He silently picked up the paddle and turned the boat to allow the sun to shine on the red patch by his navel. He noticed my staring. "Just wait, you will get it too, or something else. It is not fun getting old, not always. The sun and water are both good and both bad. But the pain slows the dripping of the clock gourd. And a young woman speeds it up." His eyes followed a snake as it slithered off a fallen branch and headed toward deeper water. "That snake reminds me, there was once a young warrior, Heb-teb. Have you heard of him? Not, of course. He knew little or nothing of history, art, music, dancing, writing, only of hunting, fishing, fighting, racing, olive wreath crowns of Siwa, and he sensed his destiny. He was the swiftest runner in his region, and swam as well as that snake. Once he bet with four soldiers that he could beat them crossing the river to a target landing, he swimming and the soldiers in a reed boat, all paddling. Guess what happened." I haven't heard this, but knew the outcome, at least roughly, by the tone of his words.

He waited a little, looking at my face, while I threw a small stick toward the snake for diversion. "Yes, you get it, if you think. Indeed, Heb-teb won, and won big, by constantly and correctly figuring his direction arrows, the water's current arrow and his own cross-current direction arrow, getting his proper reckoned arrow from those two thought arrows. The soldiers refused to pay up on their lost bet, claiming that Heb-teb cheated. Isn't that brazen? He cheated by using his head. Such is life, but you learn who can be trusted. In addition to the refusal to pay, their haughty leader said, 'We will extract silence from you.' Hah! Heb-teb killed killed him for being the most stupid and aggressive, and wounded the other three, who then put up the glass beads to settle the bet. Men like that can have really bad days. What do you say?" He looked at me without blinking, while leisurely checking the edge of his flint knife, gently grazing a fingertip over the shallow dimples on the blade.

"I know a little about the reckoned arrows, Sire. Were those soldiers good paddlers?" This stopped the motion of his finger.

"What? Yes. You may know a lot more about reckoned arrows than I do. I just know it is useful in many ways. Hunting, warfare, playing ball, but how do you explain that oftentimes a stupid man can also use it without understanding any of the details of the reckoning? The cat and the cheetah and the lion can also use it, even the swallow and the ball-eye when catching darting insects. They do it faster than you can think."

"You mean, Sire, that being able to do the reckoning slowly and consciously is just an idle pleasure and not nearly as useful as a quick natural ability without understanding it? There may be something to that."

"No. Heb-teb used it consciously, I assume, by not only keeping the reckoned arrow aimed at the target, which essentially means keeping an eye on it, but also in a straight line and the shortest remaining distance at all times, which is the difficult part when you cross the river. Try it sometime. Winning the bet, he proved the value of the well-reckoned arrow, even in a slow race. But I am tiring of this difficult subject."

"It is difficult, Sire, when you talk about non-existing arrows in strange combinations, or wave your hands to describe those thought arrows for a winning crossing of the river, and seems most unusual in a …"

"Soldier? General?" He laughed, rippling the skin on his stomach.

"Yes, Sire. I am deeply honored to know the young Heb-teb, too. You are most generous and tolerant. Perhaps I could help, if you ever need it, to describe such arrows by drawing the them on papyrus, or even sand if you are in a hurry, with a little trick, no, a big trick. It is necessary, actually, to apply that trick. It has to do not only with the direction of the arrows, which is the first requirement, but also with the lengths of them, the second requirement. In the regular quiver, all arrows are the same. In my thought quiver, if you allow me to make a little joke, most often they are different, sometimes by a great amount. Please don't tell anyone yet. It's like this. If something is twice as heavy as another thing, twice as long is the arrow for it. If something is twice as fast as another, twice as long is the arrow for that. This last one is the most useful, even if used crudely, like in crossing the river fairly efficiently. The reckoned arrow is ..."

"By the smiling grace of Amun and Thoth, when I am King, I will appoint a God of the Reckoned Arrow, and you will be its highest priest, gathering a lot of sacrifice from all the people of the Two Lands and beyond. That explains many things, even what I really wanted to talk about. The reckoned arrow is good not only for racing and killing, but for planning your life, like the young Heb-teb probably did. I assume you are interested in that."

"If you tell me to be, Sire."

"A very thoughtful young man you are, and that's why I am here. Today I saw you watching all those creatures from the boat, no paddle stirring, just dreaming. Leisurely, like a king. Yes, it is healthy for a young man to dream of Ankh."

"Sire, please, I never said that." I never said it in my waking hours, but now, what did the color of my cheeks say? I studied his scars, especially a reddish set on his chest that might have been carved by four sharp fingernails, nicking his left nipple, which must have been painful.

He cut a green willow stick and began to fashion a small whistle, in the same way as I would have done it, crunching and sliding off the moist bark tube from its core, for starters. "Carver, it is all right to have those dreams. Don't worry, probably nobody else knows it, except your Master. You are safe, if you keep your shadow short. Now, the reckoned arrow of history ... to think about queens, the way you do, you also have to think about kings. They are special creatures of the gods, but they don't live forever, or even very long, in some cases. What happens then? Listen carefully. The next one is most likely to be from his personal seed, or a related seed, but not necessarily. Royal blood can be bought if you have none, if you know who the special merchants are and learn to speak their language. There are examples of new dynasties sprouting apparently from nowhere. A given reckoned arrow can come from different pairs of arrows. You know that an infinite number of pairs of arrows can produce the same final reckoned arrow. Of course, this is difficult even for the reckoning baboon to grasp, so you can be proud of yourself."

"Sire, I am not, I do not understand, I cannot." What am I saying? Where is this going? Think of another direction. What is the price of his iron dagger? What else but a woman's fingernails could have raked his skin? What else is there to think about?

"Ah, you are interested in my scars? I have a few good stories, but let's save them for another time. Now, I have other things on my mind. The most important is, just between the two of us, what would you like to be when you are my age? I could guess. But first, imagine that somewhere, in a great land, there is a young king with a beautiful queen but no offspring, and he is ruling for a few years, then he dies, expectedly or unexpectedly, a minor detail. Imagine that his elder minister, of the same blood or not, it does not matter, this old minister becomes the new king, and he marries the young widow queen, whether she wants to move to his bed or not. She is not necessarily unhappy, especially if she was not entirely happy just before, because she remains queen, with at least a chance for her to rule alone some day, and the court is full of dashing young men to entertain her for the time being, with poetry or tongue."

"Sire, the complications in the chances ..." My mouth was dry, so I dipped my hand in the water and licked it.

He tested his new whistle, blowing into it softly for a sonorous little beep, looking pleased. "If you wish to reckon with fingers, as you and your Master are most fond of, I would say it is nine fingers out of ten for this to happen, with the old man so inclined, being sort of a cross-current arrow in the reckoning. Later, in a few years, say, the new but old king dies, crushed by the weight of his years and belly, perhaps sloshing with powders in his wine. Imagine now that another nobleman comes up, of the same blood as either king's line or not, it matters little, and this man marries the young, once-again widow queen, whether she likes it or not. Again, she is not necessarily unhappy, since she might have hoped for and planned some of it, perhaps all, because you know why."

"Sire, I have got a few glimpses, but how do you aim an arrow to get the fast duck in one shot?"

I studied his spread hands resting on his thighs, short-trimmed nails, one finger bent a little sideways at its swollen joint. He slid the hand under his leg and started with a sigh, "Later, with extreme reluctance, the new king dies, and, lo and behold, the freshly-widowed queen now chooses a young reckoning scribe, in spite of his being of another blood, actually no blood, so to speak, to rise from the horizon's shadows and be her next husband and king. She is quite happy for a change because she herself has reckoned some arrows of her own for several years, and fingered the fertility charms in her well-equipped sanctuary, not always patiently. How many fingers of chance for this? Two or three out of ten, not huge, but it has happened before, more than once. In fact, I am sure that there will be yet another young scribe who will eventually put on the wall of his tomb, 'I became great on my seat beyond words,' and more, for his eternal amusement."

How does he know about young queens so much? And about me, even in the depth of the nights? I need to splash cool water on myself, but my shaking hand is a sieve. "Sire, these things require more than that, but the heat drains my strength and blurs my eyes. I am not able to think the best thoughts. What would you suggest for me to do?"

"I am not sure yet. Re will roll across the sky many times before I will tell you. In the meantime, there are plenty of other marvelous targets to aim at, some close, some far away. For any of them, you can find a good bow. Tell me about this three-layer bow, why not just one or two, or four?"

"Sire, if you forgive me, you already know much about me, more than I have said."

"Of course. All right. Let's talk about other things. I like sparks. They are like stars that you could almost grab, especially the big ones flying off the honing wheel. Those can hit your hand if you want, sting it slightly. It tells of the best iron blade, when a spark is bright in color and glows long in its flight. Are you surprised? I learned that from Rehotep soon after he discovered it. You are not his only pupil. I wish I could be like him, and deal mainly with hard objects, not with soft-bellied men. What do you know about Ay, they say he can have just five more years, at most, by looking at his crumbling teeth.

"Carver. What else could I say to gain your confidence, which I wish to do, for my own interest and the sparks I see coming from you. My promises always come as full cups. My first one, about a thing that pains me a lot, the crude reckoning going on everywhere. I promise you plenty of gold to improve that, when I am a Stronger Bull of Re, as soon as possible, certainly within four or five years. There are several new battles on my mind, and I will need a few men like you to win them. The Treasurer Maya has reluctantly agreed to support my future quests, I am sure just to keep his position when everything changes."

I was dizzy with my mind racing, and studied his scars all over again to gain time, to speak just a little, just right. "Sire, I prefer carving wood and stone, and breathing the scent of fresh papyrus, and the sight of colored ink impregnating the fibers, to the smell of blood baking in the sun."

He smiled and slapped my knee. "Carver, Great Future Scribe, and more. Yes, there are battles with swords, and other battles, without swords. Listen. Yesterday I had a dream of Thoth presenting you before my feet, all of our feet in golden sandals … is that useful to you?"

"Possibly, Sire. There is much to mull over."

"Find a wise baboon and ask him for interpretations. Now I have to leave you, to apply oils to my skin, and let a trembling delegation from Kush breathe it in. And you, keep day-dreaming of the Opet Festival, where you seize the golden oar, not long enough to get any blisters but to demonstrate your power on the kingdom's waters and, as a bonus, on the Queen's breasts, for a joyous reenactment of your wedding, with new hope for a healthy heir that has eluded so many before you."

"My Lord, I am a humble servant."

He adjusted the flint knife in his belt, took the iron one in his fist, and scanned the water all around. "I almost forgot the most important thing on my mind. What is the latest concoction of Rehotep for an itchy scalp? Sometimes it keeps me from sleeping."

133

"There is something new for that affliction. Hot beer with a dash of Good-Poison. But I cannot guarantee it for older men, and neither can he."

"How hot? And Good-Poison? How big a dash?"

"Hot enough to make you squeeze your fists. Please forgive me about the rest of it that I cannot answer, since I swore secrecy to my Master about all crucial details."

"Of course. He is right. In that case, send ten hins of that beer to my quarters, and name the price, within reason. One hin can be hot, for immediate use." He quickly scratched the back of his head, flipped a small tuft of hair into the water, and slipped out of the boat. Soon he was gone from sight, and water was oozing back into his footprints in the mud on the shoreline.

A swarm of midges swirled in front of a willow, with ball-eyes slashing through their midst faster than a rug-maker's needle. I must ask a net-maker for a small fishnet of the finest fibers, to catch live ball-eyes without damage to their bodies and wings, look at them in the eye and learn how the wings work, then let them fly off. They must have big secrets in the wings and how they twist and flap.

I used my hands to paddle softly and drift the boat to the bank. The bottom slurped and scraped to a halt, and I stayed in it silently. An invisible bird made a raspy call, perhaps an alarm. I scooped up a handful of red clay, let it drip some of the water out, and began to shape it with my hands and knife. What does it want to become? It seems to take shape as a baboon with a cube body, to make space for writings on it. Perhaps like the Wise-One of the Great Temple. I move my lips trying to imitate it. Yes, the lower lip is telling ... stretch it upward and forward, mainly forward.

24

Tut's Slippery Slopes

"Burn it! And never make another one while I am alive!" Rehotep yelled, followed by a long guttural sound of no clear meaning, after he smashed my newest and largest ball-eye wings and tossed them at my feet. "Don't you have enough important things to do, instead of wasting your time on hopeless toys? How many times should I tell you the same thing? Soon I will be gone to the Western Horizon, mainly because you are pushing me in that direction, you ungrateful Mudcarver, then you can take over and do what you want, if your memory of me will mean nothing to you. Shame. Now disappear from my sight!" He tore at his thin hair with both hands, then quickly rubbed his temples up and down, murmured a curse involving the monster Apophis, and turned away from me.

I gathered up the pieces, secretly dusting off the torn, thin papyrus wings. This was a double setback, but just as well, because the previous, slightly smaller wings were already in the dustbin of failed models. Maybe a long cooling-off period is best, then let the ideas start welling up again on their own. But why is he cursing thus when he hardly believes in any special powers of those hideous creatures of the dark waters?

"Carver! Where are you going? You have to finish setting up the sliding and greasing demonstrations for the official visitor!"

Strange and sad, this is. What is happening to him, and why? Another master would be more helpful to me, and I should start … no, I shouldn't think of such rebellious thoughts against him, but can't help choking on my anger and frustration. And there, he is raising his eyebrows, like climbing tiny stairs, waiting for a response.

My teeth and lips are making sounds that make no sense at first, I must control it better, I can't let his words be like the sand grating in the bearing until it bursts into flames, what with all the oils.

I took a deep breath. "I am finished with it, Sire. I could easily make another ten if quantity is the main idea. I thought that quality is more important. Here, every one of these blocks on the tilted boards is with its assigned grease or oil or other liquid. I assume you don't want anything from the latrine to affect the sliding of the blocks, although that could be great to hoodwink a spy. Basically, the demonstrations are ready to go and are always easy to conduct. The less tilt of the board before the stationary block begins to slide down, the better is the grease or oil for the axle bearing. There are two that are about equal, and they are clearly better than the rest, everything else being equal, such as the smooth finish of the surfaces in contact."

He waved his hand to stop me. "Fine. But can you predict any of these before you run the experiments? That's what it's all about, ultimately. Science. What is this slipping and sticking really about?"

"Sire, it's a favorite issue of mine among the impossible ones. Surely, surface roughness has a lot to do with it, but now I am convinced that it's not the whole story. At first sight, it's roughness, mainly. The rasp or plow concept. A rough rasp is harder to push over the wood than a fine rasp, because its teeth are plowing in deeper. But, why can't very glassy surfaces, with the best oils, eliminate the stickiness completely? Why is the wet tongue of a cat feel raspy on a smooth skin? By the way, if the King ever asks you about bearing problems, I would mention this cat-tongue idea, because he likes cats and will immediately appreciate our work."

He pursed his lips and waved a hand again. His voice turned soft. "I accept it, to nine fingers out of ten, but the remaining problem, especially for the less clever mind, is the rotation of the wheel. What you are demonstrating is clear for the block sliding downhill, but the wheel is rotating on the axle, a totally different motion. How can you be sure that the straight motion of the blocks going down the boards is relevant to the rotation, and convince others of it?" He wiped beads of sweat from his brow with a fine linen kerchief, though the heat was not excessive.

What should I say to him? Who is coming to see the demonstrations of my grease-secrets? Could it be one of Ay's advisors? Or Horem's procurer for the Army? The scientific explanations must depend on the mental ability of the visitor. I had noticed earlier the sweet smell of hyacinths in baskets, which had no place among my devices invented for thinking about speed, pure animal speed. There were also bowls of melon chunks and dates and figs, a mixture of good scents. Maybe he doesn't know exactly who is coming, just that it is a person of fine cloth, and he can't admit his uncertainty. And there were wet pieces of fine linen around the stems to keep the flowers fresh. Why can't I see things sooner, even under my nose?

"Sire, I don't really have to convince anybody else with complicated words, do I? Let the doubters race me, if they dare. Of course, I can also do it with additional demonstrations and words, if you allow me the extra time, because of the need to set up identical rotation situations and the precise timing to show which oil makes the wheel run longer, the critical issue at hand. The longer it takes before the wheel stops after it is started spinning on its blocked up axle, the better the oil. Otherwise, you just have to trust the wonderfully equivalent demonstrations using the much simpler straight-sliding blocks, and trust my words, to save a lot of time and gold. Is that worth it for you and any visitors?"

"Getting a bit cocky?" He wiped the back of his neck, reaching under his tunic, then worried about his fingernails. He looked around, probably for a fine stone rasp or a piece of pumice, with wrinkles turning into a frustrated expression on his face. I waited a little for best effect, then reached into a tool-basket and handed him what he needed. He didn't say a word as he tried to smooth the nail on his pointing-finger, the one splintering and bothering him most frequently. While he was working on the nail, I reached for a large chunk of melon.

"I apologize. It is just that I am fairly confident of these blocks sliding straight down the boards, and what they mean for the bearings of rotating wheels, and feel that you might spend a lot of time and gold to prove that you could have saved a lot of time and gold, it is something to think about, to remain in the favor of the King, let alone the good feeling of reckoning this matter well."

"What? Why all these words? Keep it short and to the subject at hand, but wait, don't sample the melon, it's not for you. Be patient until you get older." He took a piece and swirled it in his mouth with great noise, then swallowed it, followed by kissing noises of his lips. "Have you tried this juice on your blocks? It seems rather slippery to the tongue."

"I am sorry, yes, I have tried such juices, and they are often good, but you also have to think beyond the first successful demonstration, I mean, about the durability of the slipperiness in a bearing. The sweetness is a problem over time, causing sticking. The durability of the grease or oil requires another set of tests beyond the initial ones, lasting many days, but this also makes the use of the blocks very desirable. The blocks win every contest of this kind. Gold saved is gold earned, you have said."

He flattened a fly on his cheek with great force, causing him to blink repeatedly, with a surprised frown. He turned away to scrape off the fly and look at his hand, enough for me to put two figs in my mouth and start rapidly chewing on them before he could notice. They were the sweetest and largest Siwa figs, not normally offered by him to any apprentice. I was beginning to appreciate my day.

I was startled by soft footsteps behind me, followed by a scraping sound from farther behind. The soft steps rapidly approached, faster than I could think and turn around, then it passed me, all the way to Rehotep, leaping on him, it was a lion cub, clawing his tunic and licking his hand. He turned around quickly, trying to restrain the cub. While nearly choking, I said a quick praise to the earth-god Geb for making figs without pits. When the lion came over to me to lick my hands, I could lean down to scratch its ears and finish the chewing and swallowing. The cub's tongue, raspy, tinged with danger, like the fine-rasp of Ankh's, as can be imagined.

138

The lion cub started love-biting my ankles, while its tail was lashing the floor and stirring up dust. For a moment I forgot about everything else and tried to get him to stop without making him angry, when I realized it was a female. Scratching her stomach made her biting harder, but gathering the skin on the nape of her neck with massaging fingers was soon helpful and suddenly she became limp at my feet. Rehotep seemed frozen as I reached into a rubbish bin and pulled out a small papyrus ball-eye flier, with two pieces of strings attached. I teased the cub with the model, which was already punctured and torn. She snapped her head left and right to follow my hands' movements, finally pounced on all the wings at once with claws spread wide, making impressions in the floor, and dragged the toy into a dark corner.

There was a whirring sound starting from the door area, and it was followed by a blurred object that spun around the two of us at shoulder height, like a rope thrown on the neck of a bull from a respectable distance, then a shrill laugh erupted. The object was a returning-throwing stick that luckily just looped around us without causing any damage, possibly on purpose. The thrower was reaching far for the stick on its returning path but missed it, almost causing him to lose his balance, and stopping his laughter. The miss in recovery may have been a lucky event, saving his hand from injury.

"Too dark in here?" He yelled as he stepped closer and tugged at his clean white charioteer's tunic.

"My Lord, it will be brighter in an instant, as you command," said Rehotep, reaching for two lanterns and lighting them with unusual difficulty.

"Dreadful, this early twilight?" He pushed back his close-fitting cap and rubbed his eyes with both hands in red gloves neatly tied at his wrists. As his fine-fringed and gold-spangled shirt folded back a little, I noticed his thin arms, but his voice was slightly deeper than I remembered from my most recent encounter. "Where is my throwing stick, where is that stick?"

I leapt and found the stick and returned it on the run, bowing deeply. "And the other stick?" He shouted and sighed and leaned on a shelf. I ran back to the door and found his walking cane, one of his least decorated ones, and delivered it to him at falcon speed, bowing even deeper than the first time, noticing beads of every color and much detail on his papyrus sandals. Each foot trampled on Nubian and Asiatic faces and nine small outlines of bows, representing his enemies, but one set of bow images was slightly more worn than the other set, perhaps betraying a difference in putting weight on his feet. His big toes were at least a finger-width longer than mine, and we were of the same height at three fingers short of four cubits. I wondered if he was also measuring himself weekly, perhaps after hanging by his hands from a cross beam, hoping beyond hope for more growth by the pull of his weight.

He extended his hands to Rehotep, one by one, for untying his gloves. My Master did that carefully, even a bit ceremoniously, and bowed. The King scowled. "Stop it? Unbend yourselves. Unbend, and don't call me big names today, no long names. Call me just Sa-Ra. Son of Re is a good enough name today." He adjusted the spotted leopard-skin strap of a scribe's small menhed outfit slung over his left shoulder. The menhed was surprising to me. What does it mean that he carries it? It was a beautiful little set, one that I had never seen before, nor one that I could afford. It was certainly too small for a real scribe working for a living, but complete. The egg-shaped alabaster palette was set in a gold frame, and it had four holes for the pigments, as opposed to the customary two. The tiny water jar of blue glass was inlaid with rubies, and I wondered how it was made, probably the rubies were set tightly and glued for extra holding strength in drilled holes. I did not envy the person who had to drill those holes, neither for the huge time necessary, nor for the risk of chipping, let alone breaking the expensive glass. The pen case was made of electrum in the shape of a short straight horn, clipped to the palette frame, and there were three ivory-handled thin reed pens in it, more than usual.

Rehotep did not know what to do with the gloves, uncharacteristically, because he was normally on easy terms with the King, and he twisted and turned nervously, folding and unfolding and smoothing them, finally settling down to enjoy the feel and scents of the leather, while the King examined his cane from end to end, pulling lint off a gold spangle and scraping some dirt off from its bottom tip using a long fingernail. Does the Queen also get nervous from this kind of royal behavior, not to mention the strange words and shifts in mood? I rescued my Master by pulling a cord that ran to the servants' resting room, and soon a maid came to him to take the gloves, after I signaled to her secretly. The girl put the gloves on a drying rack without hesitation, and left, eliciting a dark glance from Rehotep, clearly meant for me, but why?

At a post she slowed to reach up and sweep away a spider web while looking back over her shoulder. She moved in a fluid, tall reach, with a dancer's rhythm, confidently. What was her name? A flower, no, two different flowers, a bit unusual, yes, Mehmeh-Saam, Mehmeh-Saam. I should talk to her privately. The King followed the alternating hind ripples of the girl's tunic, his face brightening and broadening, and strangely I also noticed her fully rounded ball-eyes for the first time. What a blooming of desert flowers in a day or two, how they would bounce from floor to ceiling with a little practice on a chariot in the shed, and I recalled her flower-like skin while my eyes and the King's eyes merged on her like rapid streams. I cupped my left hand showing the lotus form to her and wiggled my dangling right pointing-finger by my side, unseen by the other men, and perhaps also by her. The King reached for a handful of melon chunks and stuffed them at once into his mouth, which caused him to spit and cough. He wiped his face with the back of his hand, and licked his spidery fingers by drawing them through his mouth sideways. Rehotep tried to offer him a cloth several times, in vain.

A fleeting thought said that I could see the girl any time, when the King mumbled a few words, and at last more clearly, "Hedgehog country, hedgehog land, Two Big Lands, all mine. To Sobek with Ay. What did he say? Call me what? Sickly? Dump old Ay to Sobek!" He suddenly ripped off the menhed set from his shoulder and threw it against the wall, shattering the alabaster palette, perhaps jerking his neck because he grabbed it with both hands as his eyes rolled up to the ceiling. His left hand twisted into a gnarled shape and went from his neck to his left ear, visibly pressing hard with three long fingers on his left cheek by the ear. His lips tightened and beads of sweat rolled down his face. I handed him a wet cloth that he used on his head, breathing unevenly. He burst out, "Drown Pentu in this! Drown every priest and potion, right now!" I noticed that Rehotep was thinking hard to say something, to no avail, while I was happy to be small and barely visible.

The King, seemingly recovered a bit, limped over to the wall, picked up and ground the pens of his menhed set into the floor, cutting a few strands of his papyrus sandal. I was thinking ahead to secretly rescuing the remains of the menhed and restoring it to near perfection. He stepped close to my test objects that I almost forgot about in the last minutes, and poked the slide-block on the top of an inclined board with his cane. "Good? Say something?"

"My Lord, Sa-Ra," said Rehotep, after wiping his own brows, but unable to continue.

The King pointed at the boards and laughed, head thrown back like a pigmy actor, as if he suddenly understood everything. "My friend? Is this a good block for me?" The King poked at it again, this time starting the block to slide down on the board, causing him to shriek with delight. He beat the fallen block with his cane and continued to whoop along the slashing. "I know, I know it truly, a great day by Thoth, I will tell the Queen, and show her everything! I alone. Make them all go down, now!" I hesitated, but Rehotep impatiently flicked his hand toward me, so I lunged forward, moving faster and faster, tripping every block, one by one, each at its required tilt for its own oily condition. At the end I ventured to point grandly at the winner and say, "This block, My Lord, reveals the best oil for the bearing, because it started the most easily, on the smallest incline, everything else being equal, like the size of the blocks and the smoothness of the boards."

He slashed the air with his cane as if fighting several attackers, smiled broadly, or was it a pain on his face, and jerked toward Rehotep, making a clucking noise. "Oils and juices, then try mine?" There was no sound save for a large green fly sampling the liquids on the boards as the King looked around. He found an empty jar, examined it and threw it down. My Master tried to give the King another jar and bowed, but he waved it away, pointing to the menhed by the wall. I picked it up, briefly fondling a smooth hole in the broken alabaster palette, wishing that it were deeper. I handed it to the King while looking at his frayed sandal, wondering how long it might last, and how I could possibly repair it in a very short time under his impatient eye, but no glue in the world was quick enough for that.

He waved the piece high in the air, touched the hole with his two stylus-fingers, giggled and turned away from us, reaching under his tunic with one hand and struggling with his loincloth, which must have been too tight for a one-hander. I shifted sideways to see better, in spite of my Master's glaring eyes and frantically waving arms, on account of a recurring curiosity about the royal family's undergarments, even if this opportunity was only to see his. Perhaps the material is the same for the Queen's, if not the construction. I must catch a willing servant girl alone with Ankh's noble linens in the washroom, not an easy task. Slightly twisting his head backward, toward us, the King dribbled into the palette, his arm shaking vigorously, periodically, perhaps because of the tight loin-piece. He was mainly speaking to the wall, but loudly, "Only the First Queen may see the Living Obelisk. Unless he wants others?" He threw his head toward the ceiling and roared, "At my will, Hekau's obelisk magic. No mortals allowed." He shook his hand a last time and handed the overflowing palette to Rehotep and dipped his hands in a melon bowl. "Try mine? I want to go faster than mortals." He pointed a long wet finger at the best-sliding block as my Master sucked his teeth and carefully passed the palette to me. It felt unexpectedly heavy.

My head burst from the clashes of ideas, but there was no time to think, and I mindlessly began to mumble and chant some silly childish words for a distraction, and I moved my hands fast all around the test setup so the King could not see where his palette was emptied, just next to the intended track on the inclined board, and not a foul drop on the real path. I hastily tripped the block, encouraged its start with a tiny flick of my thumb, and it slid down the slope with great ease on the original oil, and he followed it intently and shouted triumphantly, "Magic, magic. Good work with the royal juice? Can you make the obelisk trick bigger too? I will order Hekau and Thoth and any other gods you wish to help you." He took another handful of melon chunks. "Where did you get this? Why can't I get the same ripe fruit? Deliver the rest to my kitchen. No, not the two of you, I had enough of seeing you. Have that hedgehog bring it, but where is she? Right now!" He took a few shuffling steps in the direction of the side door where she had disappeared, and looked down at the front of his tunic. "The live obelisk, not just for the Queen, jubilee, jubilee."

Mehmeh-Saam kicked the door open and returned with a new bowl of melons, in an instantaneous response to the King's demand. She must have been waiting with the replenished bowl behind the door. Her lips were quivering, either in fear of the King's loud words, or, more likely, because she has just swallowed a chunk of melon and she was licking her lips. A tiny sound distracted us from her, it was a mouse leaping out of a box, followed by a snake, which suddenly stopped a few cubits from us, then slowly raised its head, as if spiraling upward. It was a moment of sudden tension, broken by Mehmeh-Saam, who dumped the bowl on the snake.

"Why waste my fresh melons?" The King shrieked and stomped his foot.

We all looked at one another. Rehotep cleared his throat several times before he found the right words. "My Lord, it's a sacred snake, cannot be killed here. The cool juice, it's the only way, and perfect... it cools the little god, slows its heart, makes it harmless for a while." He motioned to the girl to bring another bowl, and to me to scoop up the snake and take it away.

"Yes, yes," said the King, smiling broadly. "I did order the fruit sacrifice for him. He likes it. I will feed him some, make him a bigger king, as he deserves to become. Hold it for me!" In the next step he stumbled, lost a sandal, and grabbed a loose block and a slide board, trying to steady himself. I wondered if the rumor was true about Ankh putting more and more of a pinch of potion in his goblets of wine.

We leapt to him, my Master taking the King's elbow, as I was handing him his cane. Mehmeh-Saam brushed the snake into a pail and took it away. There was a long silence except for his deeper and deeper breathing from his heaving pigeon chest. He shook his head as if coming up for air from a deep dive, and he started to smile and laugh and nod repeatedly. "Friend? It is rare for a mortal to see Pharaoh loosen his obelisk, never before to Thoth's purpose, to drive faster and fly higher than any scribe before. You know, Thoth and I like each other." He leaned down to pick up his lost sandal before either one of us could jump for it. He wobbled during straightening up, studied the frayed sole, with his forehead alternately wrinkling and smoothing, and put the sandal on an inclined board. "Make it happen. Make it slide on the floor easier, better than any snake, no mortal scraping anymore. Make it happen, and I make you a god. Or let Seth curse Seth."

He tried to break his cane, and failed three times. He handed it to me, looking encouraging. I thought for a moment, pretended to try to break it several times, gave up, and reached for a saw. He almost put his long fingers around my wrist, but recoiled. "What? Give me my best cane, now! I cut this piece, it's mine, Queen-beater strong. Friend? Make him give it back." I complied so fast that I hit the palm of his hand with the stick, while he was still uttering his last words.

His surprised look and step backward scared me, especially because now he lost the other sandal, and I could only think of pulling the cord for the servant. Luckily, she appeared soon enough and that was good for a diversion of his attention, but nobody knew what to do with her. My Master closed his eyes for the longest time I had seen him do that standing up, and she ignored him. Mehmeh-Saam came close silently, hands properly at her side, while I slipped out of my sandals. She noticed the four sandals lying about, a very smart girl, deserving of a fine ball-eye-dress-up with a royal garment in a good future year, if not First Queen, Amun willing. She picked up my sturdy sandals and kneeled down to put them on the King. He smiled broadly, a strange effect with his overbite, and he scratched her back with the tip of his cane, starting from the neck and going lower and lower. She trembled almost imperceptibly, but I could imagine bigger trembles from her fleshy parts caused by my fingers.

He put his cap on the girl's head and patted it. He looked down on his feet, perhaps amused by his longest toes being bent over the front edge of the soles, as if gripping them. He twisted and slid his feet around a little, making a scraping sound. He took one sandal off and scratched its sole with a fingernail. "Rough traction soles! Good? Better yet!" He spit on it and tested it again. "Better yet!" He whooped and dipped both sandals in the spot of melons where the snake got drenched. "Rough and wet, rough and wet, better!" He fished around for the biggest chunk of the melons on the floor and swallowed it so fast that his eyes bulged for a moment.

He put the dripping sandals on his feet with the help of Mehmeh-Saam, who wiped off the excess liquid with the bottom of her tunic, and he placed his cane on the floor in front of him, pointing it away. He looked around triumphantly, gloating at our puzzled faces, and pretended to swing his right leg over the breastwork of his imaginary chariot, planting his right foot on the cane, the imaginary pole. He rocked the foot a little, as if assuring himself of a good grip with the curved sole straddling the cane.

Mehmeh-Saam started to get up, but the King gently pushed her down by the shoulder, all the way to the floor, whispering something to her, perhaps to lie down flat, face down, because that's what she did, quietly. He put his hind leg on her buttocks, testing the precarious position. "Too soft for racing, much too soft, tighten the mat!" She pulled her muscles tighter, a smart girl, worthy of a fine gift later. He was pleased with the firmed up chariot floor as he proceeded to wrap the imaginary reins on his waist, and checking them for proper tension. "Bring in the horses, my best two, what are their names? No, they are too far. Friends, you two, will do for now. Hurry and step up to the pole! Bite the bronze bits to feel my reins!"

Rehotep and I stood in front of the cane, both of us shaking, and I looked back at the King as I did once at Ankh, when she played with me, making me drunk, learning to drive me with real reins on her hips. "Don't look back, young stallion! Watch your wise elder at your side. First, a little warming up, an easy straight run. Now we make a few turns, left and right, good? Ready for the big one-wheeler? Good? You run straight now. Left wheel up on the ramp, hold on, higher, higher, higher!" He stumbled off to the side, knees buckling, arms flailing, hitting his head into the slide board with his sandal lying at its bottom. We all leapt to him, but he pushed himself up on one arm to sit in a twisted form and jerkily waved us off, his eyes becoming glazed. His feet twitched, and his fingernails raked the floor. Mehmeh-Saam defied him and crept up to him to hold his ankles together and down. She later moved up and whispered into his ear, then began a lilting peasant song, barely audible.

His twitching gradually subsided, and then he closed his eyes. He mumbled something. "Hear me?" He broke into a shout, "Cooties! The horses have huge cooties, by Seth. Horus, Horus, crunch the wicked cooties, and I want Re, hurry my Re, Seth-Seth is double-darkening, where is the bright Re, where is she, the wine tastes … snake?"

25

Ankh's Bobaha Orgy

My fish net was full and clumsy to hold as I hurried along the narrow and dusty path, barefoot for silence, tripping often on a root or on the net, which had too many loose and frayed ends. Why could I not get a better net? This cursed rushing, too, always rushing, sliding, tripping, and on the last tumble I almost broke my huge kite, the biggest ever, its reed stiffeners trying to escape from the net, like a big-toothed monster of the depths, caught unintended, as they always are, but too late to free it.

I suddenly regretted bringing this kite on this major expedition, unfinished, untested, maybe forever hopeless, judging by my previous failures with other flying contraptions, though they were smaller. I must be desperate in bringing a dream to life, to lift myself into the air, out of the dust and smells and bad people, like one of my enemies dropping a rotting fish under my bed. I must get out of all this, the shortest way, to float up higher than in a flying chariot, to see what others can't see, yet be unseen. But if I try to untangle and abandon it here, it would slow me down.

Then there is the spy tube, which once before put me in a whistling high mood regarding Ankh, but too briefly, with its glass eyes precariously held in place, always seemingly out of place, the tube also trying to escape from the net, another piece of unfinished, stupid business, far from any use by peasants and carpenters and carvers. I stopped just long enough to pull it out, abandon it for later retrieval, when it turned stubborn and refused to leave the net, in spite of my rough tugging. Slow down, calm down, but no, there is no time to waste.

Now the three-cubit Anubis-ear tried to escape, but this one is precious, and more like an animal that just needs reassurance, so I instinctively petted it tenderly and whispered to it, and it seemed to help, thanks to Thoth who holds the secrets to all these papyrus creatures.

I trotted on. The royal boat Sleepy Waters came into view, rocking gently on the lapping waves. No guards in sight. I set down with the Anubis-ear's stem planted in the sand between my knees, its point near my own ear. I strained to listen in the direction of the main cabin on the boat, and twisted the ear back and forth a little to catch the elusive sweet spot of hearing clearly, maddening, like Horus must feel after committing to a hungry dive but missing the prey by a finger or two.

"Hold the charm … me … that charm …" Ankh's voice was impatient but too soft. I pulled up the ear and crept closer, to nearly halve the distance, to another choice spot found in previous practice runs, but the line of sight was less than perfect. The eternal problem of hearing versus seeing.

"Do you hear me, King? Work … I say it is time for getting them up and out and together … we must watch, closer … they like you enough already …" She laughed in a way of, what, maybe of a ball-eye-dancer at the end of her teasing routine for rowdy soldiers. I liked the memory of such dancers' movements and voices, but not the idea that Ankh could be doing it, but why not? She could be good at that dance, but for me, alone.

The strings of beads on the door parted and Tut came out, tugging on his loincloth. The slap of his hand must have been to smash a bug on his belly. What was she wearing or taking off at the same moment? A hot day, in a hot cabin, soft cushions everywhere, no doubt, she threw out a washcloth or something after him, it plopped on the deck with a spent squish, but he ignored it. Does she sweat much, and what does she do for fanning herself in the absence of servants, the breasts and the belly and the hedgehog, in particular?

I could improve on the average ostrich fan for her. A light flickered through the beads and I strained upward and sideways to see better around a clump of reeds, while the boat drifted away a bit on its ropes.

He limped to a pad shaded by an awning, and I noticed the pair of dark animals curled up and sleeping together like stacked bowls. I rose higher, my heart leapt, for the Wise Baboon, if he doesn't mind the competition, they are the bobahas, what everybody was talking about, but few have seen, myself only a couple of times, never close or long enough, but I heard a lot. Originally there were three, but one died shortly after their arrival from the Kopora forests in Maranga Land, a thousand miles away, more than a year's journey and full of monsters, the strangely-dressed dark merchant said, justifying the high price. Ankh was furious, "What if it was the male that died?" she yelled, and demanded a lot of gold back, but by then the merchant and all his tribe were gone.

The smaller one, that must be Princess Yulan, stirred first and climbed up to walk back and forth, upright, on the boat's railing, if she balanced herself with any effort, it was not obvious. She grabbed some green leaves and fruit from Tut, and proceeded to groom his head for bugs with her long fingers. Word was that they were similar to other hairy creatures from the distant southern forests, but were the closest relatives to all noble cattle, that they had human eyes and ears though flat noses, that they coupled feverishly and many times a day, after some fun of chasing around, often in peculiar wrestling positions in the best flings, and that their species was so named after the sounds they made in the wildest orgies, so will that happen now? Can this strange Princess also reckon on her long fingers like I do?

"Come here!" Ankh parted the beads, but stayed just inside the doorway, revealing a hint of her skin, streaked golden in a sliver of sunlight. "Come!" I fought off the thought that she called me, but I pressed forward, lips trembling, hands struggling with the pathless reeds, ignoring the muck swishing up between my toes and higher. Still clutching the big ear, I finally lowered my body on my shaky knees and let the water soothe my skin. "Give Count Gim sweet melon and get him going, they rested enough, and so have you," Ankh said.

Things must have happened while I replanted the ear at my feet. When I looked up, Yulan was flying off the railing, wrapping herself frontally on Gim, but I could see only their heads bouncing behind the rigging.

"Not bad," Ankh said, "there was one or two ideas that you could pick up, though with a smaller leap. It's time to give them wine. Not our best sour one, but the sweetest of figs." Tut fumbled with a lidded, humped chest in the shade. I remembered painting it full of hunting scenes as he had requested, he liked his arrows buried deep in huge leopards and lions. He lifted out a brown jug with a long neck. The creatures yelled something like "wa-hoo" in unison and walked up to him, Gim briefly sashaying like the silly Pretty Boy of the wrestlers, then they fought over the nipple of the jug. "Wa-hee!" They began a chase all over the deck, Gim caught the not too reluctant Yulan and tickled her on the belly and hedgehog, which was not visible, but it was not hard to imagine. There was loud sniffing and smacking all over, she put her right foot on his left knee, then she balanced on one foot while her other toes ascended his thigh, and suddenly he lied down on his back, she leapt high or else he threw her high above himself like some parents play with their babies, and she fell on him, coupling in a smooth single motion, then it was over in a blink or two, and they headed back to the sweet jug that was cradled and tasted by Tut in the meantime.

"That makes three or four good ones already, and the day is not over yet," Ankh laughed from the doorway. "Tell Carver to write it all down before you forget it, and he'd better do a perfect job or he will be demoted to Carter," she said while scratching herself with both hands in the sacred notch. "Which trick do you pick first, although I loved the three of them together best, the very first day, it's really sad to lose one so young, a female with excellent fingers, and so expensive. When is the next caravan from Koranga, or what's the name? Anyway, did you watch them carefully? How many times do you need to imitate the finest Count to make one healthy boy?"

He coughed nervously and spoke barely audibly, "They rush. How many months, afterward, do they have to wait?" He turned to wrestle the jug away from Gim.

"What do you mean?" She pulled the jug out of his hands. "You had enough."

"They rush. When we rush like that, we wait nine months for the prince. How long do they wait?"

"Ask them. Ask the priests. I bet it's less than nine, like most animals. Stop, you filthy beast, not on my boat!" She ran out from the shadow, almost naked, to beat off Gim who was standing on the railing and spraying the deck yellow. "Never on my boat, do you hear me?" He thrust his pelvis in defiance and waved his penis in a circle before leaping off to safety.

Tut sat down on a heap of ropes and put a finger in his mouth. "What if they also need nine? Maybe never, what chance?"

She uttered a short scream, and another. "Stop delaying. There is no time. You know what, and if you can't, I'll get him to sniff at the hedgehog you can't feed, he has already expressed plenty of interest, and he has the stamina, better than you, the fake Strong Bull. Maybe the three of us together, yes, and, listen, I like a virile Prince who doesn't speak his every thought during the main event." She pulled him up by his loincloth and pranced before him toward the cabin. Her breasts and ball-eyes swung into the doorway's darkness.

My head was about to burst, but it was the Anubis-piece that cracked in my hands. I turned away and scooped water with the ear on myself, while hesitant to touch my painful crotch, where was the easy path, the net, the stupid kite, cold beer dribbling from the top of my head into the mouth?

26

Tails Afire

He can't do it, he simply cannot do it, even after taking lessons from the virile Gim. Should I offer a bag of Rehotep's stallion-testicle extract to Tut? No. Enough of my help for him. Anybody could do better with her, and I will, by my Big Baboon. She is not at fault, she has everything it takes to make a healthy boy. He is finished, not exactly, but should be, she is done with him. It's time to look ahead, what will be next after him, after this noble jug of fig wine is finished. Where will the next one come from? There must be more on that boat, what's its Sleepy name, Gim will share it for a good scratch on his rump, he is a fine fellow, will be a better Count at Court than many human ones. Where is the moon, it wants to share my sweet drink, it came and went. It has an uncommon taste, not for peasants' tongues, did Gim perhaps spray the open jug before she stopped him? She was sparkling and magnificent when so angry, it will be fun to tame her, but I will be up to the task. I also need to run a new experiment to get the same fine taste while Gim is alive, and quickly get rich with it, though the treasury should be full, full enough for another jug. Ankh, come and taste this royal brew!

Twelve trumpets blared beyond Hedgehog Hill to announce the beginning of the Otep-Otep Festival. Each instrument was of a different horned animal of a large kind, equipped with a copper mouthpiece of my own design just for this occasion to make more noise than ever before in the Two Lands. A cloud of white doves circled above.

"The King is dead, jubilee to the new King!" the trumpets blared. "All rekhyts press forward offering new jubilee to the Queen!" The sound whipped the doves around like the desert wind tosses laundry on the lines.

Mehmeh-Saam adjusted the fresh red and yellow flowers in her hair, and approached the Queen with ceremonial shuffling steps, and handed her the sacred Kamaras bowl of oats. The Queen took it and pressed its glinting silver edge into her white-belted belly, adding ripples to her shimmering glass tunic, a bright color rivaling Nut's bluest sky. Was it really made of glass? Possibly, knowing from my playing with lots of glass that the thinnest strands can be bent without breaking them, a miracle of strength from weakness. The tunic was cut low, revealing her gold-beaded necklace, and the two emerald-green breast cups, a triumph of wispy straps and knots.

Ankh motioned several times to the daydreaming Mehmeh-Saam, who finally went to bring up the restlessly waiting shiny black stallions. The horses snorted with pleasure and nudged each other as they buried their noses in the fresh oats in the finely wrought Kamaras bowl, clanking their ivory cheek-pieces, blowing some seeds to her belly and to the ground for the benefit of jostling ducks and sparrows scurrying among the webbed feet. The huge horses with withers at the level of my shoulders preferred the oats at the bottom of the bowl, perhaps to get a richer smell of the grain, perhaps like old women in the market, elbowing one another and constantly sorting and squeezing everything, picking only the best. When the stallions were done, they waited patiently while she pinched out the seeds from their nostrils and placed them on the soft pink lips. She deeply inhaled the freshly washed stallions' scent, and stroked their quivering lips and noses and the erect manes.

She started to back away, but the horses followed her, nibbling on her hands and up along the arms, sniffing the cloud of her rose perfume. An aggressive fly buzzed around her nipples, struggling in the air blown by the horses and whipped by their ears. She stroked one horse all the way to its twitching rump, then doing the other one from tail to head, when a probing snort parted a slit in her tunic, revealing her red loin-piece, which had been rumored for days.

She signaled to Mehmeh-Saam to pay attention to me. The girl first straightened out my ceremonial outfit, tugging here and smoothing wrinkles there. What a dolt I am, that I haven't noticed her fingers before, other than her uncommon skill with all kinds of tools, in spite of Rehotep's frowning eyes. Where and when could she learn the hard tools and the soft touches with them? She proceeded to give us the fest foods and drinks to give us strength for the solemn occasion. My favorites were the sacred pumpkin seeds of my own stealthy design, since they helped me get this far, and the kurabida honey cake laced with Sumerian fly, and the brown Nubian beer flowing from three-hin calabashes. I tossed a piece of cake to Ankh, like a he-tern flicks a fish to its floating mate. She caught it and giggled, while the girl suppressed a smile, probably having stolen a mouthful of it the night before.

The beer tasted best after a handful of the spicy Give-Me-Time-Amun-But-Hurry pumpkin seeds. I savored splitting the shell edgewise between my front teeth, using no hands, then extricating the seed in whole with the tongue, and finally spitting out the shell. Another approach, much simpler and demeaned by experts, is to eat the whole thing, tough fiber and all, purportedly to attain the best jutting jaws and bowel regularities in the world, naturally favored by peasants and fighting men. Palace wags joke that the lowest class is where the men eat the pumpkin shell and spit out the seed. Thankfully, Amun gave me time.

I pointed to the heap of chariot parts under a crimson cover on the side, and Mehmeh-Saam moved to assemble them. When she pulled the cover off, a young mongrel woke from its sleep on the floor mat of tightly strung precious stone and glass beads and slunk off, avoiding the girl's halfhearted kick, who lost a flower from her hair in the lunge. She first put the five-cubit-long iron axle, not a thumb-width less, on two blocks, displaying more strength than the average wrestler. A pair of mating Meadow-Horus-Ball-Eyes landed on the axle to be warmed by the sun and the dark metal.

Mehmeh-Saam pulled the tires from their soaking tubs, and put them on the two-cubit-size wheels in proper order, first the brown, thick cushioning hide, then the gray hide for more cushioning and holding the brown one, and on top of these the finest red outer leather, partially for holding the inner layers ever more, and mainly for beauty. After the placement of each layer she paused to blow hot air on the hide to dry and shrink it, the natural tightening of hide by heat being a marvel of dead animal skin. Fringe gusts of the hot air reached my face, carrying fever, which must have also reached Ankh, who became agitated and added her own air to Saam's blasts.

I was amused by the action of the women working together as in a dream, chewed on the seeds without hurry, and downed a hin of beer without effort. Mehmeh-Saam quickly rolled the red-leather wheels to the axle, packed the naves with spicy grease, and lifted them to their bronze bearing sleeves. The fellies were of solid gold of deathless purity, and so were the spokes. Not a sliver of wood on these major parts. She grabbed the linchpins of ivory and pushed them in their axle holes, securing them with thongs of braided filaments of electrum.

I couldn't help but like these shiny deathless parts of her chariot. They were heavy and soft and useless for mortal drivers, but they should find a prominent place in my Big Papyrus for All Ages, of Big Heroes in a Big Race and Big Battle, helped or harassed by the Big Gods of the Big Mountain in the far north, if the priests are not lying. I hope another Big Poet will not steal this before I become great beyond words. But suddenly my head was spinning faster and I couldn't hold back any longer. "Wait! Seven spokes? What are you doing?"

"Sire." She put her hands on her hips, fingers backward and thumbs forward, a haughty stance. "Sire, it is an ancient idea of six pieces of spread-finger spokes, each in the shape of a flock of flying geese, bound together pair-by-pair to make a perfect six-spoke wheel, but that is expensive, it cannot be used for any more than six spokes in one wheel, and thus it is not for the future. That is why I made only straight spokes, for almost any number in a wheel. This is seven, my own sacred number, a small privilege well earned with my hands. It was easy to make and cost little, aside from the gold in the spokes and silver in the hubs. Notice also my making each spoke with an arrowhead shape in the middle, not plain dull as usual. It does not add or take away strength in the spokes, but the form is good, and people like form above all, and always will. In any case, I have reason to doubt the strength of these metals, since wood is more similar to the bones of birds and cheetahs than gold and silver is, but the written order said ..."

"Enough!"

"You can test them, Sire. May I proceed?" She drummed on her belly impatiently with her spread thumbs.

I sighed and nodded silently, reaching for more Give-Me-Time seeds without looking at the bowl. She attached the six-cubit silver pole to the axle socket, placed the silver frame on the pole and axle, and installed the elegantly curved two-cubit golden yoke with its two taut horse-equalizing traces near the tip of the pole, liberally using lashings of silver and electrum and gold braids at every junction as required in the deeply carved Book of the Chariot, written by my humble self. Where did she learn to read? What else did she learn?

She put a golden harness on the prancing stallions, jumped on board, and made a test run on a small circle around us. The red reins hugged her hips firmly, making only a shallow groove in the flesh, giving me new ideas of pleasure, and the wheels of seven golden spokes mowed the sunbeams fast. She jumped off and scratched the horses' noses and gave them handfuls of the sacred pumpkin seeds, which they ate noisily, begging for more.

I tried to protest about her wasting my best seeds, but I was sidetracked by fresh thoughts. It was her hip-control of the reins that gave me the new ideas. Clearly, she was controlling the stallions by the twisting of her hip easier than any warrior could do because her hip is one cubit wide, some three thumbs wider than mine, allowing better leverage on the reins. Thus, a new invention suggests itself, a horned belt for the average male driver with two protrusions on the side of the hips for the reins, each piece of metal or wood two thumbs in size, as if making the hips a little wider. The increased leverage will make for a greater pull on the horses' bits, and the extra effort needed by the driver is readily available from any man with a healthy spine. There is more. A fine set of ball-eyes on the girl. And her face is bright, not queenly beautiful, but her head is inclined to reckoning.

Mehmeh-Saam smiled as if she could read my thoughts, and wiped off the excess spicy grease from the bearings, she smeared it on the pink wet parts under the stallions' tails, to which they reacted instantly, snorting and neighing at a higher and higher pitch and hoeing the ground with their front hooves. Suddenly, a drumming and shouting erupted from the bushes nearby, "Give us tail-spice!" "We want to fly!" Who invited the wrestlers here? They should be sent to their Double-Darkness, first thing tomorrow.

I shook my fist at them and turned to the girl, "What in the name of Seth are you doing?"

She giggled, "It will get better, for a faster and higher ride."

"What?" the Queen and I yelled, with a seed flying out along my word, and crumbs of honey cake with hers, not in royal manners.

"It's my speed-grease, equally good for the bearings and the horses. My father trusted the secrets to me, he had a good heart for animals, buying dying nags in one village and smearing his grease under their tails just before reaching the next settlement, selling the high-strung beasts at a good price, before hurrying home."

"What is in your grease? Hurry, she is getting anxious, but don't lie."

"Seven parts. Garlic, herbs, sharp nigela-satifa, female scorpion, jackal semen blessed by Inpu …"

"Why is this delay?" Ankh yelled and threw a bowl of Give-Me-Time in our direction. A gust blew the seeds in front of the horses, temporarily making them busy. She sprinkled rose perfume on her breasts, which caused the horses to toss their heads again.

"Get the Romp-Rite going!" The Queen stomped in a stormy dance, showing her thighs. "How big are you from eating your seeds?"

"Hush! You will find out soon. If you could reckon and remember, you would know that your First-King and I are, we were, of the same height."

She burst out laughing and threw me a two-hin gourd, spilling foam on my hands. "Are you talking the same language? Can you reckon Hedgehog-Craze and the One-Wheel-Love, my High-Axle-Prince?" She laughed again and almost choked, drowning out the wrestlers, while I drank.

I pushed up my bronze arm-straps and smashed the empty gourd on the point of the axle beam. I tossed two thick sheepskins on the floor mat of the chariot and grabbed her by the waist, hiking up her tunic and feeling the Red Cloth. I threw her on the furs and tied her scented wrists to the siding posts, while she giggled, and I nodded to Saam who handed me the whip, but the horses did not wait, their tails were afire from the grease, and they took off with a jolt that audibly strained the silver acceleration braces on the pole and almost lost both of us in the first blink.

The dog sprang out and lunged at the spokes, then he pulled off our ceremonial sandals. The wind stripped our clothes off and let them flutter to the ground like colored clouds, how can I see every little cloud this day, and she tugged at my long hair, I will get a barber at last, and the furs shifted, the bounding platform began hurting my knees and toes, while I was praying wildly, as the chariot plunged forward and up and down over the rocks and ravines, bending the pole and the fellies and anything else silver and gold, but the axle is a tough new metal, worth keeping, and the dog is barking at the rattling of the deformed wheels, and she screams over the din, "One-wheeler! Up on the One-wheeler!"

I have no reins at hand, they are overboard and nipped by the dog, but the stallions hear her demand and aim for a ramp rock, and the up-wheel goes flying and we cling on to everything with sweaty hands, I must envy Gim and Yulan for balancing on the railings tightly together, I hit my throbbing head into a post, the jug was too much, and the hedgehog cries for circling the hill twice or more, beyond reckoning, and my thighs cramp from the bum knees rubbing on bare metal, learn to pray faster, but the rocks and hills keep kicking the floor and buckling the horses' legs and she bites my neck as the up-wheel hits the ground again.

27

Walls within Walls

The Master is dead, what will happen to me?

Luckily, it was just a nightmare, though I was drowning in sweat, and I banged my knees and knuckles on the wall, and was bleeding from the fingernails. Sweat and blood, equally salty, but I wonder why the crocodile would spit me out. Who wanted to save me?

It started easily enough with a normal request by Rehotep to visit him in his refurbished quarters, after his absence of some weeks, secretly visiting several small Villages of the Dead. Now he had a magnificent new Nubian doorway, with both of the uprights leaning slightly to the right to signify his impending passage to the Western Horizon, though he was not Nubian.

The exterior Bawaba doorway was decorated lavishly, including the green outlines of a pair of spread hands, the piercing yellow ball centered among thick blue lines in the Eye of Horus, a pair of dried crocodile heads with wide-open mouths, figures of fish and plants and birds in mud and white plaster relief hanging by thin twines from mysterious head-gear shapes, and a snake skull for a door handle. Cryptic writings on the wall, done in part in an ancient style, mostly forgotten, to keep the uninitiated guessing, causing just a little trouble for me: "Learn the laws of smaller-than-small numbers," and "Reckon with few fingers," and "Give the sword to him who knows how to toughen it in ashes before the Mubyat contest," and "The evil ones shall see dirty rain on their laundry."

I was cradling my gift to him, a good puzzle worthy of both of us, a board with images of chariots, small ones on the far right, increasing in size as approaching the middle, decreasing in size as disappearing to the left, like the sound of hoofs and wheels to the befuddled observer standing on the roadside, like music quickening at first and slowing to nothing at last, come and gone. I peeked inside the loose wrap, as if to see if they were still all there, and to relish the shiny black and red ink.

He was sitting on a large cushion, with a lamp illuminating half his face, giving his skin the sheen of a faded lotus. His tunic was stained, probably by sweat and shop oils and cooking ingredients, some of it certainly fresh, because he was absorbed in mixing his favorite dish in a large crock, using goat curd, garlic, figs, honey, and three or four powders and juices that were lined up in sprinkler jars within his easy reach. At least, this tunic had no moth holes in it. I put down the gift board near his big chair, making a little noise, but he ignored me. Will I be the first one to taste his dish?

It was not a good day for me, but there were opportunities every day. Like looking at a stick that is partially in water, it looks sharply broken, but when I pull it out, it's not broken.

He got up and rubbed the olive-colored folds of skin beneath his eyes, facial colors that worried me as much as the new gaps in his teeth. He went to a shelf and opened jar after jar, loudly sniffing each one, and talking to himself. "Listen. Why don't you ever listen? This dish needs one more ingredient, the honey gathered by the bee that bends the stem of the flower with its weight. First, you have to see it happen. Then you catch the bee and weigh it and dry it and grind it in. You think you're clever? Show me how you weigh the bee when it's empty, and when it's full of gold in the pouch. You claim to have ideas to measure them? Ah, the extent of bending of the stalk, compared with the bending by a grain of stone, or use the balanced straw with replacement weight? Stir it well. The less there is of something, the more you have to stir it. The Queen will like it, the only thing that will smooth her skin and also the raspy voice. She is not getting younger."

161

Will he notice me any time soon? Not yet. So I surveyed the shop, which soon could be mine, but strangely my earlier interest in being the boss has evaporated. It's funny... the matter of domains. There was a time I begged him to allow me to put up a wall inside the shop to isolate and protect my space and my secret projects from the other apprentices. He reluctantly agreed, but too late. Now, that small wall would cut through my bigger domain, and I would have to tear it down. But it's too late for that, too, the whole shop is a mere fleck in the Two Lands, my ultimate domain, if Horem is right, as he should be. Just a few more years, and I will arrive at the top. But slow down. Rehotep is still alive, though not kicking pebbles well.

He talked into a jar. "Listen. Let me teach you. Life is worthless without a dancing hedgehog or two at your fingertips. You need a fully shaved queen and one ripe servant. Ankh is magnificent, for one. Look at those fingers and ball-eyes, though late in their season. I wish I were younger, or she more inclined to watch Gim and Yulan with me, to learn from the best. But you are still young, you have time to get there. When you do, touch her hedgehog for me, too, and make it dance. But don't wait until the suns in your eyes turn to cinder. That reminds me, have you gotten the owls out of the stables? You say it's only one owl and small, but they are huge. Go, get them, and measure them for me.

"Gim and Yulan, what a pair, almost human, I want to see them again on the wild ropes before they die, they can't possibly live very long coupling so often, but don't tell my mother about them. You know where she lives, it's a small place, a shame, but it will be redone tomorrow. Take this dish to her and your new tomb-lamp, wait for the wind to sleep, so the lamp stays burning. Take a good sacrifice, fresh crusty bread's belly, mindful of her teeth, triple-pressed Siwa oil with a touch of salt and vinegar, herbs from my shady plot, water, because there is none in those high hills, plenty of soft figs, she will be sniffing them and choosing hungrily, and her favorite poem about the lovers separated by the crocodile river, read it slowly to her, words on papyrus hurt her eyes, and her attention span is down to one finger out of ten, but she still wants to scrub me in the muddy river."

28

Kick Tut over the Western Horizon

Tut gripped the lion head of his ebony cane hard. I could see the skin of his knuckles yellowing in the light of the torches, or was it my feverish imagination, on account of Ankh shuffling back and forth restlessly on the side, applying some ointment to her face, pulling her blue-starred Nut-wrap tightly around her shoulders against the cool desert breeze, revealing more of her breasts and plump ball-eyes. Did she flash a smile in my direction? And the slow lowering of the long eyelashes, saying what? Hopefully she is appreciating my new non-sting glue that can last holding for hours, and yet is easy to remove with warm water before sleeping, so as not to damage the precious imported lashes. A second little smile, she is beautiful in the torchlight, how can I acknowledge it without danger?

Just the day before, she was beautiful in a strange way, with the setting sun illuminating a tear running sideways from her almond eye, momentarily hesitating when crossing a carefully painted black line. Not knowing what's best to do, I tried to touch the teardrop with the tip of my tongue, but missed. "Don't you dare," she giggled and whispered, "to make an image of my face on your papyrus pillow, let alone showing the tear like a bump on my skin. Instead, can we row away tonight, far away in the dark? Or, at least, I will take the pillow home."

The King raised his cane to the sky, then swept it around, upon which the six torchbearers turned away from him, evenly spaced like a wheel, shielding the light with their bodies. Ay and Horem stepped up to the King in the center of the torch circle, their faces grim. "There is still a chance to call it off, My Lord, perfectly honorably," said Ay, with his lips quivering. Why were these men nervous, when the personal danger to them was minimal tonight? Perhaps just the excitement of the hunt, or facing a whole new world if the King had a misfortune, unlikely though, so I strained to hear them as I was polishing the pole mirror of gold, reaching over a horse, rubbing the metal. At the same time, Rehotep, pale but standing firmly, was calming the hooded horses that were stomping every time the smoke wafted to them. He was talking to them and stroking them, but really watching most keenly the royal center of the circle.

Ay and Horem cast furtive looks at one another, like trained fighting baboons in a slow dance just before the first ritual contact. Which one will win the biggest bout? Does Ankh favor one over the other? If I were Queen, I would pick Ay, the older of the two noble men. But, which is best for me? I will be, at the best, third in line to claim her officially. She adjusted her sparkling Nut-wrap around her hips, the finest driving hips, judging by a hundred images of famous warrior kings. I must make her see that I am the best for her fortune and fertility.

"We can do a normal and safe group hunt in the ancient fashion, well rehearsed," Ay continued though the King was not looking at him. "Please, for the sake of all of us, getting another pelt is not so important, you have enough of every royal animal." Was he serious or cleverly egging the King on and on? There could be plenty of reasons for him, either way, something worth thinking about. Horem nodded and grunted something in agreement. The Queen, a few steps farther away, also nodded and dropped to her knees and put forth her hands as if in prayer to the King. Her cheeks shined reddish as if illuminated by her big eyes, bright little torches. She dropped her tight ball-eyes, medium width at a cubit less two thumbs, onto her heels, making two fist-size dents in the round flesh.

"Enough, enough. You don't understand, and never will," said the King, stomping with his right foot and raising a small cloud of dust, which he tried to hit with the cane. "You will not touch me again. Get a child or a slave. Do you want to be a part of this?" His hissing words ended in a sharp laugh, followed by silence, except for the popping of the torches and the horses' scraping the ground.

"We will, My Lord, be assured," said Ay, as he and Horem stepped up and started to peel off the King's blue-fringed shoulder tunic and main tunic. I moved closer, pretending to check the bearings by lifting the axle tips one-by-one and spinning the wheels by hand. This has always been fun, and again the golden spokes drew my mind into the whirling patterns of torchlight broken and scattered toward the stars. I almost forgot about Tut and the old men, but the wheel came to a stop, and I began to wonder about the rumor that the King's loincloth for this event was decorated on the hind part with the face of a man, vaguely resembling Ay. Many other eyes were also trained on the King's midriff at that moment. Has Ay heard the rumor, and what will he do if it is true?

The loincloth that came to view was covered with ceremonial beads, some colored to make patterns, which were not of Ay's face, but the oval symbol of the sacred hedgehog. I looked at Ankh while she stared at the King, squirmed on her heels and dropped her head into her hands. Was she looking sideways at me? The universal hairy symbol of man's desire for pleasure, and of woman's hope for fertility signified by the plentiful quills, it must have pained her, for not producing a healthy heir to the King. My heart pounded in my throat. What did the King mean with that symbol, and was she really glancing at me?

Tut approached the nearest guard and began emptying his bladder in the dark spot behind the man. I glanced at Rehotep on the other side of the golden chariot, and he seemed to roll his eyes in bemusement. The King shuffled closer to the guard, eventually aiming his strong stream at the man's calves. The guard jerked his torch a little, but soon stood like a rock again. Tut finished the watering with the most vigorous shaking of his right arm I had ever seen by any man, including seeing him before, when he was doing likewise in our shop.

He motioned to Ay who shook a small pouch of glass beads before giving it to the guard. The clinking beads seemed to have come from the stars in the clear night. The King also motioned to Horem and spoke loudly. "He is a good guard, a solid man. Test him for the seven palace aptitudes, because he has a good future, not like you, I can smell it." He shrieked with delight. "Let's move on, why are you wasting my time?"

The Queen shuddered, dropped her wrap, got on her Hathor-chariot and drove at cow-speed around the King, periodically stopping and blowing her golden horn. My heart raced as she raised her right arm with the horn, the left one steady on the reins, and her tunic tightening and lifting her pomegranate breast a finger or two, while she aimed at each of the four points of the earth, defined by a high priest holding up a lion skin toward the King, each with a different set of painted symbols. According to tradition, he picked the one with fifty blue stars, signifying the request to the goddess Nut for good luck of the night hunt in a big leap year, seven times seven and one, perfection and completion, rare in a lifetime and hard to reckon. He stroked the pelt and examined the dangling claws. He tugged on the biggest claw playfully. He scratched both of his cheeks with the claw for good luck. Ay and Horem dabbed up the blood and draped the skin over the King's shoulders and clasped it securely around the waist, not hiding the hedgehog on his loincloth.

Tut suddenly motioned to me, but why to me? I tried to shrink and slink away, but found myself in the open. "Carver, you come with me. First, break this." He handed me his cane.

"My Lord." Ay and Horem spoke at once and stepped forward, trying to block me, but the King waved them away.

"Hurry. Smash the lion head and break the stick." I hesitated but complied, with difficulty. He whispered to me, "You will do the reckoning, I will do the driving and the shooting."

"My Lord, I am." Where is Ankh, and is she smiling in encouragement, and for what? Is she saying "Send him over the western horizon?"

He stepped on the broken lion stick with force. "I am a good shot, straight through two copper plates at once, even moving targets. I like moving targets. Finally, after the kill, you will help us do the one-wheeler without a ramp to go up, for the triumphal run. Like rocking a boat to its edge, swing your body to tip the chariot up. I have seen you do it." His words were flooding out, an unusual flood from him.

"Alone is best, My Lord. Difficult enough. Two people is more dangerous."

"Danger is for sheep and slaves and old men. Use a rope to hang out farther. I will help with the high balancing, and with the horses. I want the Queen to see this, and remember it forever. You will, too, with a fine new long name."

"My Lord, please. The lion is not a sheep. I will drive while you shoot, and you drive alone for the triumphal run, up on one wheel. The Queen will remember both."

He thought for a moment. "Good." He motioned to me to get on alone and make a short run to warm up the horses with their hunting blinders on. Filled with pride and a queasy feeling, I passed Ankh closely and put my right hand on my chest, bowing slightly. She seemed pale but her eyes were large and burning, and her lips were moving, like saying 'Do it,' or 'Get the lion,' or 'You're King?' My head was getting foggy until I again felt the tugging of the horses on my hands. She stepped back but it was too late, she was engulfed in the dust I stirred up during my dizzy moment at the reins. Looking back, I saw her shake herself like a wet dog, but smile.

The King whooped as I slowed to approach him, and he signaled to me not to stop. He leapt on board with surprising power and grace, slipped one foot into the safety strap in the first try and grabbed his golden bow, twanging the taut string to the rhythm of the hooves, as we circled once again by the Queen, a little farther than during my mishap. Ay raised his hand, upon which flags went up, a drumming began in the distance, and the horizon lit up with torches beyond the lone lion's thicket. It had been thoroughly planned by Minakh's men and approved by Ay. We skirted the thicket at medium speed several times, while hundreds of beaters with torches pushed through the bushes from the far side to drive the beast toward us. He was supposed to be of medium size and neither too hungry nor too lethargic, the trickiest part of the whole ritual. The beaters took no chances. Most of them carried a torch and a stick or spear, some of them preferring two torches, and were almost elbow to elbow, with a backup row, all screaming their lungs out, competing with the drummers behind them. Torchbearers came up farther behind us, as well, making for a large irregular string of light surrounding us in the darker center area.

Even with my trivial hunting experiences, it was clear when the critical moment was approaching, as I smelled the torches of the beaters and watched the growing exodus of running and leaping and flying and creeping creatures from the thicket, some having difficulty in trying to avoid our horses and wheels as we crossed their current repeatedly. The crunching sounds escalated and there came a roar from a thick bush, causing the horses to jerk away from the sound and make the torches recede on the far side of the bushes.

Tut pointed at the lion as it crept out from the bushes and lied down at the edge of the cover, blending into the sand and the greens. It laid its head low between the widely separated front legs, ready to move in any direction. Its tail twitched. I glanced at the King's pelt and reckoned the size of the live claws, imagining them to spread wide and dig into the ground for a good purchase, as I have seen a cat do in preparation for leaping on a fast rat.

I drove closer in shifting circles, and the King aimed his bronze-tipped lion-arrow each time. I said, 'Patience,' when he let it go. It was a miss, but no, it nicked the animal's rump, upon which it crawled back into the bush. "I see its eyes, there," pointed and whispered the King. "Get closer!"

"My Lord, it is wounded and angry now. Hiding means no fear on his part, just reckoning. It will leap, at the perfect moment for him, and it will be high, steering with its tail like a hawk. He will choose either the horses, or us. If it's on the horses, shoot at the heart from the side, I will use the spear, and you shoot again, as fast as you can reload."

"He should choose me, knowing a King's pelt." He shook his bow toward the bush and shrieked, "Me, me."

"He will. Then wait until it's highest in the air, and aim for the open mouth. I will brace the spear on the floor, and also hold the dagger ready. You can do it, My Lord."

"Yes. Go faster and closer," he said, his wide dark eyes glowing. I loosened the reins and grabbed the spear shaft, thinking that seven cubits is long enough, but what if it is not, letting the claws reach me, and worse, if the spear-tail goes through the floor under the weight of the flying lion.

There was a roar I felt deep in my chest, a low roar rising to a thunder that echoed from the hills, to which the horses bolted sideways so hard that their legs buckled and snapped, and the bushes parted and a blur flew up toward us, then floated downward, a red glint in the wet throat and a red glint on the white fangs. "Shoot!" I screamed, and Tut banged out the arrow and I kicked him in the belly to get him off the tottering chariot for his safety, the arrow hit the lion in the throat but it kept falling on my spear, pushing it through the floor and crunching it to the ground, seven cubits is too small a perfect number, claw daggers ripping my head and shoulders, spokes snapping in a dusty heap.

Faint lights appeared, several Ays and Horems and Queens were running to help the King, my throat was raked by my own breaths, I put a shaky hand on the lion's chest, no pulse. The Ays and Horems put the wobbly King on a camp throne and supported him from falling off, rubbing him down with oils and scented towels, and giving him cups of drinks while chattering nonsense. My mouth was dry, luckily a warm stream reached my lips, though I wished for a hin of beer and the soft hand of Ankh, enjoying the darkness coming from all around.

First with one eye, then with two, I saw the King wave people off from touching him. "A great kill, My Lord," said Ay, "one for the Great Temple."

"Yes," shrieked the King, scratching his belly and thighs. "And now for the triumphal drive, a huge one-wheeler, I go alone. Ankh, watch! I, alone, hear me? Bring harnesses for two horses." His grooms ran while I was thinking of a spare wheel to replace the broken one, which was poorly made by me but it helped cushion the crash and saved my life.

The King poured wine on his head and shook it off and slowly climbed on the throne, up on his knees first, holding it there and feeling his knees, and finally standing up and grabbing the backrest like a chariot's breastwork, wobbling.

"Give me! Give me the red fangs! Give me a whip, to me alone, and you, Ay and Horem, bite the bits, you fat stallions. Are you fast tonight? Oil the bearings and the fat horses. Learn to fly from me, from me alone, wheel to the ramp or no ramp. Scribes, put it in stone. See my lucky star?"

"My Lord," said Ay and Horem, choking with anger and fear, holding the bits and reins in their hands that the servants gave them. I wiggled cautiously to remove a claw from my throbbing shoulder. A bad smell hit my nostrils.

Tut made an attempt to whip Horem, who jumped to a safe distance. "My Lord, My Lord, that's all you can say? All right, I don't need you to pull my rig, I don't need you for anything, because I am the King, alone, killer of the lion. Go home and drink and sleep with your stinking slaves. Ankh, watch your husband, watch, watch the King, going up on one wheel, jubilee to the lion."

Tut yelled, "Faster!" as he cracked his whip across Ay's thighs. Ay tried to avoid it, too late, and fell with a thud and scream turning into a whimper. The King threw the whip toward the fallen man, stepped to the side edge of the chair and jerked the backrest upward, raising the chair onto its left two legs, first just a little, then more, miraculously balancing up high and yelling "Ankh!" and still floating on his one-wheeler for one, two, three, four, five, six, seven. He fell down going right-and-left at first like a falling leaf, then accelerating over the breaking armrest, shoulder boring into the ground, starry pelt slapping down on his skin.

His legs twitched, and he screamed into the stillness, "Come to me, naked, Ankhhee!"

29

Drunken Puppet with Anubis

"What did you do with the lion?"

"What? A lion, where?"

"And how many others wanted to kill me?"

Whose voice is that, and from where? Faint, but twitching my spine like the memory of the scorpion dropped inside the back of my tunic by the older apprentices, perfectly timed by them when my hands were busy with the biggest bowl I had ever spun, which was too wet and wobbly on its own. But the time will come to pay back those devils, none too soon, because some of the names and faces have begun to fade.

"Kill you? Who?"

"Carver, find your huge Anubis ear, and prepare to come. By the way, have you heard this one? A hedgehog boat comes after a long absence and ties up near the palace."

"My Lord? Is that you?" I could kick myself for saying that when surely it was his voice. Perhaps it was wishful thinking to be uncertain. Although I had nothing to fear ... he was the one who wanted the lion hunt to raise him in Ankh's eyes, and he wanted me to drive his best horses pulling my fastest wheels, and my kick to his belly was the result of quick thinking, good thinking, a necessary evil strike to save him from the dagger-claws. The Queen, too, looking at me with those big eyes, preferred me as the driver that night. And I liked him all along, and always wished him well, if it hadn't been for her eyes and singing voice, and the best ball-eyes, and he not being able to make a healthy heir.

"So, the boat ties up, and the king, not I, and a wrestler and a priest come up."

"My Lord, it is you, eternal glory be to Amun, for your voice is full of something rich, in fact better than the last time."

"So, these three men think it may be the last time for the boat to come, and they want to make a big run, spend a lot in a long night, like a high-flying one-wheeler."

"I warned you of the dangers."

"A kill is a kill, in the hunt, but some are more." His voice trailed off, and I strained to hear. I swirled the jug to feel the liquid remaining.

Something cracked, maybe glass, then another. An hour ago, I had the first sense that I missed him. Did Ankh miss him, too, equally surprisingly? If I could undo that small kick. Vaguely, the cracking sound reminded me of my frustrations the day before when I tried to hit the nasty fly that hung around the sacred standard measuring rod of electrum, strangely, because there was no food on the stick or in its lined case. Perhaps my hands left a residue from my snack of roasted goat meat basted with fig juice and oil and spices. Perhaps the fly was really a spy, or sent by a clever one, either trying to steal the measuring science, or the secret spices. The repeated slashes and slaps with whisks and linens and hide straps and rolled up papyrus were all in vain, increasing my frustration.

"My Lord, the story?"

"Ah, the boat. All right, come to the boat."

"The boat? Which? In the dark?"

"You are acting confused, or, is it something on your conscience?"

"No. No, not exactly." I coughed, trying to rid my throat of a bug, or something.

"Everybody has something, and everybody will pay, now or later. Could be interesting to watch, for years, though time means nothing. Except, now you have to get going, on the double, darkness is closing in, perfect. Good? Leave the girl for daylight."

"Where am I going? Are there any scorpions there?" I shivered. What I should have said, "Are there many?" because of the rumor that several sacks of scorpions were dumped there before the entry was sealed, to keep the robbers away. How long would those insects survive in that hostile environment? Would they multiply? Must do some experiments on them and tell the King. More important for me is to learn of their poison and the cure, since many in the palace would like to know that. They would pay plenty.

"No scorpions on the boat. The hedgehogs would eat them, ah, that's a good line, I should work on a joke around that. You could be a part of it, for better or for worse. So, hurry up, here are the directions."

Is this a trap? I smell something. "Sorry, I am quite busy, and should rather stay around the shop."

"You think you have a choice?"

"That's it, Sire. Your voice, well, if you allow me to say it, there is a touch of anger in it."

"Anger, no. A bit of cool revenge, perhaps, for many deserving people, seasoned with the challenge of a good spell or two, to last for years. You should find it exciting, no matter what. It involves your favorite women. Get going."

"Please. It's impossible. My kite can't fly through a mountain of rock. Besides, it's guarded heavily, being freshly finished, for your eternal safety. It was sealed to last a million years, said King Ay."

"Yes, it should be, but it is not yet. I hear footsteps, good, you are on the way. Or is it just the guards? Hurry. Bring your improved light, and the two biggest mirrors from your secret room, and the two hungry baboons."

"My Lord?"

"Amun scratch me, you are slow tonight, and Rehotep says you are the best."

"Yes."

"First, you will see the guards. They are huddling by the fire, drinking and making stupid jokes at my expense, but they will pay in the long run. Eleven of them, since one ran away from the smelly rock when the gust I sent made him wet both his legs, nonstop. It was just a test as a curse, not even to last a thousand years."

"Sire, what about the hungry baboons?"

"Relax. You need only a few things."

"Those baboons you want, they are not hungry."

"They will be, just in time."

I was more worried about being stopped by Rehotep, what with the required lamp and mirrors and animals in my hands. "It's a big load, it will take a while. And how can I keep them silent?"

"You surprise me. Take the sleep-hoods for their cages and soak them in beer, but what should I know about that? You exhaust me."

I moved like a whirlwind in the beginning, gathering everything and setting off on the trek, but soon the heavy load and the winding, narrowing, rocky path made me stop often. I added oil to the lamp and made sure it was fully closed. I couldn't help but try one of the mirrors to reflect starlight onto a rock face, thinking about the strange issues of mirroring things. The baboons were quiet for the moment, but their weight was a problem, with the rod pressing down on my shoulders when walking, and the cages swinging and bumping my aching bones. I sat down and ate a little of the spicy fruit I brought to get the baboons' attention later, when the time was right. The stale water did not quench my thirst. In my bustling, I forgot to refill my gourd. And another concern resurfaced. What am I doing here? And how is Ankh's new marriage going to affect me? Ay, what to do with Ay?

Two jackals growled on the opposite side of the valley, probably fighting over a bone. Would Ankh like this dark hill when her time comes for her eternal home? And what about me? Let her sleep tonight, if Ay lets her. It would be a step forward if I could hide behind her curtains. I checked the light through a tiny gap I could open briefly on the lamp, before resuming the trek. The light was like a one-eyed jackal a wandering storyteller once had on a leash by the brewer's hut in the artisans' village. The light was more than a simple eye, perhaps a glimpse of how the oldest god, Ptah, created Re-Aten, the Big Light in the sky, from pure thought.

At last the fire came into view, and the dark figures around it, eating and drinking and throwing dice. Only one was talking, a priest, probably telling stories, while the cups were raised to the lips frequently.

"My Lord, what next? Should I rush the guards for a big scare on them? I could not sustain it. They have weapons of strong metal, while I have none. My Lord, you wanted me to come here, so, please help."

I waited for a respectable length of time, but there was no answer. I thought that the jackals should growl again in the hills, soon, and they did, as if I commanded them. A small quarrel arose at the fire, probably over the game, but soon it subsided into teasing and laughter. Probably every one of them is a non-reckoning man, as if he had no fingers to count. I must pray to the Babbling Baboon to plant images in the minds of the guards, but what images? There is a vast darkness in the valley, with pinpoints of light possible, and angry sounds mimicking Anubis, a two-headed one, for good effect, but what is that sound exactly, and how to do it?

I started moving like a drunken puppet at the harvest festival, my mind empty. Moving faster and faster, I set things up. The two mirrors with big, uneven surfaces, I hung them from scrubby bushes, where the breeze was just strong enough to shake them a little. I opened my light to shine on both mirrors equally, then I set the two cages a few cubits apart, removed the sleep-hoods, placed a little food in front of them, and waited for the baboons to awake. The first one stirred and moaned, and this woke up the other. Without any good reason, I imagined rapid shooting from a single bow. I watched the guards, who erupted in a loud and vicious dice-and-fist-throwing. I tossed the biggest chunk of food toward them, upon which my animals growled like a huge Anubis, two-headed, and charged toward the guards' food satchels, while the mirrors were flashing a hundred prancing lights all over the site. One fighting baboon, flying over obstacles, hit a guard's bag of trinkets with a bang, the other in its mad dash for food mistakenly touched hot coals and screamed as loud as the guards, the valley echoed as a trapped thunder, the men ran onto the narrow dark path away from the mirrored lights, tripping and piling on one another and each of them stabbing blindly and furiously to be the first to get away.

30

Tongue on Fire

The last moan and gasp from the pile of guards subsided, so I went around to gather up and hide the mirrors and the cages. By the time these chores were done, the baboons were half asleep by the fire, their stomachs extended with food, their eyes flickering from the cheap wine and the excitement. A tail was curling and uncurling, periodically slapping the ground, as if to an ancient, slow music. All my life, I have spent hours watching these creatures. They will find their way back to our place on their own, when the sun rises, if they care to continue the employment. If not, there are younger ones waiting, eager to learn what I have to offer. In any case, they will not talk much.

"My Lord, I am ready. What should I do next?" My words stumbled and sounded strange to me. Did I miss him? Not the husband of Ankh, no. Perhaps I miss his good touch on his horses' noses, or a crude joke for the drivers and grooms, followed by a hearty laugh. Yes, it is that laugh, though rare, because, as rumor had it, he had often been admonished by his mother when he was young that such a horsy, peasant laugh was not becoming of royalty. Will I ever hear it again?

My thin light beam fell on the main entrance, below the steps to his tomb. One, two,... sixteen steps. Why am I counting them when I know this number well? It is three sacred numbers in one. Of course, ten is sacred, based on two perfect hands. Six is great, coming from the bee and the wheel. And, I will never forget the glow turning into a glaze in the eyes of Tut, when Rehotep explained to him the third and biggest secret of the number sixteen, to be used as part of the architecture of the King's tomb, namely, that the number ten can be expressed as the number one at the next higher level of thinking, so, sixteen is not just ten plus six, but also the Second-Significant-One plus six, which is now seven, which is another sacred number. This is also the reason for the seven whiskbrooms by the sixteen steps, which the Sweeping Priests will never understand, another practical joke by my Master. Some may say this is crazy, but they don't realize how much fun this can be, like dipping a hot toe into the river, or like swishing my counting fingers in a sea of numbers.

"My Lord. Where should I go, down these sacred steps?" No answer. I picked up a broom and swept the first step. Sand and stone chips... those lazy priests should be flogged. The main entrance at the bottom of the steps was blocked, considering my lack of heavy equipment. I reviewed the architect Maya's design sketches of the tomb's entrance area in my memory, but it was not helpful. Still, I liked the man. Maybe Rehotep is just jealous of him, a common trait of the most talented.

The flames of the fire were out, but the red glow, also reflected by the animals' smooth bottoms, allowed me to check the rocky slope for a possible tunnel. A silent shooting star pointed briefly off to the side, a good sign. In time, a rock yielded to my prying and leveraging with a spear shaft, revealing a smaller stone that was a plug, just bigger than the size of my torso. I crawled in, and was soon in a larger tunnel, just inside the main entrance. The smell of fresh plaster and paint and burned-out torches twisted my nostrils. How long can I endure this air? I wondered about Tut's nose. I opened the door of my light wider, and surveyed the corridor. Yes, this is it, about four cubits wide, gently sloping downward into the belly of the mountain.

There was a lot of debris, a sign of a rushed job, a shame. Maybe it was always done this way, because a great tomb takes many years to complete, or on purpose, to hinder would-be robbers. The sight and the smells made me feel tired and nauseated. What am I doing here and why? "My Lord?"

I smiled. It's amazing to be conscious of smiling, being alone in such a dank place, when my light beam fell on an ostrich feather and a three-legged folding chair, his favorite camp chair with red leather, a chair whose stubborn hinges I worked on at one time, to very good effect. It felt good to sit down on a fun chair that I could only try in secret before, hoping in my feverish dreams to legally own one. I sat like a King, with knees wide open, when the Queen glanced at my underwear. I moved a bit to give her a better view, but the chair creaked and I jerked to my senses. It is a shame to send him on a long journey with squeaking hinges, so I pulled out the plug from my oil jar and lubricated all the hinges of the chair with the care that he deserved, even though in life he was not the favorite of many people in power. Did anybody miss him now? His young lion does, surely. The Queen? Any hedgehog? Who else?

I played my light on the inside of the entryway, filled with stones and mortar and beams of wood, musing about the silence on both sides of it. I watched a flock of dust particles dance in my unsteady light beam. I sneezed and that made them leap, and that reminded me to talk to the new acrobatic dance teacher, she has a fine long neck and legs, I could offer her to carve her image on stone, for some new acrobatic pleasure together. Tut liked her, too, and that makes her more desirable, but beware of his reaction, because kings are known to be revengeful, especially from their tombs.

There was a sharp clang. A gust knocked my lamp over and blew it out, no, it was most likely an owl, but an owl, here? I strained my eyes. This should not affect me at all, I am not guilty, not really. Tut wanted me to be here. The lamp, it was just an accident, or just a test. Yes, a test by the King, and he has the right to test all visitors.

"My Lord, watch me!" I pulled out my tiny bow-drill spark-board. I could feel its wonderful lines. I moved confidently, and my lips turned out a tune that the laundresses liked a lot. This should please him, because he liked the soapy-clean girls. My device had only one starter hole, but there was fresh friction-resin in it, proof of my preparations. There was a new fire-stick in the spinner shaft, and everything fitted perfectly. I inserted the stick's tip in the hole, looped the string on the shaft, and started the deliberate sawing motion with the bow to spin the drill-shaft. The expected sparks appeared in due course from the board's side slot, and I gathered my breath, ready to blow on the tinder as it began to smolder, but it didn't. I let the air out, and started to spin the bit again. There were sparks, but not a steady enough succession of them. After three or four tries there was still no flame. I fiddled with the lamp, for diversion, and sat back, thinking that this is a sign from the gods, maybe I should come back some other time.

Thinking more and more of fire, my bladder felt full, which was always a strange cause and effect. Maybe Rehotep knows the reason. I got up, moved away ten steps, found a good spot on the wall, and watered it. Why exactly on the wall, on his wall? I felt stupid.

"Go ahead and finish with the little fellow, I won't laugh."

"My Lord?" I choked and looked around, my eyes feeling a bulging, straining in the dark. "I will wash it, when I can."

"All right, fix your stupid light." He laughed, and it trailed off, with the echoes coming from the ends of the corridor.

I retraced my steps to my sparker, which worked easily on the first attempt, even though my hands were not dry. The lamp oil was heavenly, fragrant with essence of lavender and ostrich fat, and inhaling it reminded me of the fine linens of Ankh.

My belly was empty, my knees shaky, my nostrils dry. I sat on the chair, rocking, to help me think. I ate a little, saving some for the long haul. The garlic sausage was the best, if a bit risky, on account of the rumors that the King was not fond of it, but I assumed it was not a matter of taste buds, but trying to be fully presentable to the Queen at all times, which would not be of concern here, either for him or for me. Feeling better, I looked at my perfect sparker drill, thinking about the riches it would bring.

I relaxed. I slid off the wobbly chair and tucked my feet under my thighs, in the Asiatic cross-legged position, which is good for sensitizing the sweet spots in the ball-eyes, and to beautify the arch of the foot. I rested my hands on my spread knees, which were not shaky any more, and mulled over my immediate options.

How could I forget it? I took out the small pouch, a gift of soft red leather with several inner pockets that Ankh gave me, in appreciation of a special gift from me, the fertility charm made of the dung of seven different fast animals, stallions and lions and such. For a moment I worried that my hasty movements might have damaged the priceless, thin Asiatic tube, smaller than a breath-giving reed for diving in the river, but the lined pouch had protected it. The piece was doubly priceless, considering Ankh's handwriting on it, showing much progress with her hand on the stylus. The tube represented a difficult medium, both in the material and the shape. My lips shaped her cryptic words aloud, as if savoring a large, gritty fig,

taste the dream-tube with the tongue on fire

What does this mean? There might be several possibilities, but I got distracted. I could imagine her hunched over her board, balancing it on her knees, her fingers periodically losing control of the stylus. I have taught her much already, but it was a long trip for a female scribe, what with the secrecy she wanted, and my desire to make her feel progress while delaying the writing to the last possible scratch on the papyrus, for my own benefit. Her feet protruded from her tunic just enough to make me enjoy the crimson nails, the blue veins competing with the golden straps of the sandals, the twitching of a big toe when her hand completed a difficult line. The tunic shifted a little on her shoulder each time, too, giving me new ideas.

Hot, that's it, with the tube, too. How simple it can be, with the mind on the right track. I took out the flame cradle from the lamp and put the far end of the tube, with the word fire closest to it, into the flame. Cautiously, I sniffed the near end of the tube, with the word *taste*. I put my lips to it, taking a small gulp of the hot air coming through. It was not good, but rather bitter and harsh. My mind turned to the misty cool air over the river, at dawn or dusk, always better than smoke, and to the cool air over the hot skin of laughing Saam, why did her face pop up here, her freshly shaved skin next to mine, touching, gasping, as the boat rolls with every movement of a head or hand or foot or lips without words, aware of the red fish leaping again, without seeing it.

31

Hedgehog's Rocking the Boat

My hand touched a hot part of the lamp, and this brought my mind back to the little tube. It was smooth and warm, reminding me of Ankh's hands. Maybe the hot end could be improved, but how? I scanned around me with the lamp. Precious objects mingled with debris. I threw a piece against the wall and listened for the echo.

My light fell on small model boats in the corridor, left there haphazardly by the last workers. They were fully peopled with reddish figurines of boatmen and plump nobles eating and drinking as if on a festival excursion. On one of the boats a handful of pomegranate seeds represented a huge pile of ripe fruits. Clever idea. I took a few seeds and jammed them inside the tube, and proceeded to heat the assembly.

I sniffed at the warm air emerging from the taste end of the tube, ever so cautiously, remembering my preceding bad experience. It was even worse than during my original attempt, but something made me try it again and again, noticing some change each time. What did they soak these seeds in, or what magician's cauldron was used? "You are indeed an excellent cook of this simple dish," a laughing voice erupted behind me. It could only be Ankh, I turned quickly but not fast enough, she was already gone … what was she talking about?

The smoke from the tube turned sweeter and sweeter, no, not exactly sweet but something deep and red, ripe pomegranate-red, and it became the morning fog, soon a messenger appeared from Tut, telling me to be ready before dusk the same day, for the King will show me his new papyrus boat and a fast oar, just for me, just for me.

I spent most of the day preparing, thinking, and leisurely washing my clothes, and thinking more, about the stubborn stains I tend to pick up. While washing the linens, I decided to wash myself extra clean for meeting the King, who was known to be yelling about urine on his walls and such. With nobody watching, I did a thorough job, probably overdoing it, for he was not likely to sniff me out like a dog. It felt good, too, and I let the sun dry me leisurely. I should do it more often, royal visitor or not.

At the appointed time, I was surprisingly calm, waiting at his boat, a little ways from the harbor, fairly hidden amongst thick reeds, but I was not touching anything that he might want to show off. The boat was big enough to hold four or five people, and I wondered how much he was going to contribute to the paddling. A light breeze rustled the reeds, and the low sun painted them green-gold. It would be good to have a twin brother to leave here by the boat to meet the King, so that I could circle back and join with Ankh, to offer her a pair of gold-laced sandals, since she loves new things for the foot, and to put them on her, tickling her crimson toes, working her soft soles, helping her shed everything but the sandals, she likes to stand on new ones, and she says, "make a neat pile, no wrinkles."

Sharp claws tore into my tunic, bringing me back to reality, to the King's young pet lion, Bastet. Of course, he would let her run ahead to playfully announce his arrival. It was big and rough for a cat, but small for a lion, a small strain, and very rare, from the far south, with an uncommon black mane. I liked this creature a little, but swore to train my pets better, when the time comes. Tut was not far behind, using his paddle as a cane. It had a sharply pointed leaf, elegantly carved, including flaring veins and painted with his many names. The thin handle was practically useless, if it did not incorporate some metal bars...that's an idea worth exploring at another time. I recalled Rehotep's clever words about making things perfect, "If it looks strong enough, it is. Much better than that, make it strong enough while it appears weak." The King waved the paddle toward me, perhaps as a clumsy greeting. Royalty are awkward when alone with people of much lower standing. He adjusted the small cobra on his headband, and brushed his blue-striped shoulder wrap and bottom half-tunic that had gold wheel motifs on a narrow strip.

He opened his mouth but was interrupted by more noise from the path through the reeds. His entourage, no doubt, I thought with some irrational annoyance, but in disbelief, my eyes fell on Ankh, a sight never encountered before, first, the noisemakers, glittering sandals striding and forcefully slapping the wet sand, causing a bounce of her exposed left breast, which was not supported by a strap at all but by her right arm reaching across to the left shoulder, a strange way of walking, but perhaps to hide her two slightly crippled fingers on that hand. The presumably new sandals were getting dark from mud, highlighting the crimson toes ever more. The right breast was as blinding as the sun near the horizon, it was the nipple with a small flower, by the edge of her tunic's strap, just peeking out from the cradle of her arm, this one was not bouncing, but firmly fixed in space. The tunic was a masterpiece by Klimtuu, her most envied dresspainter, many flower motifs on the chest, as if to confuse the viewer of the flowered nipple, as if the two differently presented breasts were not confusing enough. The tunic rippled as she walked, with several elements dancing on the linen, nested pyramid shapes, squares, swirling spirals of mysterious meaning, half circles, nested hedgehog ovals of gold lines and crude meaning, stylized names of the Two Lands in gold and silver.

Her large dark eyes were burning and laughing, making me feel glad about my washing of everything, while my tongue was aching in my parched mouth. A servant boy behind her carried a large basket of food and jugs. In a single sweep of her hand she made me take the basket and dismissed the boy, whose eyes were rapidly scanning each of us, but mainly feasting on the Queen. "Good," yelled the King, who must have noticed the boy's feverish eyes. "Let him go. I will send him to Kush on foot, so he will never return." He slapped his thigh in delight, which made me more uncomfortable, standing between the two of them. "And take Bastet with you," called Ankh after the boy.

I saw that her arms had muscles, emanating from the pointed shoulders. Not overly muscular, but well defined, like minor hills and valleys at sunrise. It was attractive, being a sign of healthy flesh, but how did she get it? Were the rumors true that she played regularly with the wrestlers? And that she always had her way, because she gave them a weakening drink before the games? I envied the wrestlers, a stupid thought, but I wanted to touch her, to feel those hills and valleys.

She motioned to us to carry everything to the boat. He was first, scrambled with his oar to the prow, stood on the seat leaning on the oar for support, and looked around proudly, over our heads. I carried the basket and the real working oar, and, under her eyes' command, helped her tunic over the edge while he settled down, looking eagerly forward, slowly, ever more slowly, a feather touch on her smooth skin, my blood began to heat and pound in my neck. "Start dipping, up front," she said to him over her shoulder, but facing me in the back. "Find the quiet spot, your thinking spot." She nestled down on cushions.

I had to do all the serious paddling, but it was good to occupy me. She started on the food and the wine, first handing him a drinking horn. "How is your oar dripping?" she said. "I like the drops off the pointed feather, sharp. The drops grow but disappear, did you see? See that duck ahead, I will give him wine in bread." He talked fast at first, then slowed down, sipping his wine. She put a red pillow under her feet, and gave me a cup of wine from a different jug, brown, long narrow neck, and she drank from the same jug, sweet and warm, while he slouched sideways and backward. I fished out his oar, and the boat became wedged in reeds just when he pointed at open water through a gap, then she refilled his horn, too much, he spilled it on his hand, and squealed with pleasure. Did he lick it?

I was at a loss for words, and soon for thoughts. "Is your oar still dripping or stopped?" she asked him. There was no answer. His breathing was louder than the rushes in the breeze. I aimlessly fingered his thin oar, when and how to get it back to him ... she smiled ... but where should I put my hands?

"Your lips are moving but I can't hear you. See my feet? Come. Pick the mud out from those toes, wash it with wine till the crimson comes out shining, a small tickle is fine, but easy, no carving there, Count Carver." She refilled my cup, spilling some on her hand, which she slowly wiped across my lips, her tunic shifted a little, revealing a long slit, where did that come from, more magic by Klimtuu, and a glimpse of a knee, am I awake, images of Gim and Yulan flashed through my mind as my hand jumped like a mad ape from her painted toenails to the knee, my mouth dried to a crisp, a white skull is looming in the desert, help me live, Ptah, and survival came from the wine she poured on my head, both of us suddenly laughing, a sweet stream running down my face and chest and belly and thighs.

She kicked the red pillow toward my legs, good for my temporary ease, pray to eternity, and my hand slipped from her knee, softer and warmer every finger of the way up, she squeezed and pulled on my splitting head, hurry, find the Isis-Charm hidden in the darkness among bittersweet lavender and quills.

32

Endless Spells

I licked the last pumpkin seed, the spices were rich, then worried about not leaving enough flavoring for the flame, so I put it back and rolled it in the spicy dust in the bottom of the pouch. Ready for the tube with it.

There was a bang, then silence, from a side corridor, that must have been the rock sealing Ay's tomb. Too bad, with all that fine wine, but there should be a way to penetrate it, leisurely, some other time. But where is the freshly widowed Ankh, widowed for the second time? How many more will she have? And where is Tut, ah, that must have been he, slipping through the group of tricky Amdu Apes on the wall.

Ay liked Ankh's wines, just couldn't hold it.

"Count Carver, help me, remember me?" Her voice is dry, cracking. "How is your choice of new names coming along? It's time for you to settle down, enough of all those servants and princesses. Let's settle down with a plan, there is no time to waste. Remember the red cushion on the boat?" She is choking, the voice is old and raspy, but she will not cry, or will she?

I squeezed the crusty seed into the tube and touched it to the flame. Did the Amdu Apes stir on the wall? "Carver, have you heard this one? A wrestler and a priest and a scribe go to the hedgehog boat, in disguise. What's its name, yes, the Sleepy Waters. Awfully

186

crowded, I hate it. But the three men should have a fun night, with the shaving and brushing of the hedgehogs, three on one, it's called. And the drawing of the lots, also fun, with all the noble daughters there on the boat."

"There is a scribe now in your story? What happened to the king?"

"Yes, there is always a king, but he is dead, tired of hedgehogs, but the spell-making is good for him, it's a new sport, the only sport now. Playing hard, lobbing the long and penetrating spells, for friends and relatives. When they run out, I can try it on strangers."

"I didn't mean to kick you so hard." I hoped for my light to go out so that I could slink away, never having to talk with him again.

He made a sound, like rubbing his hands. "Do you hear the wailing ahead? A fine wedding, it will be. You're breathing like a fish in air? Try sniffing dry Anubis dung, there is some of it hidden in my shoebox. I learned how useful that is for many maladies. Yes, I learned that under my mother's knees. "

"Whose wedding is that?"

"Ankh and ..."

"Ankh? Wasn't she and King Horem recently celebrating?"

"You mean, the passing away of King Ay? And crowning the new one? That's old news. Where have you been the last two days?"

"Where?"

"Yes, and doing what? Never mind. You will get half of what you always wanted, well deserved."

"Half? Which half?"

"Good. The ceremony is about to begin in the corridor, you can resume thinking of a new name for yourself, and of healthy infants, though it won't help with your future, given the lasting developments in the spells."

"I would rather see it some other time, any time." I looked back, into the dark, reckoning the distance to the sixteen steps of the entrance.

"It's no trouble, today. Just be careful, your papyrus boat can get stuck in the hedgehog channel of reeds again, and the more you rock it, the deeper it gets."

"Which half?"

"Here comes Horem, scratching his red belly button or something, but, doesn't he look good for his age?" He dropped his voice, "The new King easily has another twenty five years to go, a very strong soldier, fresh hedgehogs aplenty, careful eater since yesterday."

Horem motions the wailers and the apes Gim and Yulan, how did they get here, into a circle. The happy red and yellow paint on their faces was streaked with black, especially on Gim. They broke into wide smiles when they parted, that's crazy, Ankh enters, closely followed by Mehmeh-Saam, and Tut whispered in my ear, "That's another friend of yours, very elegant and desirable with the new cobra head-gear of her own, where did she learn to carry it so well, maybe practicing in secret when she was a sweeper in your shop, but apparently the best ball-eyes can help one balance the crown."

Horem, of medium height and build, but imposing in this crowd, took Uncle Qed's elbow, how did he get here, he was long gone, and pulled him into the circle. Qed raised his long whip and said, "Good, finally, to settle, so you can pay for your education." Tut giggled, "Don't worry, the sky is not going to fall, not here. You can always drive a cart, earn a new name, or, simply, push a cart. Carter, Carter. It has a nice ring to it. How do you like it? Then your uncle will find nothing to reclaim from you."

I looked at Ankh, and saw her wrinkles that must have multiplied and deepened in a few days. Saam's face was more rounded than Ankh's, and pink fresh as a morning-opening flower. Saam, taller than the shrinking Ankh, was richly dressed in an imitation of the Queen's latest style of spirals and tiny pyramid shapes, or was it actually from the royal wardrobe?

Horem handed me a cup and made me drink the wine, the same he gave the women of the twisted-smiling red and yellow faces and sour voices, perhaps spiked with Asiatic powders. What did Horem say in passing about the marriage qualities of all his daughters, just in case the wine does something to Ankh. My stomach began to turn. He handed us rings of dandelions, which were shedding flying seeds with every move of the hands, a thousand tiny white kites.

Tut is poking me in the ribs, "What is this reluctance? You are old enough for Ankh, if inexperienced. Concentrate on the technique of the virile Gim for fun on ropes and ladders, unconcerned about climbing great heights or getting feeble offspring. Ankh, take him as your new husband."

She and I look at each other. Her black eye-liners are broken lines now, running in streams down her cheeks. We are strangers, both empty-handed. I feel dizzy, the wailers' smells are mingling with Saam's heavy perfume, her ears are delicate and should be good nibbling, they are throwing pomegranate seeds on us for luck and fertility, but the ducks are going after them under foot, and what about Ankh, we must live with the wrinkles, all eyes are on Gim as he slowly dances with his mate, loosely holding her wrist high up as she is turning round and round, uncharacteristically walking tall and unhurried, when will these apes spring into coupling worth learning, I can't wait here forever.

"You have lost it," said Tut, "and the flame is out. Out." I can't see him, and Ankh has also disappeared, but I see King Horem in faint light, holding Saam's hand, they are smiling and giggling. How old is Horem? He has wrinkles, I should count them, add to them. How old is he, the old mentor number two?

Where did my hot tube fall? I struggle through the crowd, my foot finds the tube but cracks it flat, then I get a new sensation, no, a replay of an old one, Queen Saam's long fingers are trolling on my ball-eyes, again and again, her fingers sliding slower and warmer on my cool skin. I must give her an excellent fertility charm, ball-eye wings and lively tails rolled into firm stallion dung, then meet at my papyrus boat in thick reeds ... there is another world out there where the sun goes down over the misty river, my favorite.

33

Tears on My Papyrus Pillow

She is asleep.

How can she be so relaxed? She should have sensed this would be the last time for us in my boat. When should I tell her my wish with finality? Maybe Ankh does know me, after all. The tear welling out of the corner of her hastily painted eye lines says something. I study the drop of water, is it rolling like a tiny wheel, or sliding, or both? The light is not good for deciding the question, but leaning close to her face, I find her scent is as rich as ever, and the wrinkles not too deep, for the moment.

She sighs after passing a faint smile, her face is again beautiful for an instant, why at this late hour in our lives, and the tear falls on the papyrus pillow, staying on the surface, quivering from the fall, I imagine.

I chase a mosquito from her neck, but it persists. What will be her life after losing her second King, Ay? Horem will not want her, most likely, what with her failures in production of healthy boys for Tut and Ay. Her hip seems wider than before, so she could steer her horses more easily, but will she have any horses and wheels, being out of the palace? What good could she do for any man on his way to the top?

I look at the papyrus rolls in her basket. She could be a court scribe with those fine long fingers, but only in another world, where men are gentle. Why did she bring these rolls here, and not even want to talk about them? Maybe later, though I know what she wrote about the three of us. The three of us, still? How much longer?

I see another tear falling off her beautiful cheek, landing near the first one on the pillow. A frog begins to sing in short bursts, and soon another answers. I could also lure them into singing, but leave it for another time. Did she play with frogs when she was young? She should have, for better luck in fertility. She is now out of her Scented Soft Room, and the girls are singing new stories in the laundry room. And is she still getting a big shave, and by whom? Yes, her skin feels one-day old. She got a full lathering and scraping with an excellent blade, but by whom?

The mosquito returns to her, heavy but insatiable, and I tighten a roll for the kill. I inch closer and smash the insect on her hip, lightly enough not to wake her, and watch the spot of Ankh's blood being sucked into a small word by the fibers of the papyrus. I listen to her breathing while reading a little, skipping around. How did she ever know and imagine us in this kind of detail, putting words on my lips, and did she get a huge cramp every day in her stylus finger?

The meanings of *ankh:*

The ubiquitous word and symbol ankh may represent life, breath of life, air and water, regeneration by water, bow, stick figure, floral bouquet, mirror, sexuality, sandal strap …

About the Author

Bela I. Sandor is Professor Emeritus of Engineering Physics at the University of Wisconsin-Madison (www.engr.wisc.edu/ep/faculty/sandor_bela.html). He is a technical expert on chariots, having researched their surprisingly sophisticated design, such as springs, shock absorbers, complex wheels, vibration control, and a stupendous anti-roll mechanism. These findings, enhanced by analyses of artistic works from Egypt, Greece and Rome, provide new clues to our understanding of ancient technology development. His seminal paper "The Rise and Decline of the Tutankhamun-Class Chariot" in the Oxford Journal of Archaeology, May 2004, is accessible by non-specialists. His work includes studies of the people of the ancient world, their art and literature, religion and sport, initially mentored by Professor Lanny Bell.

Bela Sandor's poetry writing was mentored by Ron Wallace and Dave Clewell at the University of Wisconsin-Madison. He studied fiction writing with Judy Bridges and Norb Blei at The Clearing in Wisconsin.

Bela lives in Madison, Wisconsin, with his wife Ruth of 40 years. He has four daughters and seven grandchildren. He is an active competitor in US Masters Swimming, twice a national champion, and currently holding the national record in the 200-yard breaststroke in the 70-74 age group.

Printed in the United States
141525LV00002B/1/P

9 781440 112669